Ben Pastor, born in Italy, has lived for thirty years in the United States, working as a univers the author of other novels *The Water Thief* and *The Fire* the most talented writers in In 2008 she won the prestig ......gola for best historical fiction.

LUMEN

Ben Pastor

BITTER LEMON PRESS
LONDON

BITTER LEMON PRESS

First published in the United Kingdom in 2011 by
Bitter Lemon Press, 37 Arundel Gardens, London W11 2LW

www.bitterlemonpress.com

Copyright © 1999 by Ben Pastor
This edition published in agreement with the Author through
PNLA/Piergiorgio Nicolazzini Literary Agency

The moral rights of Ben Pastor have been asserted in accordance
with the Copyright, Designs, and Patents Act 1988

A CIP record for this book is available from the British Library

ISBN 978-1-904738-66-4

Typeset by Alma Books Limited
Printed and bound by Cox & Wyman Ltd, Reading, Berkshire

Lumen

Good does not lead less strongly to Good than Evil leads to Evil.
Even if I do not commit any evil deed, if my will is to do evil,
I carry the weight of sin as if I had committed that deed.
But if my will is to do good, I carry its merit in the same measure.
And in doing good, it does not matter if I apply it to small or great things,
because there is no difference between a drop and the sea..

Meister Eckhart

1

The Polish words stencilled on the plaque read, "Take Good Heed", and the Hebrew script below them presumably repeated the sentence. Coloured pictures illustrating the alphabet were pasted on the wall around the plaque. For the letter L, the picture showed a little girl pushing a doll carriage.

Suddenly the odour of mangled flesh was sharp, crude. It came to his nostrils unexpectedly, so that Bora turned away from the wall and walked towards the middle of the room, where an army medic stood in gloves and surgical mask. Behind his figure, flooding the classroom with light, three wide open windows let in the afternoon sun and a lukewarm afternoon wind.

Six desks had been joined by their narrow ends, two by two, and the uniform-clad bodies lay on top of them, over tarpaulin sheets. Blood had dripped down the ends of the desks, from the little spaces between sheets. The larger puddles were coagulating, and reflected the light of the windows on their surface. Bora stared at the reflection before stepping closer, nodding to the medic.

After looking over each body, he pronounced a name in a low voice, a collected and controlled and forcibly boxed-in voice. The medic was holding a pad, and wrote down the names on it.

When he lifted his eyes from the third body to the wall ahead, Bora met with the colourful print of the little girl pushing a doll carriage. It read, *Lale. Dorotka ma lale.*

9

"We thought you'd be best suited to identify them, Captain, since you were in the car right behind them."

Bora turned to the medic. He didn't say anything. For a moment he looked up and down the medic's grimy apron as if wondering what either one of them was doing here. What, indeed, any of them – dead and alive – were doing in a Jewish day school on Jakova Street in Cracow.

He felt sweat run under his arms, down the middle of his back.

Bora said, "Yes, I was."

Major Retz waited below in the army car. He was smoking a cigar, and the air in the car was hazy with it, because he had all the windows rolled up. When Bora opened the door to enter, a bluish cloud floated against him with an acrid odour of tobacco. He took his place in the driver's seat.

Retz said, "So, of course they were Lieutenants Klaus, Williams and poor Hans Smitt. Had they been wearing their identification disks, you wouldn't have had to go up and look at them. How bad are they?"

Bora started the engine, avoiding Retz's eyes in the rear-view mirror. "They're in shreds from the midriff down." He lowered his window, and with the motion of the car the smoke began to blow away.

They drove down the deserted street into a square, Bora following the direction signs hastily put up in the last few days over the Polish names of streets and bridges. Retz made some trivial observations, and Bora answered in monosyllables.

The afternoon light shone lavish and clear, it drew long shadows from the trees flanking the street and the tall city blocks. Overhead, the sky was thinly raked by aircraft flying east, delicate trails like pentagrams without notes.

"That's no way to go, is it – blasted on a mine."

Bora kept silent, so Retz cracked the window to toss the butt of his cigar out, and changed the subject. "How do you like Intelligence?"

This time Bora looked up into the mirror. Retz wasn't looking at him. His arrogant, crude face was averted, and there came the rustle of a large sheet of paper being unfolded.

"I think I'll like it."

Retz's eyes met his. "Yes. They tell me you're the student kind." Bora thought Retz probably meant "studious", but "student" was what he said. He felt a curious little surge of insecurity at that assessment of him. More crumpling of paper followed, and a badly refolded street map was tossed on the front seat from behind.

"Our lodgings are supposed to be close to the Wawel Hill in the Old City. I'd hoped we'd lodge closer to head-quarters, Bora, but that's what we get for staying longer than most on the field of battle. I hope there's indoor plumbing, and all that. Drive to the office, I want to check where exactly they're going to house us."

14 October

The German Army Headquarters on Rakowicka Street overlooked a formal garden, and, past the gate, across the sidewalk lined by trolley tracks, sat a grey Dominican church. Pigeons flew to its roof, alone and in pairs, fluttering.

Bora listened to what Colonel Hofer was explaining to him. All the while, he thought that in comparison with Richard Retz, his commander was an introverted and sullen man. Hofer's hands sweated, so that he wore talcum powder in his gloves to absorb the moisture. His palms retained a dusty appearance, like fish floured in anticipation of frying. Of an unclear age (Bora was young enough to misjudge the age of anyone older than himself but not yet white-haired), the colonel had a small nose; a womanly nose, almost, with wide nostrils, a sensitive mouth and narrow teeth. He wore spectacles only when he had to read something, but his squint gave the impression that he needed them even for simpler tasks, such as looking at people while talking to them.

After an intense morning of briefing Bora on his duties, Hofer took him aside by the window, and for some time didn't say anything at all. Fixedly he stared beyond the flowerbeds into the street, oblivious to Bora's nearness. At long last, he focused his circled, watery eyes on the younger man.

His eyes seemed weary, Bora thought, as in one who doesn't sleep or sleeps poorly – something that could be said of all of them in the past furious weeks. Except that the young officers didn't look, or probably didn't even feel tired.

With some envy, Hofer was drawing a similar parallel. Bora stood by him with a fresh, prim countenance, disciplined into not showing his eagerness but yet very eager, as his record showed. Hofer could shake his head at the enthusiasm, at the eagerness, but it was a time to encourage, not discourage those excesses.

He said, "Captain, how familiar are you with the phenomenon of the stigmata?"

Bora showed no overt surprise at the question. "Not very, sir." He tried not to stare back. "They're wounds like those received by Christ on the cross. Saint Francis of Assisi had them, and some other mystics."

Hofer returned his gaze to the street. "That's true enough. And do you know how Francis and the others received them?" He didn't give Bora time to answer. "It happened during ecstasy. Ecstasy did it." He nodded to himself, with his fingernail scraping a little spot of dry paint from the glass. "Ecstasy did it."

Hofer walked away from the window and into his office. Bora stayed behind long enough to glance at the roofs of the Old City churches, rising to the left like distant ships' forecastles behind uninspired new blocks. Directly ahead, pigeons still flew to and from the Dominican church, seeking the sunny side of the roof. Spain, only six months before, had been an exultation of crude and dazzling light.

What did the stigmata have to do with anything?

He thought no more of it until after the lunch hour, when the colonel again stopped by his desk. Bora had been familiarizing himself with the topography of south-eastern Poland, and now stood up with a red pencil in his hand.

Hofer took the pencil from him, and laid it on the desk.

"Enough map reading for the day, Bora. Tomorrow you'll go out on patrol. Your interpreter is Johannes Herwig, an ethnic German, and he'll tell you the rest in the field. A good man, Hannes – we go back a few years. Come, now. I want you to take a ride downtown with me."

"I'll fetch the Colonel's car."

"No. Let's use yours. I want you to drive."

At Our Lady of the Seven Sorrows, a musty, waxy odour hovered in the convent's waiting room. Light came in through a set of three windows lined in a row, high, small, squarish, with deep slanting sills from which one couldn't look out, even on tiptoe. There were three doors and all of them were closed. The silence was so complete, Bora could feel absence of sounds like a void against his ears.

Startlingly real against a blank side wall, a life-size crucified Christ hung in agony, his torso contorted and bleeding, eyes turned back to half-hide glass pupils under his lids. It reminded Bora of the bodies in the Jewish schoolhouse, and he nearly expected to see blood on the floor at the foot of the cross. But the tiles were spotlessly clean, like everything else. No marks on the walls, no fingerprints, no streaks on the floor. And that waxy, musty smell.

Waiting for Hofer, who had disappeared into one of the rooms down the hallway, Bora paced the floor. The quiet orderliness of the room forced a comparison with the wreckage and noise of weeks past – villages torn open, fields rolling by, speeding by, convulsed by drifting smoke and the fire of big guns. Bora admitted now that he'd pushed through havoc with the mindlessness of a sexual rush, awed and drunk with it. All the more he marvelled at the sterile peace of this interior.

He'd been waiting for over an hour (the light was changing in the small windows, turning pinkish and less strong) when one of the doors opened and a priest walked out of it. Their eyes met, and the two men exchanged a noncommittal nod of acknowledgement. The priest wore clergyman's trousers, an unusual sight in this conservative country. He went past Bora, down a hallway and into another door.

Later a nun came gliding by, was gone. The light in the little windows grew lilac as the shadow of the late afternoon filled the street. Bora measured the floor in slow steps, trying to tend his thoughts and boredom. At last the priest entered the waiting room again.

He said, in English, "Colonel Hofer tells me you speak my language."

Bora turned rigidly. "Yes." And, recognizing the American accent, he relaxed his shoulders a little.

"He sent me to keep you company while he concludes his meeting with Mother Kazimierza."

"Thank you, I'm all right."

"Well, then – *you* can keep me company." With an amiable smile, the priest took a seat on a lion-footed bench, but Bora didn't imitate him. He remained standing, hands clasped behind his back.

The priest kept smiling. He was a man in his fifties, or so Bora assessed, big-shouldered, big-footed, with wide freckled hands and extremely lively, clear eyes. His neck, Bora saw out of the corner of his eye, emerged from the Roman collar as a powerful bundle of muscles, like the neck of a wrestler. The combination of his alert glance and strong frame recalled the pictures of warring peasant saints, cross in one hand and sword in the other.

But the priest was telling him, in the most unaggressive tone, "I'm from Chicago, Illinois. In America."

Bora looked over. "I know where Chicago is."

"Ah, but do you know where Bucktown is? Milwaukee Avenue?"

"Of course not."

"'Of course'? Why 'of course'?" The priest's face stayed merry. "Consider that for most of my parishioners the important landmarks are precisely Bucktown and Trinity church, Six Corner, the memory of Father Leopold Moczygemba —"

"Are you teasing me?" Bora asked the question, but was beginning to be amused.

"No, no. Well, what I meant is – you and I would be at war if I were British, but I'm of non-belligerent nationality."

It was true enough. Bora found himself relaxing more and more, because he was in fact tired of waiting and not unhappy to make conversation.

"Who is Mother Kazimierza?" he asked.

The priest's smile broadened. "I take it you're not Catholic"

"I am Catholic, but I still don't know who she is."

"*Matka* Kazimierza – well, *Matka* Kazimierza is an institution in herself. Throughout Poland they refer to her as the 'Holy Abbess'. She has been known to foretell events in visions, and has apparent mystic and healing powers. Why, several of your commanders have already visited her."

It came to Bora's mind that Hofer left the office early every afternoon at the same time. Had he been coming to see the nun, and was he embarrassed to be driven to the convent by his chauffeur? Bora took a long look at the priest, who sat and continued to smile a cat-like smile at him. Friendly faces were not an everyday occurrence in Cracow. He thought he ought to introduce himself.

"I'm Captain Martin Bora, from Leipzig."

"And I'm Father John Malecki. I was put in charge by His Holiness of a study regarding the phenomenon of Mother Kazimierza."

"What phenomenon?"

"Why, the wounds on her hands and feet."

So. That's what the stigmata had to do with Hofer's talk. Bora was thoroughly amazed, but all he said was, "I see."

Father Malecki was adding, "I've been in Cracow these past six months. In case you were wondering, that's how I happened to find myself here when *you came.*"

It was as unadorned a way as Bora had heard anyone describe the invasion of Poland.

"Yes, Father," he spoke back with faint amusement. "We did *come.*"

Later, it was impossible for Bora not to think that the colonel had been weeping. Hofer's eyes were red when they came out into the street, and although he wore his visored cap, the congestion of his face was still noticeable. He laconically indicated that he wanted to return to headquarters. It was late in the evening, but he walked straight into his office and locked himself in.

Bora gathered his papers for the trip on the following day, and then left the building.

15 October

The muddy sides of the dead hog were already drawing green clusters of flies.

There was little shade on the isolated farm, because September had been unusually dry and the trees' shrivelled leaves afforded hardly any protection from the sun. Bushes along the unpaved roads were dusty and white as if covered by snow; there was no wind, no breath of air. The patrolling soldiers spread around in a fan, blinking in the blaze of midday.

Bora walked back to the army car trying to remind himself that this was war also, killing the livestock of those who harboured Polish army stragglers and deserters. A far cry from the excitement of winning towns house by house, door by door. It seemed to him that the glorious days were already past, and now the business of war – another month at most, no doubt – would go downhill from the exhilaration of the first three weeks. He even wondered what he'd do with himself for the remainder of his life.

On the doorstep, the farm wife was weeping into her apron. Absent-mindedly Bora listened to the interpreter remind him that seldom did a poor household butcher the hog. He leaned over to get a clipboard from the front seat of the car, and then slowly turned around to face the little man Hofer had appointed to him. Like a patient instructor, he gestured with his gloved hand to the right, where, brown on the sparse grass of a treeless incline, two bodies lay sprawled.

"Don't give me that, Hannes. Remember what's up there."

Bora's men had killed two Polish stragglers a little way up from the farm, as they ran up the mild rise after firing a few shots at the patrol.

From the arid pasture north of the house, one of the soldiers now walked back pulling a red cow by the rope around its neck. Hoofs and marching boots raised a low wake of silt on their trail, blurring the hilly horizon behind them.

The farm wife heard the sound of hoofs. She lifted her face from the apron and came running, hands outstretched, to Bora. "*Nie, nie, panie oficerze!*"

Bora pushed her back, annoyed. They were killing farmers elsewhere in Poland. She ought to be grateful that he only had these orders.

"It's a nice cow," Hannes added, to Bora's irritation.

Bora turned to the soldier. "Kill it, Private."

"Yes, sir. It's a shame, though."

Bora took his Walther out and shot the cow in the ear.

"Now burn the hay."

As the fires were set, Bora stepped away from the threshing floor. He was resentful not for the farmers, but for himself. This job was beneath soldiers: beneath *him*, at any rate; beneath soldiers like him. Quickly he climbed the incline to the place where the bodies of the two stragglers lay.

They still wore the dirt-coloured baggy clothes of the Polish army, but were barefooted. Had they flung off their ill-fitting boots in order to ease their escape? Bora thought so, by the bruised and pinched appearance of their toes.

Flies clustered on the dead men's long, drawn faces, and their pale eyes seemed to have cloudy water in them. The blue collar patches identified them as infantrymen.

Bora crouched to search their tunics for papers. He hadn't handled dead bodies since his volunteer days in Spain – the past, victorious spring of Teruel. The weight, the coldness of death surprised him anew. The flies took off from the bloody clothes, landed again. Far away, artillery shots were being fired, perhaps as far as Chrzanów. *It's hot,* he thought. *It's hot and these men no more feel it than they'll ever feel anything again, until God raises them.*

Bora found no identification disks, no documents, surely all disposed of along the way. But there was a folded photograph in one of the men's breast pockets. When Bora took it out and unfolded it, it broke in half.

By the signature, he recognized that it was a black-and-white portrait of Mother Kazimierza, standing with hands clasped in prayer. Bandages were wrapped around her hands, and dark stains were visible through the gauze padding. In the upper right corner, a crude photomontage showed an engraved heart surmounted by a flame. Around the heart a crown of thorns squeezed it until drops of blood oozed from it. A crown surmounted the heart, and from the crown a tongue of flame rose. The letters *L.C.A.N.* were printed over the flame in a semi-circle. Bora looked at the back of the photograph, and read that the letters stood for *Lumen Christi, Adiuva Nos.*

Light of Christ, succour us, indeed. Some good it'd done to the man carrying it.

Rifle shots at the foot of the incline startled him, but it was only a soldier firing in the air to keep the woman away from the burning haystack. Bora stood up, slipped the photograph into his map case and walked down.

Light of Christ. Really.

He had no sooner reached the threshing floor, than a wild, close burst of machine-gun fire sent the soldiers scattering. Bora himself dodged at random, because smoke from the haystack obstructed the view. "Watch out!" a soldier shouted, and it was seconds, fractions of seconds: shooting, smoke, dodging, the soldier's cry. Suddenly Bora made out a man's ghostly figure surging through the smoke, and fired. "Shoot!" He called out. "Shoot, men!"

Ghost-like, the armed man turned to him from the flames of collapsing hay, but Bora was quicker. Quicker than his soldiers, even. Two, three times more he shot into the smoke.

The machine gun let out a last burst, skywards. The man dropped on his knees as if a great weight had felled him, crumpling into the scented cradle of hay fire.

Right arm still extended, Bora released the trigger. "He almost did us in! Didn't you see him?" He was angry at his men, but other than that, the danger had jarred him back into a state of tight control. He even felt better because of it, as if his task here were somehow redeemed by risk. "Search the other stacks," he ordered, and for the next five minutes closely supervised the jabbing of bayonets into the smouldering hay.

Loud weeping came from the farm wife, crouched on the doorstep. Head buried in the fold of her arms, her disconsolate heap of clothes shook with fear and grief.

"Hannes, tell her to shut the hell up," Bora said. He kept his back obstinately turned to her as the soldiers went poking into the deep sluice behind the barn, behind and into a pile of manure, chasing horseflies.

At headquarters in Cracow, Colonel Hofer had a headache. He hid the letter from home under an orderly pile of maps, only so that he wouldn't be tempted to read it again, when it did no good. Again and again his eyes went to the wall clock. He tasted a surge of resentment at the thought that Army General Blaskowitz would visit at four this afternoon, when the abbess had granted him an appointment at four thirty.

He'd uselessly tried to negotiate the hour with Blaskowitz's aide, who had informed him the commander-in-chief might spend the whole afternoon in Cracow.

"You must pray much," Mother Kazimierza had warned the day before, speaking in her precise, book-learned German. "Your wife must pray much more than she does. How can Christ listen to you if you don't pray? Only uninterrupted prayer opens God's doors."

Hofer reached into the top drawer of his desk, where a booklet on spiritual exercises written by the abbess – useless to him in Polish – contained as a bookmark a small square of surgical gauze sealed in hard transparent plastic. At the centre of the gauze stood a perfectly round bloodstain.

Hofer could weep in frustration. "You may only come see me during next week, and then no more," Mother Kazimierza had told him on his way out the day before.

His heart had cringed at the words. "Why only one more week?" he'd cried out to her. "I need your prayers – why only one more week?"

The nun wanted to say no more about it. "*Laudetur Jesus Christus.*" She'd signalled to Sister Irenka to escort the visitor out, and he'd had to leave. Hofer sighed deeply at the recollection, and tears welled in his eyes. It was becoming more and more difficult to hide his emotions. Luckily, Captain Bora was naive, and hadn't noticed.

Like most men of his political generation, Bora was hard to figure out, but at least there was some traditional solidity in him, a trustworthiness that had little to do with party allegiance. He knew how to keep things to himself.

The only trouble with Bora, Hofer glumly considered, was that fortune treated him well.

Out in the country, the smell of charring flesh came from the haystack, where the flames continued to smoulder and the fermenting core of the stack burned around the body in black compact clumps like peat.

Bora looked up from his map and called to the soldiers squatting near the threshold of the farmhouse.

"For Christ's sake, pull him away from there! Can't you see the poor bastard's starting to cook?"

16 October

Bora didn't return to Cracow until Monday. He met Retz at Army Headquarters – Retz was in the Supply Service, and was now cursing over the phone about some late shipment of bedsheets – and at the end of day they drove to their apartment together.

It was a fine three-storey house on the Podzamcze, directly below the formidable bastion of the Wawel Castle. Against the pale yellow stucco, freshly painted shutters and wrought-iron balconies stood out, and from what Bora could tell, a narrow garden of evergreens lined the back of the building.

He followed Retz up two flights of stairs, to a door which the major opened on an elegant interior.

"Just our luck that we'd billet here." Retz disparagingly said, pulling back the key from the lock with an ill-humoured jerk. They'd been talking of Colonel Hofer on the way to the house, but now the very act of walking into the apartment seemed to renew his contempt for the assigned quarters. Entering ahead of Bora, he added, "Did you see what's on the door frame outside?" He referred to a small, half-torn metallic container which Bora had already noticed. It seemed to have been pried open with the point of a knife, and right now it resembled nothing but torn metal. "Do you know what that's supposed to be?"

Bora said he thought he knew.

"But do you know what it means?"

Bora looked away from the doorpost. "I think it's called a *mezuzah*. It's supposed to contain some holy script."

Retz unbuckled his belt and holster, and tossed them on a chair. "If the place weren't so nicely set up, I'm telling you, that thing would be enough to ask for relocation."

Bora hadn't yet crossed the threshold. He saw that, although the brass nameplate had been removed from the door, the family name printed under the electric bell was still readable, and it was a Jewish name.

Retz had gone into the bathroom. Through the half-open door, the sound of urine falling into the bowl could be heard. He called out to Bora over the trickling noise. "Look around – your bedroom is in the back."

Bora took his cap off. Unlike Retz, it was the first time he'd stepped into their quarters. He glanced in the direction of a room straight ahead, a carpeted parlour where the shiny corner of a grand piano was visible to him. He was soon standing in front of it, and some nimble fingering of keys followed. Retz joined him leisurely.

"So, about Hofer. You've been driving him back and forth for a week and you didn't know that his son is as good as dead? Has some dire disease, and he's only four or five years of age. Late marriage, late child – the only child. The old man has been beside himself for the past year. The doctors told him there's nothing they can do, so he lives day by day like he's the one on death row." Retz leaned with a sneer against the shiny frame of the parlour

23

door. "Well, I see *you* won't have a problem adjusting to a Yid's house." He watched Bora eagerly look through a stack of sheet music. "Why don't you play something? Can you play any of Zarah Leander's cabaret songs?"

20 October

The abbess's voice came distinctly through the door, addressing a sister no doubt, because Bora recognized the Polish word *Siostra*. Hofer stood two steps away from him in the convent's corridor, white-faced. The thin layer of sweat on his balding forehead was not justified by the temperature of late October. The outside walls of the convent were massive and successfully insulated it from the heat and cold. Warm, it was not. When Hofer nervously checked the buttons of his tunic, Bora saw his hands shake.

Because of that, and because sunny days seemed to be scarce in Cracow, Bora would much rather be outside. Careful to show no annoyance, he lifted his eyes to the closest small window filled with sky and cut out like a cloth of gold in the bare wall. The abbess kept them waiting. The open air would be cool and brisk, with plenty of light left to drive to the river past the Pauline church or beyond the bridge towards Wieliczka, something he hadn't had time to do so far. He imagined walking in the tender oblique sun through venerable streets.

Hofer addressed him harshly, with a tone of sudden strain in his voice, as if he could be harsher than this but chose to curb himself.

"You have no worries in the world, do you?"

Bora was taken aback by the words. He had tried not to look distracted, and was embarrassed. When he removed his eyes from the window, a greenish square floated in his vision after staring at the bright window. "I'm sorry, Colonel."

"That's not what I asked you."

"No, sir." Bora overheard some imperious command from the abbess beyond the closed door, still he looked at Hofer's resentful face. "I have responsibilities," he said. "And I miss being home."

"You have no worries." Hofer said it as if it were Bora's fault, with envious bitterness. He glanced at his watch, took a rigid step forwards and then returned to utter immobility, the cramped immobility of one who awaits the verdict in a physician's office. "How long do you think it's going to last?"

Bora didn't mistake what Hofer meant. "I'm sure life tries us all, sooner or later."

"Sooner or later? Sooner than you think, be sure." Above the door hung a framed lithograph of Adam and Eve in the Garden, and Hofer pointed with his head to it. "That's you, up there."

Bora urbanely turned to the picture. Adam's nakedness stood behind a providential arching branch. He looked stolid, wide-eyed, a well-built yokel to whom a flirtatious Eve was presenting a very small red apple.

"This war's going to give you the apple, Captain."

"I expect it will. Still I think I have a choice —"

"Oh, you'll bite into it. Don't you think yourself superior: when it's shown to you, you'll gobble it whole."

The noiseless turn of the door handle was followed by a rustle of black and white, and a plain-faced nun cracked the door, only enough for her to look out.

"*Pulkownike* Hofer." She invited the colonel to enter. "Please. The abbess will see you now."

"Wait in the other room," Hofer tossed the words to Bora. As he walked in, through the widening swing of the door Bora caught a glimpse of another woman in three-quarters view: a tall, starchy, regal nun, whose eyes levelled a cold look on him. Then the door closed like a denial.

Walking back to the waiting room under the escort of a nun who seemed to have materialized out of nowhere, Bora paid closer attention to the sparse images on the walls, set off by the clarity of perfectly washed, drapeless windows along the corridor. The Stations of the Cross followed one another inside black frames. At a bend of the corridor, a colourful plaster statue of Our Lady of Lourdes stood on a doily-covered wooden pedestal. Despite the solidity of the building, when Bora went by, his booted steps made the metallic stars around her halo tremble and tinkle.

Although he'd come here every day he'd spent in Cracow for the past week, Bora still couldn't figure out the ground plan of the convent. Rooms seemed to be everywhere; narrow hallways and steps leading up and down confused the visitor until one appreciated the silent, gliding presence of the nun to guide his steps.

21 October

"She was the classiest lay in Poland," Retz reminisced after work over his tilted liquor glass. Eyes on the fifteen-year-old stage magazine spread on the coffee table in their apartment, he simpered, "You haven't seen class and single-mindedness until you've see *her*. Look there."

Bora looked. It seemed that in the 1920s critics had sworn by Ewa Kowalska. Picking through the printed words of the Polish magazine, Bora understood that her rendition of Dora in *A Doll's House* was unrivalled, and men had loved her in Pirandello's *It Is So.* She displayed strength, technical self-assurance, flair, et cetera. She promised to be a Polish Sarah Bernhardt and Eleonora Duse rolled into one.

From what Bora had heard elsewhere, less than twenty years later, Ewa Kowalska didn't seem to fit the promises any more. She hadn't adapted well to changes in style and interpretation, and in the end had argued her way out of the Warsaw theatre scene. It was on the provincial stages that she could still play the prima donna, and probably only because of the war she'd found herself once more in demand in Cracow. She rounded her income by doing translations from the French on the side, but, all in all, the officers said that her flat on Święty Krzyzka was still cosy in winter and had fresh cut flowers in the summertime.

Bora listened to Major Retz speak, and was actually curious to meet her.

"I don't think she would be much interested in someone your age," Retz dismissed his interest.

Bora wouldn't argue the point. He'd already concluded from the odd array of bottles and smears on the sink that Retz dyed his hair to look younger, so he added nothing that could be interpreted as a wish to compete with him on matters of women.

Retz said, refilling his glass, "I'm meeting Frau Kowalska here next Saturday, Bora, so make sure you stay out until very late that night."

"Until what time, Major?"

"Oh, I don't know. Two, three in the morning." Retz had a meaningful grin. "I haven't seen her in twenty-one years."

Lack of an answer hinted at some unspoken doubt in the younger man. Retz felt it. He added, "I'll reciprocate, don't worry."

"I have no difficulty staying out, Major. It's the matter of security."

"'Security?'"

"Fraternization."

Retz laughed. In his mid-forties at least, strongly built, he was handsome in a coarse way, self-assured in excess of any certainty Bora felt right now.

"Because I take to bed a Polish woman? Loosen up, Captain. I know what fraternizing is, I don't need Intelligence to remind me." After gulping the drink down, Retz put his glass away, and corked the brandy flask. "By the way, how's your Polish?"

"Not good. I only know a few sentences."

"Well, you're doing better than I. Call this number and schedule me an appointment with Dr Franz Margolin, here. Of course I 'know he's Jewish', what do you think? Now that he and his kind have been brought back to Poland, I might as well take advantage of it. Jew and all, he used to be the best dentist in Potsdam."

"Won't he speak German, then?"

"I wouldn't be asking if he did, would I? Polish is what he speaks. Unless your Yiddish is better than your Polish, stick to Polish. Tell him I have a cavity or two to take care of."

Bora had no idea what the Polish word for cavity might be. He dialled the operator, and managed to ask for the dentist's office. The phone rang long and empty. Bora was about to hang up when finally a woman's voice answered.

"*Margolin? Jego niema w domu. Kiedy on wraca? Nie, nie moge odpowiedzéc na to pytanie. Nie wiem kiedy.*"

"*Nie rozumiem,*" Bora said in return, because he hadn't understood a thing except that Margolin wasn't in. It took ten minutes of mutual explanation for him to realize that Margolin was not expected back at his house or office ever.

"Just my fucking luck." Retz disappointedly slapped his knee. "Now I'll have to go to one of our military hacks. Do you realize how inconvenient it is to walk around with two cavities?"

Bora, who had no cavities, didn't think it was the time to say so.

23 October

In his rented room on Karmelicka Street, Father Malecki awoke from his afternoon nap with the anxious impression that he shouldn't have fallen asleep. Heart pounding, his eyes opened on the green striped rectangle of the shuttered window and he could tell by the amount of light filtering through the slats that it was past four o'clock.

Holding his breath, he tried to control the palpitation in his chest. It wasn't like him to wake up in a cold sweat, especially when he hadn't even had a nightmare. He sat up, reaching for his wristwatch on the bedstand.

Four thirty-five. He yawned, slipped the metal band around his wrist and stretched. Why did he feel that he was late for something? There wasn't much for him to do until this evening, when he'd join the sisters at the convent for vespers.

The sting of anxiety made no sense. Malecki drank a sip of water to wet his dry mouth. He hadn't felt such discomfort since the arrival of the Germans in Poland. Sure, news every day managed to make him sad and appalled in turn, impotent before the excess of violence, but this was no vicarious anguish.

The room was quiet. The ticking of a clock just outside his door was all that broke the silence until Malecki left the bed and the springs moaned under the mattress. His heart no longer pounded, and maybe it was just a matter of giving up coffee, or going back to a decent brand of American cigarettes if he could find them on the market.

He went to open the window, and looked down the narrow old street. There was no traffic. A German army truck slowly rode in from the centre of town. Malecki turned his back to the sill, frowning. It was no use blaming coffee or cigarettes. The anxiety was still here, noxiously lodged at the pit of his stomach.

In the armchair, as in a fat lady's lap, his clergyman's vestments lay limp. Malecki put them on and began buttoning them. The idea of calling the convent bobbed up in him and he discounted it at once. How could he even think of it? There was no telephone there, and at any rate he had nothing to tell the sisters.

Disturbed by the movement of cloth, dust motes danced around him in the light that sliced across his room.

He sat at the narrow desk by the bed and tried to read his breviary. Words skipped about under his eyes, confusing the lines until he closed the book. He then began writing a letter to his sister in Carbondale, but didn't even get halfway through that. Finally he opened the door of his room and called out to the landlady.

"*Pana* Klara, is there anything in the news?"

Just then, in the east end of the Old City, Bora knew he'd have trouble parking in front of the convent. He'd barely stopped by the kerb to let Hofer out, when a growing din of steel chains and engines filled the opposite end of the street. With the car still running in idle, he craned his neck out of the window to see.

Tanks. Could anyone be as dim-witted as to do this? There was no room in this narrow street for tanks to operate. Still, jangling and rumbling on cobblestones, panzers blundered towards him from the curve ahead, where the front steps of a Jesuit church further reduced the sidewalk. Dinosaur-like, they emerged in a stench of fuel, rattling lamp posts and windows and the rear-view mirror in Bora's car. Whatever asinine thinking had made them choose this route, on they came, blind and dumb as all machines appear when their drivers are invisible, seemingly unaware that the sharp corner facing them would pose an obstacle.

Judiciously Bora drove the car onto the sidewalk, and for the next five minutes he was as much part of the deafening manoeuvring, backing up and squeezing past as the tanks themselves.

The last cumbersome vehicle was still churning the corner with its mammoth flank when Hofer unexpectedly stumbled out of the convent door. Seeing him stagger on the sidewalk caused Bora to rush from the car, sure of a partisan attack. By the time the grey-faced Hofer made some frantic gesture for help, Bora was already by him. Pistol in hand, he straddled in a protective stance, turned to the street as if the unseen danger should come from there.

"Inside – inside!" Hofer's choked voice found a way out of the cavern of his mouth. He rudely pushed the younger man ahead of himself into the dark vestibule.

For a moment it seemed to Bora that flimsy ghosts were milling around him, gowned and wailing. Then he recognized it was the nuns, whispering and sobbing in their incomprehensible language.

Hofer kept pushing him, and they hastily crossed plain rooms, past black crosses, long tables, starched linen, chairs, a hallway, steps, and then a green burst of light and the odour of watered dirt.

They were standing at the edge of the cloister. A perfectly square overcast sky opened above, and the different greens of small trees and potted plants crowded the view on all sides.

"Look, Bora!"

Mother Kazimierza lay face down by the well at the paved centre of the garden, arms spread to the sides, face turned away from the viewer. Part of her wimple showed white. That, and the black robe gathered around her legs, made her look like a strange, overgrown swallow, felled from a great height. ⎯⎯

From under her tall body a thread-like red line had come snaking in the grout between the bricks, to the edge of the paved area. The long, sinuous ribbon seemed to reach out for the men and women standing at a distance. Past the edge of bricks, it had been absorbed by the moist dirt, like a river that disappears into porous soil.

Bora lowered his gun.

To his left, pressing both hands on her mouth, one of the young novices began to shake convulsively, but would not weep. When a breath of unseasonably cold wind swept over the cloister, round yellow leaves, no larger than coins, rained in from the trees outside. No coherent sounds came from the staring group until Hofer stammered to himself, glassy-eyed.

"She's dead, she's dead – the saint is dead."

With his eyes, Bora followed the trail of blood to the lacy edge it formed at his feet. It had already happened to him in Aragon, two summers ago. The dirt had drunk it all, but small black ants were racing towards it, and back and forth surveyed the bank of what must be a nourishing, drying river bed to their infinitesimal size.

2

25 October

"What is your professional opinion of Colonel Hofer's state of health?"

SS Captain Salle-Weber stood planted behind the colonel's desk like a roughly hewn, insignia-strewn tree. Bora looked ahead of himself rather than directly at him.

"I have only served with the colonel two weeks, *Hauptsturmführer.* As a subordinate, my opinion is by necessity limited, perhaps even irrelevant."

Salle-Weber had Bora's folder in front of him. He glanced through it. "How long have you been a captain, Captain?"

"Three weeks."

"Well, you're a big boy now. Leave aside the matter of hierarchy and give me a dispassionate assessment of your commander. We wouldn't ask if we didn't feel it were relevant."

"I believe the colonel is under great stress."

"Aren't we all?"

"He has personal reasons, I'm sure you know."

"All I know is that he's got no nerve."

Bora glanced at Salle-Weber, and then once more ahead of himself. "He must have *some* nerve, given that he volunteered for Spain two years ago."

"What of it? So did you and a shipload of airmen. So did Schenck, and even your jug-headed interpreter."

"Well, then. With all that we're in hostile territory, Colonel Hofer doesn't bother to carry a gun, unlike you and I. How's that for nerve?"

"That's not nerve. It's idiocy." With pretended indifference Salle-Weber opened the top drawer of Hofer's desk, started rummaging with his hand in it. He pulled the prayer book out. There was a packet of letters, and he took those out as well.

Bora followed his movements with a needling sense of being personally intruded upon. "Is this an investigation?"

"Just answer the questions, Captain. Hofer had a total breakdown two days ago, and this is hardly anything we can afford in the middle of a campaign. You were with him when he took sick, so be good and report accurately on it."

Bora did.

Salle-Weber listened in silence, without taking notes, keeping his eyes nailed on the younger man. "You're an observant fellow," he said in the end, not in the way of admiration but acknowledging the fact. "It's a virtue, you know." He finally removed his eyes – like Bora, he was green-eyed, but the measure of eagerness was different in his glance – and put Hofer's things back into the drawer. "What's the nun to him? What did he expect to gain from visiting her every day?"

"She had the reputation of being a saint."

Salle-Weber laughed. "A stone-dead one! There's no such thing as saints in Germany today."

"We're not in Germany."

"There's no such thing as saints in the *General Government* either."

"I said she 'had the reputation', *Hauptsturmführer.*"

"Well, good enough. Don't go anywhere after work tonight: I want you back here to give me a detailed account of what you saw when the body was discovered."

Bora resigned himself to the thought. "What will happen to Colonel Hofer?" he asked before leaving the office.

"Oh, he'll return to work when he gets his nerve back. We'll have you keep an eye on him from now on, how's that?" Salle-Weber locked the top drawer of Hofer's desk with a key, which he pocketed. "Your interim commander is Lieutenant Colonel Emil Schenck, and I believe he has orders for you already."

Halfway across town, Father Malecki walked back from the American consulate in a despondent frame of mind. He'd just wired the Vatican the news of the abbess's death and would be back this afternoon to hear the official reply. The shock of her death was still with him, nearly forty-eight hours after the fact. With the removal of the reason for his presence in Poland, everything was tilted off centre. Thinking ahead fatigued him, and he refrained from it.

He glumly walked down Franciszkańska and then took a narrow, winding street to reach the convent church, whose façade opened on the sidewalk with a flight of baroque marble steps. He'd been saying mass here every day since the titular priest had volunteered for the army, and had gone the way of thousands of prisoners of war.

He didn't expect to find a German army car parked in front of the entrance. There was a driver waiting in the front seat, so he realized an officer must be inside. Atop the flight of stairs, in a recess of the pilaster-flanked portal, a soldier stood with submachine gun slung on his stomach.

Even before crossing, Malecki decided not to attempt to go directly past him. He had in his pocket the key to one of the side doors, and without so much as pausing on the sidewalk he continued down the street, took the next perpendicular alley and approached the church from behind.

*

"Ewa?" The red-haired girl stuck her head inside the dressing room they shared in the city theatre. "Can I come in?"

"Come."

"Someone left a card for you. Here it is."

With both hands carefully pulling the silk stocking up her leg, Ewa Kowalska wouldn't risk a rash movement. "Open it and read it to me. Who's it from?"

The girl held it out for her to see that the address had been typed. "I don't know," she said with a little smile. "But the private who delivered it isn't wearing a Polish uniform."

"Don't be a prude, Kasia. Read it to me."

Kasia ripped the envelope and looked inside. Her heart-shaped mouth pouted. "Oh, crap. It's written in German."

The church by the convent was empty of worshipers. Bora was blushing, but did not stop doing what he'd begun, namely taking the open missals one by one and ripping out the page with the hymn *God Who Saved Poland.*

Father Malecki watched in impotent anger, while the sexton twisted his hands. "*Jaka szkoda, jaka szkoda,*" he moaned. "What a pity!"

Bora threw the missals into a pile, resentfully. "I was told that you had a whole week to get rid of this page, and you didn't. Now I have to do this."

Malecki kept his temper under control. "Did you expect me to tear pages out of a missal?"

"You had specific instructions to do so! It's not going to do you any good to refuse us collaboration. If the song is sung tomorrow, we'll close the church down."

Malecki swallowed an improvident word, by force. He could see that the German would carry out orders, and there was no speaking sense to him just now. The missals fell one after the other, some landing open, others bouncing on their edges. Like red-and-black serpent tongues the bookmark ribbons flicked out from the pages.

Malecki began retrieving the missals and stacking them behind the soldier who handed them open to Bora. When Bora had nearly finished, he started gathering the crumpled pages as well. With a thud, the spur-clad boot landed close to his hand.

"Leave those alone, Father. We take *those* along."

Malecki did not pull his hand back, still holding on to the one page. He didn't look up at Bora. His eyes stayed on the sheen of black leather. "Surely there are things an officer of your upbringing could be doing other than this, Captain."

Bora dropped the last missal at his feet, and stepped back.

At his command, the soldier swept all the crumpled papers inside a canvas bag. Malecki stood slowly, and confronted Bora's hand extended towards him.

"Do not force me to pry your hand open, Father."

Malecki opened his hand. Bora picked the torn paper from it, and gave it to the soldier. Politeness of demeanour and voice belied his resolve to intimidate, but he said, "You know nothing about my upbringing, Father Malecki. And my upbringing has nothing to do with the things I have to do."

28 October

At noon on Saturday, Salle-Weber blasphemed in the receiver.

"Where?" He stretched the telephone cord to reach the map of Cracow on the wall opposite his desk. "Where the hell is that? Oh, I see it, I see it now. Why, how many? Was it our own or was it the army? Well, I should have known! How can you tell me an SS platoon was caught off guard? And in the presence of army officers, too!"

The incident did not elicit such anger in the army hospital, where army surgeon Lieutenant Colonel Nowotny was about to go to lunch. Leaving his office, he caught sight of the army officer waiting a few steps away in the corridor. There was a prodigious amount of blood on his face and collar, and down the front of his uniform.

Nowotny decided to delay his lunch. "This way, Captain." He hooked his forefinger to invite him in. "Let's take a look. Did you get X-rayed?"

Bora said he had.

After flashing a light in his eyes to check the reaction of both pupils, especially concerned with the left one, Nowotny wiped with cotton and looked inside Bora's right ear for evidence of internal bleeding. Bora winced.

"Well, you drove yourself here and walked on your own two legs, so you're not as badly off as you could be. Do you remember what happened?"

Bora told him, complying with the physician's request to hold out his hands. Nodding, Nowotny leaned over him. A robust, greying man, with healthy skin and a careless five-o'clock shadow, he had good humour written on his face, in his warm, dark eyes. And if powerful noses mean character, he enjoyed a no-nonsense, prepossessing one.

"Shake my hand. Now with the other hand. All right. Look straight at me. Follow my finger with your eyes." As if the nature of the incident struck him as humorous just now, Nowotny began to laugh. "All I can say for you is that you must be from Prussia or Saxony, judging by the hardness of your skull. It's a miracle if it didn't crack. It sure bled enough."

Bora said nothing. He had switched to a pain-control mode during the probing and cleaning of the wound behind his ear, while Nowotny chatted about how handy it was that German haircuts made it unnecessary for him to shave the skin.

"It's a good-sized hole, and the edges have retracted. You're going to need stitches, so it'll sting a bit. What were you doing, were you in the middle of a 'spontaneous manifestation of welcome'?" Bora looked up as much as he could, irritably, and got his head pushed back down for it. "Stay put." Blood started pouring again, and Bora had to cup his hands to keep it from soiling his breeches.

"I hope you won't consider yourself a casualty because of this."

"I don't consider myself a casualty."

Nowotny handed him a cloth to wipe his face, and continued his work. "So, who throws rocks at German officers?"

"I don't know. It hit me from behind. I didn't see who did it – there was plenty of rock throwing."

"Were there arrests?"

"Yes, there were arrests."

While they waited for the X-rays to be brought in, Nowotny washed his hands in the sink, looking over his shoulder as Bora put his tunic back on.

"So, have you been playing the piano for many years?"

"Since I was five. How did you know?"

"I heard you play the other night, during the reception at Headquarters. Schumann, wasn't it?"

"From his concerto in A minor."

"You have a gift." Nowotny nodded with his head towards the sink, for Bora to wash up. "I can tell piano hands when I see them. You have a good span, good muscle control. I'd give my left hand to play Schumann the way you do

– but then I wouldn't turn out to be much of a pianist, would I?"

Bora dried his hands before buckling his belt. After a knock on the door, a nurse peered in with the mottled images of the X-rays in hand. Nowotny held them against the light for some moments, attentively looking at them. He shook his head afterwards.

"Well! I guess you got close to getting a wound badge after all. Your skull is fractured." He pointed at a serpentine line on the hindmost quarter of the temporal bone. "There isn't much we can do about it, save giving you painkillers for the time it starts hurting in earnest." He handed Bora a small bottle. "Call me if you need more than this to sleep at night. Otherwise come back a week on Friday and we'll have the stitches out."

At Bora's entrance that evening, Retz stared.

"What the hell?…" He averted his face from Bora's bloody uniform, and wouldn't let him finish explaining. "Take it off, take it off! It looks awful, take the damn thing off!"

He heard Bora walk to the bathroom and turn on the water in the sink.

"Wash the sink after you're done!" he cried out after him. "I hate the fucking sight of blood, and don't want it there while I shave!"

Bora changed before joining the major in the living room. He now noticed that there were flowers in a vase, and a bottle of wine on ice.

"That's better," Retz said. "Do you remember what day of the week this is?"

"Yes, I know. I'll stay out until late, Major." Bora was beginning to have an atrocious headache, but added nothing to what he had said. He sat in the armchair and rested his shoulders against the padded back of it. When he closed his eyes, fragmentary images of the incident down the street from the convent flashed before him. A meat-chewing animal seemed to eat in spasms at the right of his head.

Retz wouldn't look at him. "Well, you obviously expect to be asked. What's happened to you?"

Bora told him.

"You don't say! What did we do about it?"

"The SD shot five men against the wall of the Jesuit church."

"Well, thank God for the SD."

Bora opened his eyes. Major Retz was turning the bottle inside the ice bucket. "*Schloss Vollrads*, 1935 vintage. She's worth it."

Making leverage on the back of the armchair, Bora turned to leave the room. He was groggy with blood loss and beginning to feel nauseous. Retz's impatient glance at his watch didn't help. "I'll be out of here in a moment, Major," he said. "Just the time to wash my face in cold water one more time and figure out where I'm going to spend seven hours."

"You should have thought about it earlier!"

"Yes, Major."

Five minutes later, Retz hammered with his fist on the bathroom door. "What the hell are you doing, Bora? Are you throwing up in my damn bathroom?"

Bora was too sick to talk back. He held on to the rim of the toilet bowl with both hands, and his icy, clammy forehead on them.

"Hurry up, and wipe it clean afterwards!"

Bora had to give in to another heave of sputum before shakily lifting his head to answer the insistent hammering.

"Goddamn it, Major – will you let me vomit in peace?"

*

The wire from the Vatican, signed by the Secretary of State, instructed Malecki to remain in Cracow until further notice, and collaborate with any official investigation into the abbess's death.

Father Malecki lit himself a cigarette. It was a German brand he'd obtained through the landlady's son, a pale yellow five-count pack marked *Sondermischung*, with an Army seal. Collaborate with the investigation. It was more easily said than done. In the confusion following the incident he'd been unable to determine if Polish authorities would be involved in the case. German cars were cordoning off the convent when he'd arrived for vespers on Monday, and although he'd seen neither Hofer nor Bora he'd been told by Sister Irenka that they were inside.

She'd expounded on the tragedy at length. "The colonel's in a terrible state," she'd added. "He passed out in the waiting room and the young captain had to all but lift him off the floor. We're terrified at the thought that we'll be blamed for his getting sick, as if losing the abbess weren't enough!"

Five days later, Malecki knew no more about it, and they hadn't been able to assist him at the Curia or at the consulate either. The news had been kept from the local press, but was starting to circulate by word of mouth. He worried about the notebooks on Mother Kazimierza he'd left in the library of the convent; they were written in English, of course, but Bora spoke it like a native.

And Mother Kazimierza, Mother Kazimierza – killed by gunfire in the enclosure of her own cloister! There was something more terrible than just death in this. Hard-faced, Malecki rested the cigarette on the edge of the window sill. Murder. It was murder, naturally. He shook his head in anger. What's natural about murder? And would the Germans – biased, heartless killers in their own right – be the ones to investigate this murder?

Without eating his food, Bora sat at the table in the smoke-filled restaurant as long as he could, and then walked out, up the stairs to the street level.

The fresh air of the night was actually edging towards the cold of winter. It'd be raining and sleeting soon, he could smell it in the air. The temperature and grey skies of Cracow were much like Leipzig. It'd soon sleet in Leipzig, too. There were no stars out, or else they were cancelled by the glare of street lights.

Laughter and voices loudly speaking German came from the restaurant behind him like from some happy nether region. Bora stood on the sidewalk breathing the night air as one drinks water.

He doubted he could drive himself home. His head pounded with blinding intensity, but it was mostly the medication Nowotny had given him that lowered his alertness. The phosphorescent hands of his wristwatch indicated only eleven o'clock. Christ, he thought, that was all – eleven o'clock. He had no idea what he'd do for the next four hours.

Against his better sense, he got in the car and drove out of the Old City, straight past the river. It was his intention to go to Wieliczka, but he missed the left turn and found himself well on his way to the mountain resort of Zakopane before an army patrol halted him at a roadblock. Bora didn't argue with the soldiers' reasons for stopping him. He backed up the car to the shoulder of the road, and turned the motor off.

The soldiers were a little surprised that an officer would choose this place to sleep off a hangover, but wouldn't do more than wonder.

Jewish forced labour were washing the side of the Jesuit church when Malecki passed by the next morning, bound for mass at the convent. This church and the larger complex of the convent stood at the two ends of the same narrow street, as if to bless its length.

With brushes and buckets steaming in the cold air, old men with armbands scrubbed the bloodstains of yesterday's execution from the tender pastel colour of the stucco wall. Soapy, reddish trickles of water already ran off the basalt kerb of the sidewalk into the drain. SD soldiers stood guard. Malecki thought they'd ask him for papers, and went as far as getting them out of his wallet. They didn't ask, but with a tight heart he walked past the silent work detail.

Novices were singing in the small chapel when he arrived at the convent. Their high-pitched, thin voices travelled the vaulted spaces of hallways and rooms like ghosts of sound.

The nuns flocked to him. They told him they'd heard the shots of the improvised firing squad and had feared for him.

"No, no, I was in church," Malecki reassured them. He followed Sister Irenka to the room where the coffin was still laid, and asked to be left alone to pray.

At the same time, across town, Bora turned the key in the lock, opened the door and listened for noises from the interior of the apartment. The radio blared some inane little song that went, *Nur du, nur du, nur du.* Noise of rushing water in the bathroom meant the shower was on. The door to Retz's bedroom was ajar, but the shutters in it were still folded.

Without moving from the vestibule, Bora tried to sense if anyone else was in the apartment with Retz. His head had considerably cleared overnight, and other than that he was sore for having uncomfortably slept in the car, he felt rather well. He sniffed the air, as if he could tell the presence of a woman by it. Ewa Kowalska would have to have worn a pint of perfume for him to detect it through the smell of stale smoke. The rush of water stopped.

Bora closed the door noisily, and at once Retz's voice came from the bathroom. "Is it you, Bora? What kept you so long?"

A surge of anger went through Bora, so that the pain in his temple awoke and startled him. "I'd like to take a bath when you're done, Major."

The gurgle of the bathtub drain preceded Retz's coming out of the bathroom. Stark naked, he was pink-bodied and thick around the waist, with much blondish hair on his chest and groin. He was vigorously rubbing his head with a towel.

"You'll have to wait a couple of hours, I've just finished the last of the hot water."

Cursing under his breath, Bora walked to the living room, where the ice bucket was filled with water and the bottle beside it sat empty among glasses on the coffee table. Cushions had been bunched on one side of the sofa; on the other, a wet bath towel lay twisted, and was darkening with moisture the fabric below. Retz's boots, his breeches and shorts formed a trail on the floor between the table and the door. On the gramophone cabinet, a record was still on the turntable, but the radio was no longer blaring, *Nur du.*

Bora waited until Retz poured himself a brandy and went to dress, before picking up the towel with two fingers. Stepping towards the window to open it, he knocked over one more drinking glass with his foot, and heard it circle around itself on the floor. As morning light poured in through the wide-open panes, he stooped to pick up the glass, closely inspected it for breakage, leaned over and threw it in the street below.

30 October

When Lieutenant Colonel Schenck came to see him privately after lunch, Hofer knew already that he had been replaced in his job. He harboured no resentment towards the wiry, youthful Schenck, and made it clear from the start.

"So, you're my successor," he mildly addressed him. "It was a good choice, I heard of your record."

Schenck was polite. He wouldn't sit down, wouldn't discuss Hofer's breakdown, but did say he'd come to talk over the death at the convent.

"As you know, we successfully kept the local police from the case. You understand we needn't add to the complications of military rule by allowing a religious hysteria to build up around this." He said the words with eyes averted, not wanting to give Hofer the impression that he was speaking about him, though Hofer understood it anyway. "Frankly, my first impulse was to sandbag the entire incident, but I realize this is a hard-line Catholic country, and General Blaskowitz advises that we make an effort to show concern. It is out of the question to allow Polish authorities to delve into this, all the more since we do not know which direction the inquiry might take – *who* the culprit was." Schenck extracted a personnel folder from his portfolio. "You have a young officer under your command, new to Intelligence but well-schooled, with a brilliant record in combat so far, and a little too gifted to be used just to lead a company over a trench." Schenck handed the file to Hofer, who nodded in acknowledgement of the contents. "Personally, I like the fact that he struck the *Adelsprädikat* from his name. We needn't be reminded of titles or ancestral privileges in a modern army. I intend to assign the case to him, and unless you know details about his nature that would make him unfit for the job, he'll start working at it as of tomorrow."

Hofer gave back the folder. "I have no objections. I'd probably have done the same. I only hope you will not take him altogether away from the field."

"Oh, no." Schenck straightened to his full skinny length, smiling. "Young mules do best with heavy loads."

A few streets away, Kasia laughed too much to keep the eye pencil straight, and smudged the thin arch of her left brow. "And he's gained weight, too?"

Ewa Kowalska embraced her shoulders. She threw a critical look at the mirror, although the diffused light in the back of the dressing room made her face look taut and attractive.

"He's still a good lover, if he doesn't drink too much."

Kasia's eyes met hers. After unscrewing the top of a rather worn stick of lip rouge, she rubbed her forefinger on it and then dabbed her cheekbones with it, sucking in her lips in to mark the blush zone. "It's easy to laugh, but I almost envy you. German officers make good money."

"Money has nothing to do with it."

"Then what does, nostalgia?"

Ewa shrugged, without letting go of her shoulders. "I don't know. Power."

"Power?"

"There's power in it – in getting a man back."

"Is he married?"

"Yes. No children, but he's married. His wife's a sow."

Kasia laughed again. "Did he tell you that, or did you see a picture of her?"

"Neither. But I'm sure she's just a sow. Most women are stupid sows."

"Well, Ewusia! Where does that leave *me*?"

Ewa came up to Kasia's chair and embraced her. "Not you, darling. But you know that most of them are."

1 November

Father Malecki didn't say what first came to his mind. He looked at Bora standing at the other end of the convent waiting room, and had to make an effort not to bring up the issue of the torn missals.

Bora was leafing through a loosely bound typescript, but his eyes were on the American priest. There was a stern, challenging look on his face, unless of course it was a form of defensiveness.

"I was assigned to this investigation, Father Malecki. I didn't ask for it."

"Oh, I understand that."

Because the priest's eyes stayed on the document, Bora made a point of continuing to scan each page quickly. "Some utterances of the holy abbess were politically significant."

Malecki kept a straight face. Today Poland had been officially incorporated into the Reich, and he had to be prudent. He was especially careful not to stare at the sutured wound on Bora's head. "Their interpretation was, anything can be made of oracular responses."

"I'd say that 'Cross-marked flags from the West' identifies us rather clearly, Father. What amazes me is that she referred to 'The Round City and the Ram' as leaders of the flags. Our army commanders are in fact von Rundstedt and Bock. It's remarkable that she said this as far back as a year ago."

"Well, I see that the good sisters have given you my notes. What do you think of them?"

"Technically, that your typewriter has a defective 'R'. You have consistently tried to avoid words with 'R' whenever possible: 'Might' instead of 'power', 'benevolence' instead of 'charity' or 'mercy'. From the theological viewpoint, I would not hazard comments – I don't know enough about mysticism. Judging by your scepticism, though, I'd say you attended a Jesuit university. Wasn't it St Ignatius who said, 'No novelties'?"

Malecki grinned in spite of himself. Sunken in his broad face, the bright blue eyes revealed the quick labour of his mind. "I did attend Loyola University, and I *am* a Jesuit."

Bora didn't smile back. "I had some Jesuit teachers, but you know us Germans – our Catholicism has a monkish bent. And I'm not much for compromises, even though I can relate to the obedience and discipline of a 'soldier of Christ'."

"Well, that's that. What will you do now?"

By a questioning gesture of his head Bora asked for permission to take along the typescripts. Since he was already placing them in his briefcase, Malecki could only nod in acceptance. "I have to go back to work now. If you care to walk me out, Father, I'll ask you a few questions."

2 November

Doctor Nowotny didn't expect Bora back so soon. He asked him how the wound was coming along, and lectured him when he heard of the nausea.

"You should have called me at once about that. Don't you know that vomit can be a very serious sign after a head injury? It could have been the build up of intracranial pressure."

"Obviously it wasn't, Colonel. The reason why I'm here has nothing to do with my head." Bora spoke for perhaps five minutes, during which the physician listened on the edge of his chair, half-intrigued and half-amused. When he could no longer keep the curiosity to himself, he interrupted.

"So, what's with this sainted nun, other than she'd dead? Do we have the body, at least?"

"No."

"Well, we'll need the body."

Bora had a frustrated look on his face. "It won't be easy to have it released to us. I tried for the past two days, and got nowhere."

"How high did you go?"

"I called at the Curia. The archbishop refused even to see me."

"Well, how high did you go on our side?"

"I'm expecting to hear from General Blaskowitz's staff this afternoon."

Nowotny grunted. "Hans Frank is the one you want to go to."

Bora didn't answer. He let the issue fall, with a stern setting of lips. Nowotny couldn't say if the reaction was due to his dispensing with Frank's title of Governor General, or because Bora didn't care to follow that avenue; he put a cigarette in his mouth and let it dangle from his lips.

Bora sat with stock-still rigidity. Nowotny smoked Muratti's. He was now studiously standing the long, flat cigarette box on end at the centre of his desk.

"This is an official investigation, Captain. Without the body…" Nowotny flicked his finger at the box, and the box fell over.

"I know. I'll try again."

"It's been twelve damn days. Unless she's like Jesus Christ and has got up and walked off, you had better get the dead nun here before too much longer."

An hour later, Father Malecki said he certainly didn't have the authority to have the body exhumed. Bora had a drumming headache, and grew angry.

"I don't understand why you have to be so reticent. All courtesy has been extended to the sisters so far, and you're giving me some lip service about authority! I could get the SS involved and *have* you give me the body."

Malecki felt it was an empty threat, and tightened his jaw. "Apparently you will have to do just that."

As it turned out, at the SS command north-west of the Old City, *Hauptsturmführer* Salle-Weber didn't seem interested at first, but eventually began paying attention to what Bora was telling him.

"Well, that's a good one! I'd just like to know what the nun did, that someone put a bullet through her."

"None of us know. That's why I've come."

"To get the muscle to enter the nunnery, eh?"

"Yes. The sisters have dispensation to bury their own in the vault of the chapel."

"Now then!" Salle-Weber rocked on the soles of his shiny boots for some time. "Are you sure you don't have other reasons to want to get in?"

"What other reasons could I possibly have?"

"That's what I'm asking. What should any of us care about a Polack nun? We'll end up having to kill a few in time. Maybe there's something worthwhile in the nunnery that the Army knows about."

"I know of no such thing."

"Precious manuscripts, holy vessels – hidden Jews?" Salle-Weber smirked at Bora's impatience. "Well, then? The novices, maybe."

"I'm not interested in those either."

Fists on his sides, Salle-Weber stepped to the wall map of Cracow. "Only because I'm curious, Bora. We'll get you the dead nun."

"What methods will you use to enter?"

"That's none of your business. We'll handle things our way. Just wait outside with an army ambulance, and I promise you, you'll have the carcass before this evening."

Seen from behind on the sidewalk, the girl had a nice round crupper, and very nice calves even in her cotton stockings. Retz pulled in close to the kerb and rolled down his window.

"*Dzien dobry,*" he greeted her gallantly. "May I offer you a ride?"

The girl didn't answer. She stopped, however, and gave him the impression of debating with herself whether she would accept.

"Thank you," she said in fairly good German. "You could take me to work, maybe?"

Retz opened the car door for her. "Sure, come right in. Just tell me where, darling."

She gave him the address. He looked at her legs and started the car. A mischievous hostility lined her smile when he asked, "What sort of place do you work in?"

She moved his hand away from her knee. "A busy one, Major. The city morgue."

*

52

At the convent, Father Malecki rushed out of the main door in a distracted manner. He looked around and saw the German staff car and the ambulance next to it. Bora rolled up his window in the time it took the priest to come striding from the threshold to the car.

Bora let him fret for some time, but when his driver asked if he wanted him to remove the priest, he said, "No, no," and came out of the car.

Within moments he was arguing with the American. "Well, you could have given us the body the easy way! I told you we needed it."

"Do you know what the penalty is for those who break church rules by forcing their way into a convent?"

"I doubt very much that the German SS worry about excommunication."

"I'm talking about you: *you* are Catholic!"

"And if you notice, I haven't entered the convent. If I were you, Father, I'd go back inside and see how things are coming along."

It took two hours, and it was Salle-Weber who came out first, followed by two of his men. He had red spots on his face and was short of breath.

"Why the devil did you get me involved in this, Bora? There's no damn body in there!" He ignored Bora's attempt to say something. "The coffin's empty, and so's the wall hole in the vault. We checked the place from top to bottom – huge, damn place it is, too. Kitchen, refectory, cells, the garden, attic, cellar, church, chapel – I don't know what in hell they did with a rotting nun, and I don't care if they shoved her down the latrine at this point!"

Bora took a sideways look at Father Malecki. He stood a few steps away and might not have understood the exchange, but bore an indefinable expression that seemed to him one of relief.

It seemed impossible, but an idea made its way into Bora's mind. "Where were the other nuns?" he asked the SS.

"They all flocked to kneel before the altar, the geese. The chapel was packed with them. The coffin was in the vault all right, but the damn body was not."

"And they were all kneeling?"

"Yes, yes! All kneeling, that's what I said!"

Bora would not remove his glance from the priest. He told Salle-Weber, slowly, "You should have asked all the nuns to stand up."

Salle-Weber blasphemed, and was gone again. This time Bora followed him in.

4 November

Nowotny laughed when he heard the story. "They pulled the dead nun out of the coffin and got her to kneel among them? What precious hypocrites these holy folks are!"

"I'm really interested in the preliminary results of your examination, Herr *Oberstleutnant*."

"Sure. Here it is." Nowotny handed him a form, handwritten in minute Gothic script, resembling chicken scratches on the page. "It was a Polish bullet that did her in. Pierced the left lung from a few feet away, and lodged right in the heart. Death was instantaneous, though by now we can't pinpoint the time of death." Nowotny grinned, placing the bullet on his desk. "I'm going to play with it for a while – the body, that is – to see about these stigmata and the *miraculous* phenomenon of its reasonably incorrupted and pliable state after two weeks. If I had the time and the equipment, I'd take a good look at her brain to see what was in it that was so holy."

Bora stared at the bit of metal, then put it in his pocket along with Nowotny's form. "We already have an official protest from the archbishop. I'm afraid we have to give the body back at once."

At Headquarters, since Hofer had come to move his things from the commander's office, Colonel Schenck invited him to hear Bora's first report. Hofer sat through it with his head in his hands, listlessly following what was being said.

"It's true that no weapons were retrieved so far, but the convent is a large complex of buildings, and there are more nooks and crannies than one can count. No shell casing has turned up in the cloister or in the upper balconies around it. In any case, I found out that on the morning of the day the abbess was killed, there were outsiders in the convent."

"What do you mean?"

Bora turned to Schenck, who had asked the question. "It seems that a stray bomb had damaged the roof of the chapel during the invasion, so workers were called in to repair it. I doubt very much that we can trace them now, but I'll do my best."

Schenck made a wry face. "Ha. So, there's a chance that Polish workers killed a *saint*."

Bora could see the words annoyed Hofer, and was careful to defuse the tension.

"Whom else do we have to suspect, Colonel? 'Everybody in the convent *loved* the abbess,' the nuns tell me. Father Malecki doesn't seem to have been wholly convinced of her mystic powers, but I doubt his Jesuit scepticism would bring him to kill her. Besides, he wasn't in the convent at the time of her death."

"They could have shot her from the outside," Schenck suggested. "After all there are tall buildings around the convent."

"I'll do the rounds of the neighbourhood, to see from where a shot could have been fired. However, the bullet entered her chest straight on. Hardly the angle that would suggest a shot fired from a distant vantage point."

Hofer, who'd been slouching, sat bolt upright, as if words said before were just now reaching him. "What do you mean, the priest doesn't believe in her mystic powers?"

"Well, he's an investigator in his own right – he shouldn't be biased to begin with."

"But disbelieving is a bias all the same. What do *you* believe, Bora?"

Bora knew Schenck was curious to hear the answer as much as Hofer was, and weighed his words. "I don't know. I don't think it's important what I believe about the abbess. The German command wants to know who killed her, and I'm trying to figure it out."

"But you must believe in miracles if you're Catholic!"

Schenck inwardly smiled when Bora kept silent.

3

Colonel Hofer's departure was as quick as it had been predictable. Bora went to see him off at the Cracow Glowny station on Tuesday. He was himself on his way north to question ethnic Germans on their complaints about violence by retreating Polish troops.

Hofer seemed to appreciate Bora's presence. Pale but composed, he let his bitterness through by commenting on how a "hair-line crack causes the whole pot to be thrown away".

"I hate to say I'll be better off in Germany, Bora. I know how your generation hankers to expand. I don't expect you to understand."

"Colonel, did the abbess give you reason to think that she feared for her life, or that she might die shortly?"

Hofer's composure gave way a little. "No."

"But do you think she *knew*?"

"Please let us not speak of it, Captain. I cannot add any piece of information that will help you solve her murder. I'd rather not speak of it." The train was preparing to leave, so Hofer boarded. Without leaning out of the window, he added, "Goodbye, Bora. When you talk to your farmers today, keep in mind they'll tell you what you want to hear."

Bora saluted. "It's unlikely, sir. I don't know myself what I want to hear."

"Hopefully the truth – whatever the truth means to you." Hofer cleared his throat. "Try not to be more self-assured than the situation calls for. It won't serve you well." Slowly he answered Bora's salute, as if raising his hand to the temple were too much for him, or he no longer cared for the gesture. "Remember Adam and the apple."

The train began to move. In the time it took Hofer to leave the Cracow metropolitan area, Bora and Hannes had already taken the road into the countryside. When the train stopped in Kielce, Bora was sitting on the rubble wall of a fly-infested farmyard, surrounded by disgruntled Silesians who wanted to have their say.

9 November

"Was *L.C.A.N.* the abbess's motto?"

Father Malecki didn't need to look at the photograph Bora held in his hand to answer. "Yes, it was her Latin maxim. You may know it translates into 'Light of Christ, Succour Us'."

"Yes, I know."

The evergreens in the cloister gave an illusion of spring which the low temperature dispelled as soon as the men walked out into it. Bora regretted his decision not to wear his greatcoat this morning, since he was soon uncomfortable in his woollen uniform. The news of a failed attempt on Hitler's life the day before had thrown the military establishment into such confusion, the wearing of a coat seemed a superfluous preoccupation.

Bundled around the neck with a bulky scarf, Malecki wore nothing over his cassock, but had already taken care to wear long johns underneath.

Although no photographs had been taken of the body, Bora remembered the position in which it had been found. He walked to the well, and with a twig showed Malecki approximately where the head and feet of the nun had lain.

"Had it been up to me, I wouldn't have let them move her," Bora said as he leaned against the rim of the roofed well. "It was clear that she was dead, still the sisters hauled her inside to try to revive her. They wouldn't have let me help even had I been so inclined."

Malecki watched Bora pensively rub the metal-clad toe of his boot on the grout between bricks, where a dark residue was all that remained of the blood flow. He told himself he was putting up with Bora at this point. Resentment for a military presence in the convent found no open expression because there was nothing in this situation over which he had control. The archbishop of Cracow felt very differently from the Vatican on the issue of collaboration with German authorities, but he, too, had to keep it to himself. So Malecki had resolved to be here whenever the German visited, in hopes of keeping a check on him.

Bora knew it, and accepted it for the time being.

"Captain, you must believe me when I say that if you're looking for culprits within this convent, you're making a colossal mistake."

"Am I?" Bora lifted his glance to him. Under the brief shade of the visor he had a look of quickly controlled animosity. "Judging by the angle of entry, the shot was fired from a few feet away, by someone standing somewhere between here and there." He pointed to the south side of the cloister, where an arbor vitae sat in a massive clay pot. "As best as I can reconstruct the series of events, Colonel Hofer was let into the convent shortly after half-past sixteen hundred hours. Though he has no precise recollection of the time lapse, he probably entered the cloister no more than two minutes later. He had an appointment, and you know the sisters automatically let him through. When he walked into the cloister, he saw Mother Kazimierza's body. The shock was such that it took him a few minutes to gather his wits enough to run out for help. It was fifteen minutes to seventeen hundred hours when he made it out of the convent to call me. Somebody did the abbess in just before our arrival, Father: make what you will of it." Sensing Malecki's disgruntlement, Bora added, "By the way, Father Malecki, I read your annotations very carefully, and I believe there are some parts missing. There's no history of the abbess previous to her entrance into the convent, and more importantly there are no personal observations on her character. You live on Karmelicka Street." Bora took out a notebook and flipped through it. "Number 17, third floor. I imagine you keep the rest of your papers there. I had no intention of being disrespectful, and resisted the temptation to go see for myself. May I impose on you to get the rest of the documentation for me before tomorrow? I noticed you number the pages of your notebooks, so I'd know at once if there were any missing entries."

"I see." Malecki felt his teeth creak in his mouth, by the tightness of his jaw. "And where do you want them delivered?"

"Kindly bring them here. I'll be back to pick them up at sixteen hundred hours, by which time I hope to be able to start interrogating the sisters." Bora walked away. Only after reaching the porch did he turn around to see if the priest had followed. Seeing that he had intentionally stayed behind, he retraced his steps to the well. He stood facing the priest for perhaps a minute, something which might make the American uneasy, although – unwilling like many soldiers to share physical closeness – Bora kept at some distance.

He said finally, as if rushing out of some unrehearsed, impulsive process of thinking, "We can work together or separately on this, Father Malecki. I'm not going to offer more than once."

Malecki felt his heart race. All of a sudden, resentment and hope and his own anguished curiosity about the death struggled in his mind so fiercely, he feared the German might hear the screaming in his head. It was one of those moments when one becomes perfectly aware of what is around: time and place and circumstances, as if a revelation of eternity within the fleeting moment were granted. All Bora had asked him was to collaborate.

He suspiciously returned Bora's attention. To him, somehow Bora looked Anglo-Saxon more than German. He had the face of good breeding but not of inexperience, a sensitive and disciplined expression, harder, yet not unlike the faces of idealistic young priests Malecki had known.

"But of course you wouldn't share your findings with me, Captain."

"I will share what I see fit."

Bora was taking off his glove to shake hands. Malecki felt for an instant that this might just as easily be God's way of offering him the right choice or an unrecognized compromise with virtue. He grabbed hold of the proffered hand much in excess of rude firmness.

Bora understood the warning, and laughed. "You shake hands like a longshoreman."

"I worked among them long enough."

11 November

"Don't be a spoilsport, Bora! It's only the third time I ask. Do I complain when you play your damn Beethoven and Schumann every night? Just stay away, no one is telling you you have to sleep outdoors."

"But what does the major expect me to do in the middle of the night in this town? I don't think it's appropriate for me to sit in a hotel room or in my car until the major is *done.*"

"Well then, I'll make it easy for you: I'm ordering you to stay away, and I don't give a damn what you do with yourself in the meantime."

Bora swept his coat from the back of the armchair, and left the apartment.

An hour later, Colonel Schenck was leaving the officers' club as Bora walked in. Bora saluted. Schenck returned the salute. He stopped on the threshold, and so did Bora.

"Do you know what time it is, Captain?"

"Yes, sir."

"I want you to be aware that I don't approve of junior officers staying up late. Are you alone?"

"Yes, Colonel."

"In that case, I suggest you order one drink and drive back to your quarters."

Bora went to the bar and ordered a cognac. Through the mirror behind the counter, he could see that Colonel Schenck had not moved from the entrance. He drank, paid and walked back.

Schenck saw him outside to his car. In the frigid rain he gave him a lecture on the benefits of a regulated life and the necessity to maintain peak levels of energy at a time when German manhood was tested at the front and at home.

"Especially with an eye to reproduction, Captain, it is imperative that easy but temporary and unhealthy habits and liaisons be avoided by the responsible German male. The step between an innocent drink at the officers' club and wasteful profligacy – even race defilement – is often too brief. I speak for your own good, as a commander and a political comrade, out of concern for your unborn sons and our great country."

Bora gave up wondering what the officers' club had to do with his unborn sons. He thanked Colonel Schenck, assured him that he would remember the advice and drove off towards the south-west of town.

Street repairs were being carried on at the corner of Święty Sebastiana, where a powerful bomb had exploded three days earlier. Army trucks idled with headlights on, and carbide lamps were also being used. The glare formed an eerie hole in the dark, where wraiths of fog drifted in front of the lights, and men working in the fog seemed infernal denizens doing their eternal penance. Men were carrying stones – kerb stones, the darkish basalt from Janowa Dolina – to an upheaved section of sidewalk.

Bora stopped the car, and for a few moments just sat behind the wheel. The interior of the car was cold. Trickles of rain mixed with ice crystals blurred his vision through the windshield. Ahead, the glare drew ghostly yellow streaks that seemed to rain and melt down the window. Bora stretched his legs. He couldn't help thinking about Retz. How Retz at this time was sipping wine, or talking in his loud voice to Ewa Kowalska, or already fingering the fly of his breeches on the sofa. Blood came up his face, a neat little surge of envy dressed in righteousness. His head ached. He felt uncomfortable and tense. Gooseflesh travelled up his thighs, making him bristle.

Impulsively he left the car and stood by it as if it interested him to watch forced labour at one in the morning.

The shadows wore armbands.

He neared the edge of the upheaved earth, where the concentration of light flooded the small area, and moisture condensed before the lamps in a cold vapour. The closest soldier saluted him.

"Has to be patched up by tomorrow morning, Herr Hauptmann."

Observing one of the workers shuffle by, a slope-shouldered old man in a ridiculously unsuitable tweed jacket, Bora felt the cold in his greatcoat and upturned collar.

"Are these Polish Jews or German Jews?"

"German Jews, Herr Hauptmann."

"All right. Carry on."

The stooping old man followed back and forth the path from the upheaved sidewalk to a heap of basalt blocks, pacing more and then less quickly as the weight came to lodge between his hands. He brought the block to someone at the edge of the hole, who passed it to a third man. Younger workers carried their stones against their stomachs without bending their backs. Each time the old man received his block, he hunched to a greater stoop.

Bora waited for him to halt outside the circle of light, in the shadow where the basalt blocks lay, and approached him.

"Herr Weiss."

Not so much that a German officer had addressed him, but that he'd used a form of respect intimidated the old man, whose first reaction was to step back and aside with head low, as required.

"Herr Weiss, it's Martin Bora."

Other workers were coming for their blocks and jostled Weiss, casting furtive glances at Bora. Weiss regained his balance, staring up at the officer. Brusquely Bora took his hands, turning them palms up. He examined them in the way of a teacher checking if a pupil has washed properly.

"How long has this been going on?"

Weiss spoke to him for the next few minutes. His breath could be seen as short, fleeting clouds when they reached the circle of light. "I only wish I could be employed to work during the daytime, you see. At times I feel I shall go down like Goethe, crying out for more light. But they move us to a camp tomorrow, a much better place, I'm told. As things are there's no complaint, really. You see? And a good street worker is as honourable as a good piano teacher. Things pass, Captain Bora, things do pass. The good times, the peaceful times come back eventually. One should see these things like intervals, shouldn't one?"

These things. Bora blushed so violently, it was merciful that he stood in the dark. What did Weiss mean – the war? The racial laws, deportation? Hauling kerb stones?

A soldier had noticed the interruption in the work chain and came cursing, rifle held butt first at an angle. Bora stepped into the light to shout him off. The soldier stiffened in mid-stride, recognized the rank and pulled back.

The truth was that Bora didn't want to be kind to Weiss, didn't want to feel sorry for him. Right then he didn't want to feel anything. Anger and shame made him egotistical. Two blocks away there was a dead nun whose murder he was expected to solve, and this little man, his old piano teacher, asked for more light. What about the light *he* needed?

"I can't stay," he said, even though he could have stayed because he had nothing to do for the next two hours. But he couldn't, he couldn't. He didn't want to stay.

Back in his flat on Karmelicka Street, Malecki couldn't sleep. He tossed and turned with an ear to the sputtering and hissing of the radiator. He had an appointment with the archbishop in the morning, and knew already what he'd be told. All papers concerning his study of Mother Kazimierza should be turned in to the Curia for safekeeping before the Germans asked for them. He'd have to confess that he'd already given them to Bora, and all that remained was Sister Irenka's log of the abbess's utterances after her mystic crises.

It was a matter of time before Bora would ask for those too, and what would he answer then? He'd remind the archbishop that the convent had already been violated once, a proof that refusal wouldn't insure safety from the Germans.

The archbishop would ask how did he, Malecki, think the abbess had died. He'd honestly say, "She was last seen alive at the midday meal and then was shot by someone, I don't know whom." How can a nun be gunned down in the inner garden of as secluded a spot as Cracow offered? *Why* – well, why, Bora was perhaps closer to unravelling that: because of her prophecies, most of which the Germans hadn't yet seen.

He was tempted to get up and risk a walk through the night streets to retrieve the log from the nuns and hand carry it to the Curia even now.

12 November

No one answered when Bora called out to Retz. The house was silent, although the shutters in the living room were open and the drapes had been drawn to the sides of the window. Bora took off his tunic and shirt, and went to draw water in the bathtub. With his hand he felt whether the water was hot, and tossed a bar of soap in it.

He smelled fresh coffee. If Retz had made a pot of it, there might be some left in the kitchen. He went there, poured himself a cup and, sipping from it, returned to the living room. While he waited for the tub to fill, he moodily started looking through the records in the gramophone cabinet.

Having chosen one, he put it on the turntable and stood listening to the music, cup held up to his lips.

"Good choice." The voice from behind startled him. He turned around, and with the motion coffee spilled from the cup, burning his hand.

Ewa Kowalska stood on the threshold of the living room in a low-necked blue dressing gown. Bora had the frantic impulse to button his shirt, at which point he realized that he wasn't even wearing one.

"I'm sorry." He groped for a magazine on the coffee table on which to rest his cup. "I didn't know, I apologize…" With a sweep of his eyes he caught sight of his shirt on the back of the armchair, and stretched his hand to retrieve it.

Ewa laughed.

"Please don't apologize. I should apologize for keeping you out at night. You must be Captain Bora."

Clumsily Bora put on his shirt. Her eyes on him were wise and amused; he didn't know what to make of them except that she wasn't offended by his indiscretion.

"*The Magic Flute*, isn't it?"

Perhaps because he needed to sleep, Bora had a kind of awkward slowness about him, very unlike him. He nodded, staring at her rather more wide-eyed and unprepared than he usually would.

His fingers had as little nimbleness around the buttons as he had wits in relating to her. Her face, colour of eyes, hair were not as immediate to him as the opening in the raw blue of her dressing gown in the morning light. The satiny blue somehow made him stare. He was passing the right suspender back over his shoulder when Retz came in with hot cakes in a paper bag.

"Bora! What the damn hell?…"

*

67

The Curia sat in the heart of the Old City, but no noise filtered through its heavy walls. Malecki said, "He's a young doctor of philosophy from Leipzig. A professional soldier, he says, but by far more accessible than the rest. He won't give in on matters of security, still I believe I can at least speak with him."

The archbishop listened to the report, stiff-backed on his chair. An unconvinced gathering of brows marked his expression.

"You Americans – let it be said with all respect, and taking into account that you are the son of Polish parents – are too ready to trust. This entire country is an open wound due to the Germans. You may be very improvident in according even a modicum of confidence to a German officer, educated or not, Catholic or not."

Malecki saw well it wasn't the time to mention that Bora was the same man who'd torn patriotic hymns from the church books. In his informal Midwestern way he crossed his legs, only to be at once reminded by an insistent stare at the sole of his shoe that he'd contravened the laws of etiquette. He sat up straight, feet joined like a schoolboy.

"It is true that we are by and large a trusting society, Your Eminence, but it has made us successful enough."

"Only because you're far from Europe."

"What I mean is, I may mistrust Captain Bora in the measure Your Eminence desires. I still have to associate with him to try to get to the bottom of this unhappy case."

The archbishop stood up, striding to his ornate desk. "Have you seen this, Father Malecki? This is a list of priests and nuns and monks the Germans have killed since the invasion. A list many times longer is needed for the names of those who are being detained, or whose fate we no longer have any hope of finding out. Your status as a foreigner keeps you from the real dangers that your Polish brothers and sisters face every day. You think – you will forgive me for saying this – you think like one whom the Germans can't hurt."

Malecki began to sigh, and halfway through decided to keep his breath in. "I submit that my special status makes me the perfect intermediary."

"The captain is in Intelligence. Do you know what his job is? He's probably writing a report on you every time he meets you."

"I did the same in regard to the abbess for the past six months."

"Not with the same aims!"

The archbishop was right. Malecki let air out of his lungs in a conciliatory sigh. "I promise I will not befriend Captain Bora, Your Eminence. With God's help I'll only do what is good for the Church and the memory of the abbess."

Bora laughed, because he was embarrassed. He had no doubt that Retz meant what he'd said, but still a part of him wanted to disbelieve it. "I'm a married man, Major," he heard himself answer.

"So, what does that have to do with anything?"

"It has to do with the fact that I'm not interested in Frau Kowalska. Not as the major seems to imply."

"I don't need to imply anything. I saw you."

"It isn't at all what the major thinks. Frau Kowalska told you I had no idea —"

"Leave her out of this! I want to hear from you, what you were doing half-naked in front of her."

Bora didn't want to repeat the story of the bath one more time. "I do quarter here, Major Retz. I was told to stay out until three hundred hours, and I assumed that by seven thirty…"

Retz stared him up and down, with a spiteful, critical cast on his flushed face. Irritation was just beneath the surface, unconcealed and lacking in arguments, which might be angering him more.

"There's nothing more to be said. Next time you get the itch, Captain, go find a place to jack off instead of exhibiting yourself here."

14 November

The farms were all beginning to resemble one another. Whitewashed log houses among rye fields, deeply rutted paths leading from one to the next, red cows, cabbages. Occasionally shooting still echoed in the distance. SD staff cars would honk and pass his VW jeep, signalling him to pull over and let half-tracks and personnel carriers go through. In the distance buildings burned slowly, nearly without flames, raising tall pencil lines of smoke. Through his binoculars Bora made out the huddled villages, a house smouldering here and there. And still SD and SS vehicles speeded ahead of him.

This place was no different. The woman wept, and it seemed to Bora he'd seen nothing but weeping farm women since he'd come to Poland. She led him to a trampled cabbage patch and showed him an area where the plants had been crushed.

"Look at the blood," she whimpered. "Look at the blood."

Bora looked at the blood. "Did they take your husband from the house?"

"No, he was hiding out here in the patch, because he knew they were coming to look for us ethnic Germans."

"And he left you alone in the house with Polish Army stragglers coming through? Didn't he think they might kill you instead?"

But they hadn't killed *her*, she wept. They had searched the house, gone out, found and killed *him*.

"Did they do anything to you?"

"No, but they took Frau Scholz down the way. I heard her screaming."

Bora made a note of the name. He'd go to the Scholz farm next. "They 'took' her: what do you mean, they 'took' her? Did they force themselves on her, did they carry her off?"

The woman started sobbing again. All Bora could make out from her broken sentences was that the stragglers had killed the Scholz men and carried the wife off for themselves.

"...But I prayed to God and to Mother Kazimierza of Cracow. So they killed my man and the Scholzes and they carried off Frau Scholz, but they didn't do anything to me."

16 November

Nowotny sneered when he heard the question. He rubbed his finger over the healing scar on Bora's head, rather more brutally than was required, so that Bora would admit it hurt.

"Of course I'm an atheist, Captain, therefore don't expect any pious statements from me. I believe none of this foolishness. Miracles! There are explanations for most so-called spiritual phenomena, including the preservation of cadavers and this mystic *bleeding*. For instance, have you ever heard of *micrococcus prodigiosus*?"

"No. It's a bacterium, I suppose."

"It's the bacterium that forms little red spots in bread crumbs, if you've ever noticed. It's also believed by some to play a part in the hysterical condition called hematohydrosis."

"'Bloody sweat'?"

"Precisely. Hematohydrosis is, technically, a 'quasi-sweat', or parahydrosis. There seems to be a spill-over of serum containing red corpuscles and the parasitic bacterium into the sweat glands. That's not to say that your nun wasn't a nice woman, or even a saintly one – whatever saintly is – but the 'blood' can be scientifically explained. In the case of that girl in Austria, the Neumann girl, even less edifying tricks have been suggested, related to much more readily available monthly blood emissions." Nowotny spoke with the unlit cigarette dangling from his lip, toying with the stethoscope on his desk. "That takes care of question number one. What was question number two – ecstasy, right? You wish to know what a physician thinks about the state of so-called 'ecstasy'."

"For my own information, yes."

"Well, I haven't witnessed any instance of it myself, but my father started his practice as intern at La Salpêtrière in Paris, where he studied hysteria and hypnotism with Charcot. I would say that in the case of your abbess we're dealing with hysterical ecstasy, a 'grand attack' which culminates in so-called passional postures. Such attacks may be followed or accompanied by lack of response to painful stimuli – technically, self-induced anaesthesia – bodily rigidity, interruption of normal breathing rhythm, et cetera. I imagine your nun underwent this routine before the prophecy stage."

"I don't know."

"What do you mean, you don't know? Haven't you found out?"

"No one has actually seen Mother Kazimierza in ecstasy."

"So, how does anyone know that she went through one?"

"By the time the bloody sweat began to appear on her hands and forehead or she started growing rigid, she ordered everyone out of the room."

"And?"

"And by the time she called her secretary in – a certain Sister Irenka – the crisis had passed. Blood supposedly streamed down her fingers and face from wounds that would close within hours, including a wound on her chest, and of course those on her feet. I did ask for gauze or bandages used to absorb the emissions, but I was flatly refused. Hopefully Father Malecki has managed to get a sample for his Vatican inquiry. Whether or not he's willing to share it with us, we'll see. Since it isn't relevant to the investigation, I expect him to refuse."

"And are you telling me that none of the nuns ever snitched a look through the keyhole?"

"Well, Father Malecki admits to have lingered behind the door at the time of one of her attacks. According to him, she let out a choked cry, and then he heard the thud of a body that falls flat on the floor. When he was let into the room again, the pattern of bloodstains on the tiles made him think she'd fallen face down, arms outstretched in the posture of a cross."

"A passionate posture, indeed."

"She could also kneel for two straight days with her hands clasped in prayer, sometimes indoors, sometimes in the garden. Once apparently she knelt through the night by the cloister well, with snow falling on her and in a freezing temperature. According to Father Malecki's notes she suffered no consequences, not even frostbite."

Nowotny finally lit the cigarette. "What are you really thinking of?"

"That it's a shame we haven't a better record of her ecstatic phenomena. She didn't always bleed, but one wonders what else went on physically and otherwise."

With a good-natured tilt of the head, Nowotny emitted smoke out of his mouth. "Pay attention the next time you have an orgasm. It isn't that different."

17 November

"Who kept a log of the abbess's prophecies, and do we have her last one?"

The time had come for this inquiry. All the neat arguments Father Malecki had planned to use in order to refuse Bora access to the document seemed immaterial.

"Sister Irenka took them down in shorthand. Would you like to come to the library and ask her yourself? She speaks some German."

Sister Irenka stood less than five feet tall, a slight woman with thick glasses and a pointed, mousy little face. Her hands peeked out from the sleeves fingering a rosary, small and nervous, white and waxy, like the hands of nuns Bora had seen before.

"I speak very little German," she said emphatically. "Very little German. Please speak slowly."

Eventually she pulled down from a shelf a voluminous log, whose pages were covered with the flowery sweeps of shorthand notes. At the top right corner of each new note, the date was duly marked. The latest in order of time had been taken the day before the abbess's death. Sister Irenka reread it to herself, and then exchanged a nervous look with Father Malecki, who sat by the library table. "Nothing important that day," she began by saying.

Bora ignored her and questioned the priest. "Why doesn't she want to tell me? What does it say?"

"I don't read shorthand."

"Ask her, then. I'll have someone else translate it if you don't."

An animated discussion ensued between Malecki and the nun. She sounded defensive and unwilling, even spiteful in her reticence, but she was possibly only scared.

"Tell her I don't care if it's political," Bora said in the end. "What's the gist of it?"

Malecki chose his words. "According to Sister Irenka, it prophesies that five years minus three weeks from that day, the 'Great City on the Vistula' will be laid waste."

Bora had to make an effort not to smile. "Warsaw? I thought we'd done that already, and besides – five years from now? The war will have long been over by 1944! Is that all it says? Nothing about her own death?"

Again Malecki consulted with the nun, who reluctantly began flipping pages backwards. Having found what she sought, she told Bora, "On God's birth – how you say, at Christmas, last Christmas – the Mother Superior says, 'God will call me through my name.' I ask her what it means, *panie kapitanie*, and she says, 'When I die, it will be through my name.'"

Bora glanced at the priest. "Why, what does 'Kazimierza' mean? Something to do with peace, right? And what was her name before she became a nun?"

Malecki shook his head. "I wouldn't put undue import on such a vague message."

"I haven't much else to go by, Father."

"The abbess's lay name was Maria Zapolyaia. She was related to the royal line of the Batorys, and took her religious name from the patron saint of Poland, the son of King Casimir IV. And you're not far from the truth, 'Kazimierz' in Polish means *he who preaches peace.*"

"Well, she wasn't killed through peace and she wasn't killed through preaching."

That night Bora went to bed early. Until about ten o'clock he overheard the chatter from the portable radio in Retz's room, and either he fell asleep afterwards or the radio was turned off. The apartment was wrapped in stillness when he awoke.

His watch marked midnight. Bora adjusted the pillows beneath his head and stared into the darkness. Why had he awakened, anyway? He was tired enough. Unwittingly, he began reviewing the events of the day, from a bloody confrontation in the village of Liszki, where partisans had been found and *disposed of* – Colonel Schenck's term – to Schenck himself, who wanted a list of alleged rapes against ethnic German women, by age, location and number of existing children.

Bora turned on his stomach, and as he did so, he thought he heard a sound like suffocated laughter, but it was probably only Retz's turning on the bed springs. Recalling how Malecki had told him with a straight face that he'd won several amateur boxing championships in Chicago, he smiled to himself. At the mention of it, he'd actually laughed. "Why, Father," he'd said, "do you plan to knock sense into me?"

The muffled noise came again, and this time his neck stiffened. He knew what it was this time. *Not again*, he thought. But he listened, holding his breath.

Retz's room shared a wall with his own. Through the partition, Bora more distinctly heard Retz speaking under his breath. A woman's whispered tone came in response, trying hard not to break out in laughter.

Bora was tempted to believe that Ewa Kowalska had arrived while he slept. He couldn't positively identify her voice because he hadn't heard her speak long enough, and it was difficult to tell from giggles and whispers. Still, he didn't think Ewa was one to giggle, so it must be one of the others.

Suddenly he was very warm and uncomfortable. He sat up, totally alert. Unmistakably Retz's groans came through, accompanied by the rhythmic squeak of springs, and for all his trying to get angry, Bora grew aroused instead.

Noiselessly he left the bed. He groped in the dark for his breeches, put them on, then wore his collarless shirt and buttoned it. The repeated thumps of the bedstand against the wall of the next room were beginning to make him sweat. He cracked the door and slipped out, making his way down the hall to the library. There he turned the light on and locked himself in.

Hands driven deep in his pockets, he paced back and forth for a while, with his bare feet meeting now the coolness of the parquet floor, now the soft bristle of the carpet. Not thinking was the best policy, so he did his best not to think. Not even about the times when he, too, after all – Ines was her name, and she squealed when he tickled her. But Spain was a different matter, and civil wars allow other freedoms. All around him, shelves lined the walls and buckled under the weight of books with German and Polish titles, and the occasional Yiddish one. By and by Bora relaxed his pacing. He'd noticed several familiar titles, classics, contemporary fiction, books on art and geography. He even recognized a series of Renaissance studies published at the turn of the century by his grandfather's firm.

Between two shelves, a framed watercolour showed a rugged, woody mountain scene, identified in pencil as "In the Pieniny Mountains". Silhouettes of Heine and of Felix Mendelssohn faced each other in black oval frames below. Between two other shelves, a case hung alone, containing a triple row of insects under glass.

It was impossible not to think. Bora's mind kept returning to Retz and whomever he'd brought home for the third evening in as many days, and what he'd do tomorrow, whether he should talk to him or just go to work. Restlessly he walked to the case of pin-impaled beetles on the facing wall, and then back again.

It was not at all a matter of sanctimony, either. Not at all. He wasn't puritanical about sex, in fact it was because he wasn't, that – no. It was an issue of propriety, let alone elementary concern for security. Perhaps some resentment, because he didn't have his wife here. Benedikta, who had erased every other experience, who was the ideal lover. No, no. It was plain concern for security.

How had the woman been allowed upstairs after hours, anyway? He'd have to check with the doorkeeper tomorrow. Bora stared at the Renaissance studies, but it was no use. The image came to him of his wife slipping out of her briefs under him, eager to be made love to, wet and eager. *God, let me not think of Dikta right now!* Bora didn't find enough saliva in his mouth to swallow.

On the shelf right in front of him, Garcia Lorca's verses, dripping with female blood and gentle sweat, were off-limits; he had better seek the Greek classics lined up next to Latin poetry, or contemporary German fiction. Bora knew Thomas Mann was a forbidden author, but he grabbed one of his novels from the shelf and with it in hand he sank in the armchair. The first line began, "He was an unassuming young man…"

18 November

It would be a cloudy day, and it'd probably snow. Father Malecki exercised in front of the open window, feeling the bracing coldness of dawn. His tendons stretched and muscles bulged in the lifting of weights, not bad for a fifty-six-year-old man. For many years, every morning he'd recited the rosary while exercising, knowing exactly that he'd lifted weights and done push-ups sixty times plus the litanies. *Gloria Patri* – one – *et Filio* – two – *et Spiritui Sancto* – three. *Gloria Patri...*

When the time came, he thought, he'd try to sit in on Bora's interrogation of the nuns. The choice of a new abbess was being delayed due to the circumstances, and they now depended on him, the American priest, for decisions.

Malecki admitted he'd never held so much sway in Chicago, where his parish of St Stanislaus, huge, damp and soot-black, sat like a widow among the workers' houses and factories of the neighbourhood. Much study and application had brought him this far. Who knows, he might end up going to Rome next, and speak to the Pope about the Holy Abbess of Cracow.

Breathing hard, he put down the weights for the last time – "A-men!" – and began running in place.

In the library, Bora spent his first waking seconds wondering how he'd come to be in an armchair with Mann's book on his lap. He'd read as far as the chapter entitled "Politically Suspect", and must have drifted off then.

His first care was to get to the bathroom in advance of Retz, who took for ever. When he passed by, no noises came from the major's room. In the hallway, a woman's raincoat hung from the rack, and rubber galoshes looked like sleeping mice beneath it.

Bora made no special effort to be quiet at this hour. He showered and shaved at leisure. He was blotting his face with the towel when he heard the clacking of a woman's heels in the hallway. There was a pause, and then the front door was opened and closed.

Less than a minute later, Retz's sleepy voice reached him through the door. "How long do you have yet to go, Bora?"

4

First thing in the morning, Colonel Schenck said, "Get ready. We're going to the university to carry out the directives of the 15 September memorandum."

Bora felt a pang of discomfort, because he remembered the memorandum well. He pulled out a file on manuscripts and documents to be seized from the university archives, and followed the colonel out of headquarters. "We're to add to the list whatever is written in German or refers to Germany," Schenck was telling him. "You read Latin, so I expect you to supply me with on-the-spot advice on worthwhile additions."

It no longer rained but it was cold outside. When Bora glanced back, the brown-and-yellow façade of Headquarters – the former Economic Academy – loomed with its statuary over the dying flowerbeds. Before stepping into the staff car, Schenck signalled for the driver of an army truck parked by the kerb to follow. The moment Bora sat by him in the car, he said, "Well, what are you finding out about the murder?"

Bora expected the question. From the briefcase resting on his knees he took out a batch of neatly typewritten pages.

"These are testimonials by all the sisters, regarding the afternoon hours of the day Mother Kazimierza died. Not all of them have checkable alibis, as was expected: one nun will vouch for the other, and we obviously have no witnesses from outside the community. Sister Jadwiga is the only one who dealt with the repairmen. According to her, they were still working at the ceiling inside the chapel when the victim died. No shot was heard, she made me understand, but on the other hand the men were making plenty of noise by drilling and hammering. And of course when Colonel Hofer and I arrived, the tanks were rumbling outside."

Schenck gave back the papers without reading them, listening intently. He had lost an eye fighting in Madrid two years earlier, and one could not tell except that the left iris, icily grey like the other, had a vitreous splendour when the light struck it.

"So. How many workers were there?"

"Three. Some time after sixteen hundred hours – Sister Jadwiga couldn't be more precise than that – one of the men left the chapel to get a different bit for the drill. The toolbox had been left in the sacristy, and he was gone for about fifteen minutes."

"Fifteen minutes to get a drill bit?"

"That's what Sister Jadwiga said. She admits she grew impatient and then nervous about his absence, because silver candlesticks and monstrances are kept in the sacristy. After a few minutes she went to see what the man was up to. She found him eating bread and cheese by the toolbox. She says she ostentatiously checked the shelf of silver to make him aware of her concern. Nothing was missing, and she thought no more of it until I asked."

"Well, what does it prove?"

Bora placed on the briefcase a hand-drawn sketch of the chapel area. "The chapel is behind the main convent church, which faces the street and can be entered from it. No access is possible to the chapel from without the convent. Here, see – there is a doorway that leads from the sacristy to a corridor. One of the windows in the corridor looks over a low wall that connects the chapel-sacristy complex to the main body of the convent, where the cloister is. It took me less than two minutes to reach the low wall from the chapel, then the roof of the cloister, and from there I easily gained access to the upper balcony of the cloister itself, and slipped down to the inner garden."

"You presuppose the man knew the abbess would be in the cloister."

"Everyone knew. The abbess prayed alone in the cloister between the canonical hours of sext and nones – one to four in the afternoon – and seldom did she break this seclusion. That's why the workers were told to proceed with repairs indoors during that time."

The staff car and truck stopped to idle at a crossroads, where military police were directing a column of half-tracks down Copernicus Street. The rumble on the sidewalk forced the officers inside to raise their voices to continue to talk.

"What hope is there of tracing any of the men?"

Bora shook his head. "They'd all sneaked out by the time the ambulance came, at seventeen hundred hours. I didn't know of their presence then, nor did I get a useable description of them, unless 'taller than the other' or 'dark-haired' is sufficient to identify them. I began enquiring with construction companies in the city, but from what I understand the nuns relied on independent journeymen and even makeshift hirelings. In this case, the nuns asked the priest of the Jesuit church down the street to find them a crew."

"Well, what about the priest?"

"His name is Father Rozek. He's been detained by the SS since the rock-throwing incident. So far, I've been unable to find out even where he's kept."

The last half-track rolled by, trailing a smudgy smell. No sooner had the car started again, than Schenck gave the driver a sharp order to stop.

"By the kerb, you idiot. There."

Under Bora's surprised glance, he strode out and made for a plain young woman waiting on the sidewalk holding one child to her chest and another by the hand. Gallantly Schenck saluted, took her under his arm and escorted her across the street to the Planty Park. Having distributed a couple of starchy pats on the children's muffled heads, he walked back to the car.

He neither smiled nor seemed more kindly disposed because of the interruption.

"Do you have children?" he asked Bora.

"Not yet, sir."

"I've been married six years. I have four children and my wife is pregnant." Schenck waved his glove for the driver to take Sienna Street into the Old City. Looking over his shoulder to make sure the truck followed, he said, "You ought to start a family as soon as possible, Bora," and then fixed his bright, real and artificial eyes on his colleague. "What about the alibis of the other nuns?"

"Well, we know about Sister Jadwiga, with the workers in the chapel. If we assume the abbess was murdered – say – between fourteen and sixteen hundred hours, during that time ten of the sisters were gathered in the refectory for choir practice. Two were apparently cooking the evening meal in the kitchen. The eldest, Sister Teresa, lay sick in bed, and is deaf besides. Two postulants were whitewashing the walls in the cellar, and Sister Irenka had left early to accompany an ailing novice to the dentist —"

"True?"

"True. I checked."

Schenck grinned. "Go on."

"We're down to the porter nun, who hardly ever leaves her post. The walls are thick, and I doubt she'd hear much that went on anywhere else in the convent. As I see it, the sisters' alibis are reasonable, but that's as far as it goes."

"Hofer said it was half-past sixteen hundred hours when you arrived at the nuns'."

"It was thirty-five past the hour. The body was lukewarm. I can't say more than this regarding the hour of death. Doctor Nowotny reminds me that within five minutes of being exposed to the air, blood begins to coagulate, and a cadaver's temperature only decreases one degree Celsius in two hours' time. I touched her wrist, but frankly couldn't tell how long she'd been dead. The doctor also explained that hysteria" – Bora could kick himself for blushing as he said it – "sometimes affects body temperature, so – being untrained – I shouldn't count on that detail."

At the theatre on Szczepanski Square, actors were re-hearsing.

Ewa leaned with her hip against the wall unconvincedly, holding the receiver between ear and shoulder. "I don't know, Richard. I might be busy tonight, I just can't tell. We're getting ready for a new production. No, it's nothing you'd be interested in." She nodded to Kasia, who stood by with her finger on her cheap little wristwatch. "Look, I have to go. You can call me later – I don't know, five, six. 'Bye."

Kasia took a slip of paper out of her pocket, and dialled the operator. "Well?" she asked while waiting for the connection.

Ewa shrugged. "I don't want to talk about it. Do you have a cigarette?"

"No, I'm fresh out. Yes, yes, operator? Please give me this number…" Kasia read the number from the slip of paper, and then reached out for Ewa's woollen sleeve. "Wait a second, wait a second. I have something to tell you."

In the Jagiellonian University, the gothic vaults of the *Collegium Chymicum* sent back the men's voices in harsh, slapping echoes. Bora did not take part in the exchange, balanced as he was on the stepladder to reach for books on the twelfth shelf. When he came down with a fragile leather-bound volume in hand, old Professor Anders had his back against the stone pilaster by the window. Schenck faced him with the list.

At closer look, Anders' leonine head and mane of white hair made him look venerable, not so much old as prematurely aged. He was saying in excellent German, "I must protest, Colonel! Haven't you taken enough? You have already removed the best in our collection. These aren't historical texts that concern Germany!"

Schenck glanced over to Bora, who had opened the book on a small table and now leaned over to study its frontispiece.

"Hartman Scheden," Bora read. "From Nuremberg – his 1480 *Chronicle of the World.*"

"Take it."

Anders charged with unsuspected energy towards Bora. "I hope you know this is outrageous and illegal, Captain," he warned, though Bora avoided eye contact and continued to check titles off his list. Schenck laughed.

"You may laugh," Anders raised his tone. "But I tell you it is stealing! It is nothing but stealing!"

A rustle of clothing caused Bora to look up from his list. Schenck had grabbed the professor by the lapels, driving him against a glassed-in massive shelf. His skinny, booted frame vibrated like a metal rod. "Watch your tongue, old man."

Anders could not hope to free himself, but held his own. "Watch my tongue?" His voice boomed under the vaults. "For *you*? You are nothing but thieves!"

Bora cringed at the words. Twice Schenck struck the old man full force with the back of his gloved hand, so that his grey head lolled from side to side against the shelf. Shoving him towards the middle of the room, he sent him knocking against the table where Bora was. Bora lunged to keep a frail book from hitting the floor, but already Schenck was summoning him.

"Leave it, Bora. Take what you have and let's get out of here."

They paused in the courtyard below, where a sickly blade of sunshine came down to cut out deep shadows in the archway. Soldiers hauling boxes came down the steps. Schenck had quite recovered his control, and stood now with fingers hooked in his belt, supervising the operation of removal. He caught Bora's fluster through the corner of his good eye, and showed no patience for it.

"Does name-calling trouble you, Captain?"

"I think it troubles the colonel as well."

"Me? Why? We *are* thieves! I just didn't want to admit it in the face of a Polack."

Ten minutes earlier, Father Malecki had got off the streetcar at the head of Franciszkańska Street, bound for the Curia. He'd noticed the two German army vehicles by the university, and wondered what new abuse was being visited upon them. In a suitcase, he carried small bundles of bloodstained surgical gauze and handkerchiefs the nuns had soaked in the abbess's blood after death; a strange load, had the German sentinel at the streetcar stop asked to see it.

The secretary of the archbishop himself threw a less than enthusiastic look into the suitcase.

"His Eminence appreciates your prompt collaboration in this, Father Malecki. There are many steps to be taken before we even begin considering the possibility of making relics out of these."

Malecki found himself in agreement. "Martyrdom is another issue that requires much investigation."

"Oh, we wouldn't mind a holy shrine in Cracow!" the secretary said with sudden levity. "We should compete with Częstochowa then." He regained his aplomb when the American failed to show amusement. "Actually things aren't as simple as that. Word of mouth has amply circulated news of the abbess's death. We're even now in the process of printing funerary notices. Her followers will readily accept the idea that God called her back to Himself, but should murder be openly suggested, we might face an outrage, even a riot."

Malecki thought of the army vehicles he'd seen parked by the university. "I doubt there's much physical chance for unarmed folks to revolt."

"The people would automatically see the Germans' hand in her death, all the same."

"We don't know that the Germans' hand isn't in it."

The secretary led Malecki to his well-heated office. He showed him a black-bordered poster with the abbess's name, dates of birth and death, and the *L.C.A.N.* motto.

"By tomorrow morning you'll find these pasted up and down the streets of this city. If you are asked about the circumstances of the abbess's death, mental reservation might come in handy."

"So, I should lie."

The secretary seemed peeved at having to spell it out. "Yes, Father Malecki: you should lie."

*

Sister Irenka's mousy face puckered. She seemed to smell trouble, nose wrinkled and mouth gathered tight. She swept a brief look Bora's way, immediately to return her attention on the greenness of the cloister below the balcony. Were Bora to insist on direct information about the murder, he knew she'd try to walk away from him.

"What shrubs are those?" Bora was asking instead.

Sister Irenka kept the pucker on her face. "*Jałowiec* is the Polish name. It has nothing to do with what you want to ask."

"No?" Bora paused briefly. "What I want to ask, you're not willing to tell."

"I am willing, but not certain. I think one should not."

"I see." Unaffectedly, Bora leaned over the balcony. "*Jałowiec*, eh? *Wacholder* is the German name. Of the juniper family. Down there, by the well – that's boxwood, isn't it?"

Sister Irenka followed with her eyes the direction to which Bora pointed. "Our Mother Superior was a saint," she blurted out, and Bora recognized an inflection of pretence, or a curt concession to someone to whom it's useless to explain things anyway.

He waited a moment before observing, "I imagine saints are not easy to live with." He stared frowningly into his notebook as though something in it were more interesting than the matter at hand. His nonchalance in flipping pages concealed his interest well enough for the nun to keep quiet at first, accepting the comment.

Then she said, with a little voice, "It takes a saint to live with a saint, yes."

Bora admired the cleverness of the answer. He looked up and met the cool demeanour of the nun, the firmness of her eyes. He said, very directly, "I have an outsider's impression that the whole convent revolved around her routine, not necessarily to the benefit of the community. I'm sure donations came in because of her, but how well does a stream of visitors fit in with the contemplative life?"

"There were days when nothing ever got done, not even praying, because of the visitors."

Bora rested the notebook on the ledge of the balcony, and his hands on it. He had such punctilious calm built around himself, Sister Irenka could read nothing more than mild agreement in his face.

"We loved her, naturally," she added.

Bora nodded. With the tips of his fingers he ran the cover of the notebook up and down, as if to smooth invisible wrinkles on it.

"But did she love *you*, Sister?"

21 November

When her turn came, Sister Jadwiga didn't want to talk. She was shy, or reticent, or both.

Only afterwards, during his afternoon visit to the convent, Bora learned from Father Malecki that she had borne the brunt of the holy abbess's mood swings.

"But as we say in America, Captain, it was no big deal. I don't want you to have the impression that Mother Kazimierza was actually unkind. Like all unique and gifted people, she had her ways."

Bora maintained a remorseful face. "I'd say she did. In one of her prophecies, she covertly referred to Polish Marshal Śmigły-Rydz as a traitor."

"You read that." Father Malecki sighed deeply. He sighed as one who wants to expel all from himself: air from his lungs and a moral weight from his chest. He still resented Bora, because Bora spoke unadornedly to him and chose not to use diplomacy, which Malecki would find more palatable. Bora was too direct. Youth had much to do with it, or lack of humility, even though it wasn't really arrogance in Bora's case. It was a conviction, zealous and intolerant, something more missionary than military, more spiritual than firmness of character alone.

"In the end," Bora was saying now in his unaccented continental English, a well-educated, upper-class speech, "In the end, Father Malecki, I found out that the holy abbess was not so loved after all. She remained a princess aside from and beyond her position as head of the convent. Some of the sisters, you will forgive me, seem to have hated her outright."

"Hate is a strong expression."

"Death by gunfire is a strong expression."

Malecki made a rash cutting gesture with his hand. "Here you go again, suggesting that one of the sisters... it's preposterous!"

"I'm not suggesting anything. I don't know how the abbess died. All I know is that envy and resentment ran deep among her subordinates. I'm a long way from making suggestions yet."

When the priest reached into his pocket for his Polish cigarettes, Bora prevented him by extending to him a pack of Chesterfields. Malecki took one, and Bora lit it for him.

"I don't think I'm telling you anything you didn't know, Father, by saying there were Polish 'patriots' hiding in one of the houses nearby. The SD flushed them out thoroughly on the day after the abbess died. Just before I came here today, I climbed to the top floor of that house over there." Bora pointed at a tall building across the street. "You were in the cloister, Father Malecki, and very visible to the naked eye. Even with my ordinance pistol I could have easily shot you through the head or put a sizeable dent in your frame."

Malecki didn't appreciate the humour. "Good of you not to have done it."

"I had no reason, God forbid. As I suspected, any shot fired from the neighbourhood would have penetrated the abbess's body at a very different angle. In other matters, I have come to admit there was a remarkable lack of bias in her prophecies. She stated facts that would or might happen, without taking an open nationalistic stance. That attitude might have irritated the Poles as well as others."

"'Others'? You Germans, you mean."

"We'd find less blatant ways to dispose of politically troublesome church people. But let's say yes, for the sake of impartiality." Bora smiled. "Without sharing it, I understand the neutrality of a true saint in matters of political ideology. There's no objective good or bad in the Godhead, if the Godhead transcends the mere game of relative opposites."

Malecki pricked up his ears. "That's a dangerous speculation, Captain. Are you trying to equate the principle of evil with the principle of good?"

"I'm saying they're necessary value judgements, but value judgements none the less, time-bound and contingent."

"You confuse value judgements with values of obligation!"

"Why, Father Malecki, it's the Jesuits who say that the end justifies the means, and that all that leads Godwards is good. That kind of theology isn't my cup of tea, but it might have been the Holy Abbess's."

On Thursday, one month after the incident, Bora was riding with Hannes to the countryside west of Cracow with the nun's murder in mind.

With an eye to the rainy countryside, he pulled out of his map case a plan of Our Lady of Seven Sorrows convent. It was over fifty years old, he'd wrangled with the archbishop's secretary to get it, and the newer buildings in the neighbourhood didn't appear on it.

Even though the interpreter did his best over the bumpy country lanes, it was impossible to read the map in the car without incurring the risk of tearing the flimsy paper. Bora put it away in despair.

"Hannes, how far is it?" he asked.

The jug-headed, dwarfish Silesian turned back just at the time necessary to drive into a hole that sent them both tumbling on the seats. "Another half-hour, Captain."

His first thorough interrogation of a Polish superior officer lay half an hour away, Bora thought, and he couldn't get Mother Kazimierza out of his head.

26 November

She was still on his mind on Sunday morning, when he and Retz were riding in the major's requisitioned BMW back from breakfast at the officers' club.

Retz had been jabbering for some time, and now said, "You have to come, Bora. You've never been there, have you? It's educational, and before they seal it off you have to see it."

He meant the Cracow ghetto, and whether or not Bora felt otherwise, Retz was already directing the driver towards it.

"I have to buy a gift for someone. There are good deals to be had these days, and the Supply Service has carte blanche in visiting the Jewish quarter. Besides, where else would we find shops open on Sunday? You can help me out with the language."

It had snowed overnight, and uselessly the sun tried to shine after the men parked by the brick bulk of the Corpus Christi church. Rims of ice ringed the puddles in the street, and slushy remnants of snow heaped in the corners.

"Look up the Polish word for 'shoemaker', Bora."

Through narrow alleys, leprous with peeling plaster and dampness, they had reached a small enclosed square, where used clothing for sale hung from the wrought-iron fence of the synagogue. Odds and ends were piled up on blankets along the synagogue's wall, and the unevenness of the cobblestone sidewalk made some of the objects stand askew or totter at the touch.

Retz glanced at the glassware, brass and trinkets.

"'*Shevtz*'? Is that how you pronounce *szewc*?"

Bora looked up from his small dictionary. "That's how you pronounce it, Major."

"Well, all I want is a nice pair of shoes, with buckles on them."

Their coming had made an impression among the vendors up and down the irregular shape of the square. Right and left, haggard men moved away from the officers' path as they walked towards Szeroka Street. Retz said, in the manner of a carefree tourist guide, "There's a nice old pharmacy just down the block."

Bora watched the people move away, seeking the walls with faces downturned. "Has the major been here before?"

"Some twenty-plus years ago, sure. The Yids weren't nearly as skittish then."

A few steps ahead, the next storefront was no more than a deep doorway with a glassed-in shelf occupying one half of it. The shop sign was written in Hebrew characters, but the goods on the shelf spoke for themselves. Retz pored over the choice of shoes for some time, during which Bora kept a resigned eye on the dilapidated state of the houses around.

"Those are nice, what do you think?" Retz pointed at a pair of yellow leather pumps.

"They're not easy to match. That is, if the lady wishes to match them with her outfit."

"Does it make a difference?"

"I suppose not."

"Well, I like them." Retz indicated the cost in *zlotys*. "How much is that in real money?"

"It's two Polish *zlotys* per mark, Major."

"Well, then it's not a bad price, is it?"

Retz bought the yellow pumps. Outside the store, a small boy in clogs asked if he could carry the package for him, and Retz said he could. When they turned the corner at Józefa Street, Retz told Bora, "They're going to start making army boots pretty soon, did you know that? They've already begun turning out decent ghetto-made Air Force insignia and shoulder straps." When they passed a window that displayed boxed soap, cologne and cosmetic jars, Retz stopped to look. "I ought to buy something else. Maybe perfume or stockings – what do you say?"

"The major would know best."

"Why? I *do not* know best, Bora. If I knew best I wouldn't have taken you along for advice."

They entered the store followed by the boy. Stiff behind the counter like a cut-out image of herself, the shopkeeper nodded a nervous salute. She had a morbid pallor, where the darkness of her eyes made them seem like holes drilled in her face. She spoke a little German, so Retz did his own bargaining over a paunchy flask of essence, decorated at the neck with a sprig of cloth violets.

He uncorked it and held it to Bora's face. "Smell. It goes well with a young woman, wouldn't you say?"

It was the first clue Bora received that the recipient of the gifts was not Ewa Kowalska.

"Make it two," Retz was now telling the shopkeeper. "One for my wife." He grinned at Bora.

Clattering on the cobblestones with his wooden clogs, the boy behind them sounded like a small donkey. Bora continued to watch the people seek open doorways or stop against the house walls, eyes averted, faces averted. SD vehicles were stationed at every other street corner.

Retz caught Bora's attention. "I don't know how we're going to fit all the Jews in Cracow into this place. It's true you can cram them tighter than sardines, though." He put his gloves on, bending his head towards his colleague a little. "I'll tell you a secret, Bora, though you probably guessed it already. I'm in love."

Bora pretended stolidity. "With Frau Kowalska?"

"Why, no! Not Ewa. Ewa's all right. She's really all right in certain respects. No, much younger. A fresh little piece. God, how wonderful women are at twenty!" Retz couldn't detect any sign of agreement or disagreement in Bora, so he said, "Satisfy a curiosity of mine, Bora: what do *you* do after hours? That is, other than playing Schumann or studying Russian. How do you keep yourself, you know, well-balanced?"

"I drive around, Major."

Retz failed to understand the irony in Bora's words. "Well, you ought to do something else other than driving around Cracow. Doesn't it get tedious dealing with nuns day in, day out?"

"I do as I am ordered."

The boy with the packages stopped before they came back to the Corpus Christi church, which marked the west end of the ghetto. Retz's BMW waited north of the church, and, seeing the officers come, the driver opened the back door for them. The major tossed a coin to the boy, who put the packages in Bora's hands and ran off with all the speed his clogs allowed.

Bora handed the packages to the driver. The visit had depressed him, though he was careful not to give that impression to Retz. Retz took his place in the BMW and said, "You should take life less seriously."

27 November

Sister Jadwiga dried her hands with the rough cloth of her apron. She was a large nun with straggly grey hairs on her chin, something like a sparse beard coming out of prominent moles.

"*Niet.*" She spoke Russian fluently, but still wouldn't talk to Bora about the abbess. Bora suddenly came to the point of losing his temper, visibly enough for Father Malecki to interject a few words of advice, which the nun took in sullenly.

"She doesn't want to talk because she has something to hide," Bora burst out. "She's either seen something or heard something and doesn't want to spill it out. I can tell her in Russian or you can tell her in Polish, Father. I will hear what the matter is!"

Malecki showed that he understood. "*Siostra* Jadwiga." He began a stern homily that lasted a full five minutes. Bora didn't understand it and didn't care. He paced back and forth until the curt defensive replies from the nun grew longer and more tremulous. Malecki was breaking down her resistance with a steady flow of hard-sounding words, at the end of which Bora turned away from the gory crucifix and to the unexpected scene of Sister Jadwiga beginning to cry.

Eventually she led the men out of the waiting room. They went through a bare hallway, up a ramp of stairs and down an elbow-shaped corridor.

Bora remembered having been here before. He recognized the plaster statue of the Madonna with a tinsel crown of stars. Sister Jadwiga stopped in front of it to cross herself, and he was about to ungraciously urge her forwards when she lifted the statue by the elbows and without effort rested it on the floor.

"What is she doing?" Bora asked.

Malecki said he had no idea.

Sister Jadwiga dabbed her eyes and blew her nose in a napkin-sized handkerchief before removing the embroidered doily from the statue's pedestal. Carefully she folded the doily over the window sill and lifted the hollow wooden pedestal straight up.

Bora and the priest stared at the floor. Malecki didn't move, didn't breathe. Bora said something in German. The tinsel stars on the Madonna's halo tinkled when he crouched to lift by the barrel one of the hidden guns.

Minutes later, they formed a most unlikely centrepiece on the nuns' refectory table. Bora had been careful not to touch the stocks with his bare hands. Under Malecki's troubled scrutiny he laid the weapons in a row, five of them.

One after the other, he released the clip catches to check the magazines, and laid them – full as they were – alongside each gun. His movements appeared to Malecki intentionally slow or exacting. Whatever hung in balance here depended on how Bora would take the presence of weapons in the convent.

"Ask her where she found them."

Malecki repeated the question to Sister Jadwiga, and already Bora was adding, "Tell her not to lie to me. The SS searched the convent, so I know the guns were not under the statue at that time. I want to know where and when she found them."

In his second-floor office on Rakowicka Street, Retz laughed into the receiver. He balanced his chair on its hind legs, one knee against his metal desk. "I knew you'd like them, *luby*. I chose them with you in mind. Do I get to see you tonight? Yes, I know you're rehearsing, but you can find an excuse to leave early, can't you? Just tell her you have to go." He set the chair down, suddenly eager. "Come on, Helenka. You have to come. You have to come see me. Tonight, yes. Why not tonight? I'm going to die if you don't come." A knock on the door caused him to sit up and cover the receiver with his hand. "Yes, what?"

"Major," an orderly said as he looked in. "The shipment of bedsheets has arrived."

Retz waved the man off. "Later, later. Close the door. Nothing, Helenka, just someone at the door. You've never come to see me, darling. It's time. It's time. Don't you love me enough?"

In the convent's refectory, a deadly silence accompanied Bora's study of the cache of weapons. He was irritable, hard-eyed. Now that Sister Jadwiga had left, Malecki drew close enough to the table to come within the German's peripheral vision.

"Don't say anything, Father," Bora warned him.

"Well, you do the talking, then."

Bora did just that. Blood had drained from his face, so that the whiteness made him look alien and young. "These are Polish Army Radoms, Father Malecki. Their presence here is as damning as I can think of."

"Do you honestly think the sisters used any of them?"

"*Das macht nichts!*" Bora shouted. The passage from calm to anger happened so suddenly, Malecki didn't know how to react to it at first.

"What matters, then?"

"Their presence matters! Their being here and their being *hidden* here matters! Who else was here on the day of the murder, or at any other time? You are lying to me and I can see clearly that the convent will have to be handled in a different way!"

Malecki swallowed. In the face of Bora's outburst, he had a rash lack of fear. "Is it the fact that you're being 'lied to' that makes a difference? Because in that case, Captain, rest assured no one is lying to you. If Sister Jadwiga says that she found the guns on the day after the search, *I* believe it."

"On the roof?"

"Why not on the roof? The workers had climbed on it to check the damage to the shingles. The roof can be reached the same way you can walk from the corridor to the cloister, on the low wall. Oh, yes, Captain Bora. I noticed that, too."

"Are you telling me that a seventy-year-old nun climbed on a steep wooden roof in search of weapons? Do you think I'm stupid?"

"I think you're hasty in your conclusions. The icy rain might have caused the canvas bag to slip from its hiding place behind one of the chimneys. She noticed it from her window and reached for it with a cherry-picker. Why not go and check if it can be done?"

Bora furiously returned the clips into the guns, and put these inside his briefcase. "I'm going to order a thorough investigation of this. From now on you'll deal with the SS."

Malecki didn't know what came upon him but as he watched Bora begin to leave the room, he dementedly reached for him, grabbing him at the shoulders. Bora swung around, "Don't you touch me!" but Malecki held him fast then. Bora was amazingly pale. He said, "Get your hands off me, Father, or as true as God is I'm going to hit a priest."

Malecki didn't even hear him. Bora broke out of the hold with effort – the priest was strong, heavy-muscled – and made for the door. Malecki tackled him. Bora fell on his knees and was already reacting as he did. He half-turned and struck the blow of a closed fist on the priest's face.

Blood sprayed out of Father Malecki's nose. For an instant he was tempted to strike Bora back – he knew he could floor him with a professional uppercut, especially as he still lay on him.

He pulled back instead, slowly, letting the red trickle find its way out of his nostrils, to soil the Roman collar and the front of his clergyman's vestments.

Bora came to his feet also. Breathing hard, he retrieved his cap from the floor and wore it. "I warned you," he said. "You asked for it, Father Malecki."

Malecki fished a plaid handkerchief from his pocket and wiped his nose and chin. "Hitting a Catholic priest, Captain: how will you explain it to the archbishop?"

"Don't try to pull that, Father, I'm not in the mood for it."

Malecki shrugged. "Actually, if being punched in the nose convinced you that we ought to trust Sister Jadwiga on this one, it was worth it. Must you contact the SS right away?"

*

Retz was in a vile mood that night. It was obvious that he'd waited until ten o'clock for someone to come, and that *someone* hadn't shown up.

He strode to the door of the apartment's library, where Bora was studying Russian verbs.

"Bora, how many times must I tell you not to leave the blade inside the safety razor after shaving? It dulls it and makes it rust."

"I didn't even think about it, Major. We use different razors, so there's no need for the major to worry."

"It's the principle of the thing. Weren't you taught basics in army school?"

Bora said he'd pay attention in the future. Retz lingered for a red-faced moment on the threshold and then was gone. Soon he was opening the front door. "I'm going out, Bora. Take any phone messages for me."

His car had just roared away from the kerb below when the phone rang.

It was a young woman's voice, speaking German with a Polish accent. Bora said that Major Retz was not in.

"Kindly tell him that Helenka called. We're still rehearsing and I couldn't get away, because I was given the lead part."

"Is there a last name?" Bora asked.

"Yes, Kowalska. Helenka Kowalska."

28 November

The meagre frame of Colonel Schenck held up the uniform like a coat hanger, but all the same he had a look of great energy, and right now of sarcastic relish as well.

"You hit the priest in the face?" A light of geniality fleeted across his leathery features. "I hope you were well-justified."

Bora explained. The colonel found the episode hilarious. He'd already gone through the evidence of weapons, freely handling them and remarking on their obsolescence compared to German handguns.

"Well!" He disparagingly held one of the pistols by its long barrel. "Vis Model 35, the famous Polack version of the Colt Browning – was one of these used to kill the abbess?"

"I doubt it. The magazines are loaded, but the barrels are still packed with grease."

"Then we needn't make a big issue out of them. Caches are turning up all over the place, and the SS are after them like dogs in heat. We don't need to give them another lamp post to smell."

"But even if the cache was an aberration, and somehow unknown to the sisters, we must assume that *others* had access to the convent. What if they were the same who committed the murder?"

"The murder isn't a matter the SS are investigating: *you* are." Schenck snickered. "Keep it in the family, Bora. This is no bait you wish to throw out to outsiders, especially after a Wehrmacht officer smacks a priest from a non-belligerent country over it."

"I'm very sorry about embarrassing my command, Colonel."

"Sorry? In your place, I'd have knocked the American's teeth in!"

Black-edged posters with Mother Kazimierza's name were posted in nearly every street. The first Bora noticed covered older notices on the side of a church portal, where a wooden bulletin board had room for several of them.

The fact that no complaints had come from the Curia led him to believe that Father Malecki had decided not to report the scuffle to the archbishop, or hadn't yet done so. Actually, Bora felt little guilt over it. Walking back from the SS command, he rather congratulated himself on having finally extracted from Salle-Weber the location of Father Rozek, the priest who'd secured the work crew for the nuns. He was detained in a camp to the north-west, towards Czestochowa.

Schenck had told him to go see Rozek after work tonight, and meanwhile to take an hour off for lunch. Bora knew Schenck was priming him with a mind to take him east to contact occupying Russian forces at Lvov. He'd mentioned it in passing, asking him how his Russian was coming along. Bora couldn't wait, and looked forward to the change.

The restaurant was called *Pod Latarnie*, and bore a telltale gilded iron sign in the shape of an oil lamp. It was frequented by German officers but not interdicted to Poles. Bora had come to it with Retz once and liked it.

"I'm by myself," he told the waiter. "I'd like a table by the window."

A few blocks away from the restaurant, at the Curia the archbishop's frown seemed chiselled on his forehead for ever.

"This American way of doing things!" he chastized, facing Malecki. "We're not in the Wild West, Father!"

"The lawlessness of the times is much like it, if Your Eminence allows."

"But assaulting an officer of the occupation army, Father Malecki! Did you not think that if it doesn't reflect on you as an American, it still does as a member of the clergy? Whatever happened to turning the other cheek?"

"Had I turned the other cheek, the captain would have broken my jaw." Malecki tried to ignore his swollen nose, while the archbishop seemed to find it a focus of engrossed interest. It was best not to mention the time he'd surprised a thief with the church money box and sent him to Passavant Hospital after knocking him down. "I didn't actually strike him, so —"

"Enough, enough. We're not in a gymnasium, enough talk of striking. The matter of the hidden weapons is what anguishes me above all. What will you say if you're brought in to testify?"

Malecki didn't answer, thinking it was best to look away.

At the *Pod Latarnie* Bora was also looking away. By stretching only the fraction of an inch further, he could have caught full sight of the generous cleavage revealed by Ewa Kowalska's dress. He already saw plenty from where he sat, while she bent down to put her gloves in the spacious leather bag at her feet. He turned his eyes to the centre of the restaurant, so as to appear less than interested when Ewa sat up.

"Thanks for letting me sit at your table," she said. "I didn't realize how many people ate lunch out, and I didn't expect the place to be full."

"Well, you can see there are more Germans than your fellow countrymen here."

Ewa did not look around. "I'm actually not Polish at all." She smiled. "I was only born here. My father and mother were ethnic Germans, theatre artists in Warsaw. The name 'Kowalska' is something I chose because it is so typically Polish. My real name is Olbrycht." It was not lost on her that Bora kept his hands clasped on the table so that the wedding band showed on his ring finger. She obliged him by looking at it. "You look quite young for one who's married."

Bora swallowed. "I'm not young, really. I just turned twenty-six."

"What's young, then?"

"I don't know. Twenty, I expect."

Ewa, who wore no rings on her hands, spread her fingers in front of her. She said, quickly admiring her painted nails, "Am I mistaken, or do you mind my sitting here?"

"Not at all. I hope Major Retz doesn't mind."

"Richard is out of town today." She smiled, realizing that Bora wondered how she knew. "Truthfully, I'm not attracted to younger men."

"Yes. The major told me."

"He *told* you?"

Bora shrugged. "I understand. You're probably used to more seasoned men."

"I believe the word is 'experienced'."

"One can be experienced at twenty-six."

Ewa found Bora's stare very direct. She was sitting in the light, and knew that even the smallest wrinkle showed this way. Too bad the German had already been sitting with his back to the window when she'd come in. It was the seat she preferred.

Bora caught her insecurity without perceiving the cause. True, he noticed thin lines under Ewa's eyes, where the skin was thin and brittle. Make-up covered her skin well elsewhere, but under her eyes it only made it look more brittle if she smiled. A little sag of the chin stayed visible, even though she kept her neck straight and shoulders thrown back.

Retz had told him how old she was. She was his mother's age exactly. Had a daughter and a son about *his* age. Bora doubted Ewa had planned to meet him here, although she might have seen him through the window and decided to walk in. There was something she wanted to find out, and he suspected what it was. The waiter came by, and Bora told him to ask the lady first.

"Major Retz and you don't seem to have much in common," she remarked, pointing at her choice on the menu.

"That's true." Bora poured wine in her glass. He shook his head when the waiter offered him the menu. All of a sudden he wasn't hungry. But he drank the wine.

"You're not going to eat?" Ewa asked.

"Not right now. I don't have much time."

"Should I, then?"

"You should."

Soon the steaming plate of "pigeons" – ground meat in cabbage leaves – drew a waving partition of vapour between them. Ewa cut through one of them with her fork.

"Does the major confide much in you?"

"No."

"He mustn't, if you didn't know he'd be gone today."

"We don't work in the same office." *She is jealous of Retz, and hopes I will tell on him,* Bora thought. He took another sip of wine. It was cellar-cool and it wetted his tongue pleasurably. "I work in Intelligence."

Ewa touched the napkin around her lips. In the unkind glare of day she knew that fairness of skin, hair, eyes didn't make her look younger.

Bora put down his glass. His statement seemed not to have surprised her, or else she drew on her acting ability not to show surprise. He realized he was callously staring at her and made no effort to remove his attention.

Ewa was not deceived by it.

5

1 December

A blustery wind was blowing from the west when Bora
arrived at the army compound outside Tarnów, where
Polish army prisoners were kept. Most of their officers
spoke French, so he told Hannes he would not need him
for the time being.

"As far as I can tell," the camp commander mentioned,
leading him to the grass-poor expanse where several
prisoners stood or walked in pairs, "they want to talk about
the Russians."

Bora glanced over. Sentinels with rifles and sub-machine
guns straddled the edges of the space. The prisoners had
noticed the coming of the German officers, and turned to
stare.

"Why? Weren't these men captured during our advance?"

"No. They straggled in from the east after 17 September.
The one over there is a Lancers colonel. Was a regimental
commander in the Suwalska Brigade. He's been here a week,
and insists that he wants to talk to German Intelligence. I
don't want to tell you anything else. See what you can make
of it."

The Polish officer had been allowed to keep his ankle-
length greatcoat, though belt, baldric and shoulder straps
had been removed from it. Bora drew close. They saluted
and introduced themselves, and the prisoner's face lit up at
the sight of the golden yellow piping on Bora's uniform.

"Vous appartenez aussi bien à la cavalerie!"

Bora admitted he did. "I'm not here as a cavalry officer, however. I have come to hear what you wish to tell us about your experiences with the Russians."

In Cracow, Father Malecki felt he had achieved a minor victory by convincing Sister Jadwiga to show him the canvas bag in which the guns had been stored. She had hidden it in the pantry, where it sat in a cupboard, filled with potatoes.

"Who do you think brought the guns to the convent?" he asked her, one by one taking the potatoes out of the bag. The nun grimly placed them in a colander, flicking the eyes off them with her thumbnail as she did.

Bora was called in to report to Colonel Schenck as soon as he returned to Headquarters.

"The Polish officer retraced his way back from Białowieża with remnants of his unit," he said. "They had to walk, of course, and twice were almost captured again by Russian tank patrols at the ford east of Tomaszów. There's no question but that he sounds sincere, Colonel, even though he tells an incredible tale."

Schenck made a face of contempt. "You can't trust a Polack." He stepped around his desk to reach his chair. "On the other hand, you and I both learned in Spain what the Reds are all about. It's a matter of choosing whom we distrust less." He lowered his eyes onto the map Bora had the prisoner draw by memory. "And this 'massacre' would have taken place where?"

"Where the place is cross-marked, Colonel. It's a swampy area north of the river, with no communities of any size within fifty kilometres."

Schenck sat upright, as if pinned to the chair. He reminded Bora of the insects in the library glass case. "It's a fantastic claim, Bora. What proof does he have?"

"He gave me a list of names that could be transmitted through the Red Cross to Soviet authorities. The ranks of the dead range from captain upwards, with a number of colonels and lieutenant colonels among them."

"They could have died in battle. And all this might be just a ploy to sow discord between us and the Russians."

"I don't know what the man could hope to gain from it. He'll stay a prisoner regardless of how we get along with the Russians."

"There's such a thing as spite, when one has lost everything else." Schenck fixed his shiny false eye on the rainy window pane. "Wouldn't it be a smash, though, to be able to prove that the Reds are purging prisoners as they did to their own officer corps?"

"If it's true, close to one hundred ranking prisoners of war were mass-murdered against all laws and conventions. It may not be the only case, or it might happen again if we do not intervene."

Schenck didn't say no, but his forefinger moved back and forth in familiar reproach. "It's hardly our business to 'intervene', especially now. You know the procedure. Send the original of your report to the War Crimes Bureau, and copies to the High Command, Army Group Ic, Foreign Office liaison officer, et cetera. The Polish dead are not our concern here. If, when we travel east, we hear of anything having happened to our men, that's when I'm ready to nail the Reds over war crimes."

3 December

It took a heroic effort for Father Malecki to relate politely to Bora the next time they met. Mindful of the archbishop's words, he extended his right hand to the German.

"I confess I'm not entirely sincere, but my habit requires that I apologize to you."

Bora bowed his head as he shook the priest's hand. "We're even, then, since I choose to apologize even though my uniform requires that I do not."

"I found the bag used to conceal the handguns."

"And I found the priest who sent the repairmen to the convent. Where's the bag?"

Malecki handed it over. "Where's the priest?"

"He's dead." Out of his breast pocket Bora extracted a folded piece of paper. "His body may be claimed at this hospital."

A jolt seemed to go through the American, but he controlled himself. "Any reason for his death?"

"A heart attack."

"Father Rozek was in his late twenties!"

Bora examined the bag. It was a square, olive-drab back-pack of the type issued to the Polish infantry. No iden-tification was visible anywhere on it. He said, "Sometimes young people have heart attacks." Negligently, he gave the bag back. "Tell Sister Jadwiga she can keep it."

"It'll interest you to hear that she'd noticed the presence of the bag on the roof just before the SS searched the convent. She fretted over it, but it remained there all the while without being discovered. Trust me, the sisters don't know who put it there or when any more than you do."

Bora didn't argue the point. "We'll see. As for me, I lost my only chance to find out who the repairmen were. I hope you believe me when I tell you that I'd much rather for Father Rozek to be still alive." He took an illustrated article on Teresa Neumann out of his briefcase. It was from a British magazine, and Malecki read the title, *Saint or Charlatan?* "Because it's in your immediate field of interest, Father, I'd like to talk for a while about mysticism. I'm told this Bavarian woman is a fraud. Since you spent half a year studying Mother Kazimierza, I'm anxious to hear your conclusions about the veracity of her visions."

"The political ones?"

"The political and the non-political ones. I'm not totally devoid of intellectual curiosity in this."

4 December

The woman was young, ash-blond and too thin. She was not wearing the yellow pumps, and the low heels of her shoes were worn and scuffed. From the hall, Bora could see Helenka Kowalska standing in the vestibule with her coat folded on the crook of her arm. He'd heard Retz come in with her a moment ago, but didn't stop playing until the major actually walked up to the piano.

"Enough fancy fingerwork. Have a schnapps with us, Bora."

Bora stood, without saying yes or no. Retz had gone out to dinner with her for the past three days, but this was the first night he brought Ewa's daughter home. Sedately Bora followed him to the living room, was introduced and was handed a glass of cherry-flavoured clear liquor.

"Your health, Bora."

The manoeuvre failed to dispose Bora towards leaving the house of his own accord. It had been snowing for two hours, the roads were iced over and he didn't feel like obliging Retz on a personal whim. He kept a calm eye on the major in case he should directly suggest his departure, ready with an answer.

Next to Helenka, whose figure was childlike in the narrowness of hips and shoulders, Retz seemed rough-hewn and as though unfinished, a sketch of himself. The vicinity of a table lamp showed how her face – a triangular, high-browed little face resembling a Cranach portrait – was framed by delicate down, an impalpable glitter on her forehead and the hollow of her cheeks. Her legs were bony, but her breast – no doubt about it, Helenka's breast, like her mother's, was beyond reproach. Bora found that her blondness reminded him of Dikta a little, though his wife was taller, more athletic. More his size. Helenka was too small a woman for either Retz or himself.

"Well, why don't you sit down and chat for a while?" Retz was suggesting. "Don't tell us you have to read or study, Bora!"

Bora settled in the armchair closest to the door, at an angle from the sofa. "No, but I have to get up very early tomorrow morning."

Retz scoffed. "At your age I could stay up all night and not even know it!" He turned to Helenka, who pensively looked around the room. "He's not as hidebound as he sounds."

She said, "I knew the people who used to live here."

Bora drank half of the schnapps and put down the glass on the coffee table. He saw Retz make a face that wanted to be humorous but wasn't really.

"Why, *luby*. Yids lived here!"

"I know. And now you do."

"Who lived here?" Bora asked. Retz sat so close to her, Helenka had to lean forwards from her seat on the sofa to look over.

"Jacob Malev, the playwright. Have you heard of him?"
"No."

"No? He wrote his first play for Esther Kaminska."

"I have never heard of her either."

As expected, it wasn't long before Bora found himself out of his lodgings for the night.

Cursing as he struggled to free his car from the snow accumulating by the kerb, he felt the tires spin, and only by rocking the vehicle back and forth on its tracks was he able to get over the icy rut. Wind from the river blew a hard snow up the street, and the gigantic shadow of the Wawel Hill rose across from it above a whirling white storm. Forecasts said it wouldn't last, but here it was for tonight.

Helenka or no Helenka, tomorrow he'd have it out with Retz. He refused to choose another billet, and these night rides had to end one way or another. Bora's car skidded at the first curve, and he found himself advancing crabwise for several metres, sliding as he went along.

It was unusual for *Pana* Klara to come knocking on his door after dinner. Father Malecki had been reading his breviary and came with it in hand, a finger stuck between the pages to keep his mark.

The old woman spoke in a low voice, glancing furtively over her shoulder. "There's someone to see you, Father."

"At this hour? Who is it?"

"I don't know who he is – middle-aged, drooping moustache. A labourer of some kind. I wish you'd see him quickly and send him on his way, Father."

Malecki grew impatient. "Well, where is he?"

"I wouldn't let him come up. I'm sorry. Please go see him downstairs. Make sure the front door is closed if you have to talk to him."

Malecki knew how cold the stairs of the draughty old house were. He grabbed a woollen sweater from his dresser and left the apartment. The electric light in the stairwell was one of those that automatically shut off after a few minutes, and the bulb went out just as he started down the first ramp. At the risk of breaking his neck going down the worn steps he groped in the dark down to the next landing, where he turned the switch on again. He leaned over the wrought-iron banister trying to see who waited two floors below. All he could make out was a dark cap and the shoulders of a man with hands in his pockets.

Shivering in the chill of the stairwell, Malecki said, "Who are you, and what do you want?"

The man swept the cap off his head. He answered with what seemed to be a password, which Malecki dismissed. "I don't know what that means. Speak straight."

"*Ojciec* Malecki, we need your help."

"I still don't know what you mean."

"We were told you're one of us."

God knows why, but for an instant Malecki thought that Bora was setting a trap for him. He started to say, "I think you have the wrong person…" and the words died in his mouth. The man was holding a letter with the *L.C.A.N.* heading and the heart-and-crown device.

"We were told that we could depend on you in an emergency."

"By whom?"

"*Ojciec* Rozek said so."

The name alerted him, but Malecki wasn't given time to say anything.

"It's the matter of a bag of weapons, *Ojciec*. We desperately need them before the Germans find them."

Malecki paused. He was about to give back the letter, then changed his mind and stuffed it in his trousers' pocket. "Too late. The Germans have found them already, and it could have cost the sisters their lives. Don't you pretend to be amazed or put out with me, it won't work. Whose hare-brained idea was it to hide weapons in the convent?"

"*Matka* Kazimierza suggested it. She'd warned us that we shouldn't leave them there too long, but we could hardly show up after German officers had taken to visiting her. Damn, if we'd only – we did try to get the guns back on the day she died."

"Ha. I understand now. And why didn't you?"

"Our man was new, young. He screwed around and just lost his pluck. He took a wrong turn and ended up crawling up the wrong wall. He had to rush back and close the window before the sisters found him missing from the sacristy."

Malecki interrupted. "Your bungler wouldn't by any chance have fired the shot that killed the abbess?"

"Why would he want to do such a thing, *Ojciec*? He'd tagged along with the workers to get our stuff back, that's all. Even his toolbox was empty. The guns were supposed to go into it." The man groaned, shaking his head. "Damn. Damn, we didn't need this one."

"Watch your tongue, and count your blessings if nothing disastrous comes of the finding. Fools that you are, there's a German Intelligence officer who visits daily! What about your man, where is he now?"

"I wish I knew. I told you he lost his pluck. He's been gone since late October, maybe hiding in the country."

Malecki's tenseness was such that he was startled by the squeaking of hinges one floor up. It was probably *Pana* Klara keeping anxious watch on the door of her apartment. "You can't stay," he spoke under his breath. "Quickly, do any of the other sisters know about you?"

"I don't think so, unless she told them."

The light went out again, and this time Malecki didn't bother to turn it back on. They stood in the dark for the time necessary for the priest to discourage further visits and for the man to ask for the return of the letter from Mother Kazimierza.

"Sorry, the letter stays with me."

When Malecki opened the front door, a tempest of small hard flakes was whirling in front of the street light like an immense swarm of moths. Touching his temple, the man sullenly said "*Dobra noc,*" slipped out and was gone.

A few streets away, next door to the Jagellonian Library, Colonel Schenck didn't have the heart to tell Bora to avoid temptation and leave the officers' club. It wasn't late, and after all Bora had done no more than sit down at a table with a stack of notes.

But he couldn't resist the temptation to lecture, so he joined him eventually, sitting across from him. Bora stood at attention.

"Sit down, sit down. I didn't realize your stepfather is *Generaloberst* Sickingen, Bora. What happened to your father?"

Bora remembered from previous conversations that Schenck disapproved of divorce, so he was quick to explain that his father had died.

"I see. Did you know the general is coming to Poland?"

Bora didn't, and said so.

"Well, you ought to be glad to see him. What have you there?"

Bora showed him Malecki's notes on the abbess.

"I speak little English," Schenck removed his attention from the papers. "I understand on the other hand that your mother is British-born. She's racially pure, I hope."

Bora felt himself blush a little. "She's quite racially pure, Colonel."

"Well, and how is it that her maiden name was the same as your father's?"

"They were first cousins."

"It's not the best choice in marriage. In that sense, your half-brother is probably a better specimen than you are. Did you at least marry a pure German?"

"My wife is entirely German."

"Let's see a photograph of her?…"

Bora took a snapshot of Dikta out of his wallet. Schenck observed it closely. "You should produce fair-haired offspring, providing that as a child you were lighter than you are now. Is your body hair dark or light?"

Bora stared at the colonel. "Lighter than the hair on my head."

"These are important questions, you know."

"I realize that."

"You'll fully comprehend how vital these questions are as the war goes on. This is no time to be romantic about reproduction. Love, sentimentalism – those bourgeois luxuries are not for the German man of today." Schenck stretched his lean body on the chair. "I have no difficulty telling you that I fertilized my wife before marriage, inasmuch as I would never consider tying myself to a woman who couldn't produce children. In two weeks I had her pregnant, and the third week I married her. Unfortunately, it turned out to be a daughter, but she did better ten months later." He lightly tapped the floor with his foot, surveying the sparse population of the officers' club. "I hope you have a high sperm count. A high sperm count is essential in these matters."

Afterwards, Bora drove out of the club with a headache, and no desire to go back to his address. He stopped at the first hotel on the way, took a room and proceeded to stay awake until the time came for him to get up.

5 December

It was very early in the morning, and Doctor Nowotny knew that Bora had to have a good reason to want to see him before going to work. When he heard it, a ripple of hilarity threatened to come up his throat, but he sent it back down with a gulp of hot coffee.

"How long have you been married?"

"Four months."

Nowotny raised his eyebrows. "A-ha. And how much time did you actually spend with her?"

"Less than two weeks."

This time Nowotny laughed. "And after 'less than two weeks' you worry about not having yet generated a child for the New Germany? He, he, he. Give time to time, as my father used to say. Tell me this, have you been screwing standing up?"

Bora knew he should have not come, and should have not brought up any of this. "A few times," he mumbled.

"In a hurry, eh? Just couldn't wait. Well, haste and fertility don't necessarily go together. You ought to take your time. The missionary position, of course, is reputed to be the best for the purpose, though I'm a great supporter of *more ferarum* myself. You're a horseman – the next furlough, spend it on top of her." Nowotny drummed the desk with his fingers. "Myself, I'm not married. I have no children. I have no patience with relationships, and give me the army any day. It doesn't mean I don't like to see a young woman popping at the seams with a baby, but it doesn't have to be my own to make me happy or proud to be a German. Sure, when it comes right down to it, we'll need the replenishment. We lost over sixteen thousand in this campaign alone, and we're only at the start." He kept smiling, because Bora had a frown. "Russia's turn isn't so far away, mark my words."

Nowotny felt a sting of regret, or pity, which was as much a part of his nature as the hardness he showed others. The man before him was in so many ways untried, unaware, just beginning to be hurt. He still wore the beautiful uniform of testiness and idealism and blessed arrogance. Nowotny had an odd premonition of grief for him, as if not so far in the future the clean hard looks would be tried, and pain burst his courage. It was an ever so brief sensation, unwarranted in that he hardly knew Bora. He should hardly care.

So he said, gruffly, "What country do you think is going to get it next?"

"It is not my place to speculate."

"But I bet you think we can take it all."

During his lunch break, on a hunch, Bora travelled down the extension of Karmelicka to Salle-Weber's office on *Reichsstrasse*. After some prompting, Salle-Weber admitted a file on Mother Kazimierza existed, but was not sympathetic enough to share it with Bora. All he said was, "She was an aristocrat, from an old, politically involved family. Even had she not been a big-mouthed nun, we'd have had a file on her. There's nothing in it that would help your investigation, so don't ask to see it."

"May I at least see the folder?"

The folder was slim, only a few pages in Bora's reckoning, and on the tab the label read *Lumen*. His heartbeat accelerated.

"Why the title?" he asked.

Salle-Weber put the folder away, and locked the cabinet. "It was a codename we came up with. You're the college man here, you should know what it means."

"It's Latin for 'light'."

"There you go."

"And it's the first word in her *L.C.A.N* motto: *Lumen Christi, Adiuva Nos.*"

"Clever, eh? Now go about your business, Captain. I haven't the time to chat over dead nuns. The file is closed."

Bora didn't want to insist with Salle-Weber right now, all the more since he'd put in a request for permission to interrogate the partisans flushed out from the houses around the convent. He left the office with a sense of euphoria. Mother Kazimierza had predicted she would die "through her name". Could the codename be what she referred to? He was anxious to read Malecki's notes once more.

It was again beginning to snow when he came out of the building. Silvery flecks fell in slow spirals here and there, and the air was already below freezing. Beyond the Vistula, low on the horizon, a pale gold ribbon of sky linked the layered clouds. A shaft of light came from it and went to illuminate some distant hillside elsewhere. Bora was bound for those hills in the morning.

In the car, he flipped through Malecki's notes until he found what he wanted.

"*The abbess often referred to Christ as 'her Light'. Her favourite quotation was from Matthew 6:22.*"

The quotation was not reported, so Bora had to wait until the next time he'd see Malecki to ask.

At the Old Theatre, Retz talked to Kasia when Ewa didn't seem disposed to listen to him.

"What's the matter with her? I called her three times today, I sent her a pound of butter. I shouldn't even be out of my office right now."

Since Kasia spoke no German, the words were obviously aimed at Ewa, who sat smoking in front of her mirror, one leg dangling nervously over the crossed knee.

Through the mirror, though she didn't look directly at it, she discerned Retz leaning towards her friend with an anxious posture of shoulders and face. Kasia turned to her. "Ewa, whatever he's saying, will you listen to him?"

Her silence did not discourage Retz, although he came dangerously close to self-exposure to cause a reaction.

"Does Ewa think I'm seeing somebody else? I'm not seeing anybody else! Tell her she just has to come. My room-mate is going to be away for two days. We'll have the house to ourselves for two days. I'm not seeing anybody else, and she just has to come!"

"Ewusia, I think he needs you." Kasia simpered. "I wouldn't be so tough on him."

Ewa sucked on the short butt of her cigarette, squeezed tight between thumb and forefinger. "He can call me again after work, if he wants to."

6 December

The hefty tines of the pitchfork showed a viscous coating of darkish red, and straw had been used to absorb the blood from the barn floor.

Bora scribbled on his clipboard. No noise came from the outside except a bellow now and then from the disconsolate cow tied to the barnyard fence.

"She needs to be milked," Hannes mumbled as he was going out of the barn.

Bora ignored him. Trailing his eyes on the snow-patched distance between the hut and the barn, he noticed signs of raking across the yard. "He dragged himself here from the house," he told the unkempt, angry-faced soldiers beside him. "The dirt is mixed with blood here and there."

"Sepp wasn't found in the barn," one of the soldiers spoke back. "We found him behind there in the slop, Herr Hauptmann, with the hogs trying to grub into his belly."

Bora scraped the bloody edge of his sole against the door jamb.

"So. You all came together, the four of you. Was there anyone else but women here?"

"No, sir, there wasn't."

Having cleaned the edge of his boot, Bora stared at it. "And what were the three of you doing while Sepp got himself impaled in the house?"

The soldiers stayed stiff at attention. When Bora looked up, he saw on them the mien of wary dogs. The man who had been doing the talking said, "We'd been out on patrol all night, Captain, we were dog-tired. We took a breather of an hour or so. Sepp went inside to ask for something to drink."

"'Something to drink'? Wasn't there water in the well?"

"It's cold for well water, sir. These people keep ale sometimes. He went asking for some, and they killed him."

It required no effort for Bora to sound harsh. "I have three Polish nationals with bullets through their heads out there. Who killed them?"

"Sir, we had to do something about Sepp! They were nothing but —"

"I don't give a bloody damn what they were, Private. There are three dead women out there and I want to know who killed them."

"We just had to, sir."

"'Just had to.'" Bora placed the clipboard under his arm and capped his pen. "It still doesn't answer my other question. Where were the three of you while your comrade went into the house? You weren't around or you'd have heard the scuffle. Did you hear the scuffle?"

Just then Hannes called from the barnyard fence. "The medical examiner has arrived, Herr Hauptmann."

"I'll be out in a minute."

When Bora joined him in the yard, the physician was kneeling by the three dead women, with one hand lowering the skirts of the youngest one.

"Get me the men out here, Captain. Tell them to drop their pants."

In his room on Karmelicka Street, Father Malecki debated whether he should show the archbishop the compromising letter from the abbess. It only said that he, Malecki, could be trusted if the need arose. It had no date and was addressed to no one in particular, but still he decided to keep it to himself for the time being.

He should have thought that underground agents might have been among those visiting the abbess in weeks past. Bora had made no mention of German suspicions in regard to that, but then Bora wouldn't. Malecki regretted not asking his night visitor to put him in touch with the men who'd worked at the chapel roof on the day of the crime.

So he sat in his room with the note staring at him, tempted to burn it one moment and to keep it as evidence the next. If by any chance the strange meeting last night had been a trap set by the Germans – well, he hadn't fallen for it. But then, he could see no reason for a trap. There was no reason.

Except, of course, being accused of collaborating with anti-German forces and being expelled from Poland. Bora would have free rein in his investigation then.

Malecki rested his forehead on the window pane, careful not to touch his sore nose. Most of the snow had melted and the street below was bare and lonely except for two bundled, helmeted German guards, patrolling with equal pace on the sidewalk.

The torn, bloody cotton briefs were draped around the younger woman's knees. Her bruised belly looked like mashed snow with blond, red-streaked grass on it. Bora's lips contracted as he forced himself to look.

"I'm sorry to show you this, Captain, but it's relevant to the facts. She also has bruises and chunks of hair missing from her head. I believe this was done by two men at least." The physician waved for the medics to come and remove the bodies, and followed Bora, who had started for his car. "What you reconstructed is a sound analysis of the sequence of events: the men came to the house to ask for a drink, and whether or not they got it, they began to take liberties. The women resisted, so two of the men carried the girl out and raped her; the other two men tried the same indoors, and one of them got himself impaled in the back room. However it went, there was confusion, and by the time the women were corralled back together, everyone had forgotten about the soldier who dragged himself to die in the barn. As you pointed out, there's no mud around the women's shoes. They weren't the ones who threw the body in the slop. Where I disagree with you is concerning the guilt. I think the killing was quite more cold-blooded than you envision. The women were made to lie side by side and were executed that way. Not an angry spur-of-the-moment reaction. And the wilful removal of the dead soldier from the barn hints to an attempt to manipulate our emotions by facing us with a German soldier murdered in the dung."

Bora tossed his clipboard in the back of the car. "I will have my report by tonight. When may I expect yours?"

The medical examiner watched Bora's interpreter milk the cow by the barnyard fence. There was no pail, and the milk simply sprayed out onto the ground. "If you are willing to wait one hour, you may have it today."

7 December

"*If therefore the light that is in you be darkness, how great is that darkness!*' That is the quotation from Matthew, Captain.

It was a self-deprecating reminder the abbess used in her daily prayers. The image of light, as you probably noticed, is recurrent in her utterances."

They sat in the convent church, and Bora was only half-listening. He had his mind on the drive back from the country, with reports that were couched in the impersonal language of the military so that horror became statistics. Colonel Schenck was not one to be moved, but was a pragmatic commander. He had recommended that the army patrol be indicted and the one soldier among them who hadn't earned medals or citations during the invasion be executed.

"Have the sentence with his name and crime posted around the village near the farm where it happened, Bora. That'll be lip-service enough."

Bora's eyes now wandered up from the altar to the baroque accretions of stucco reliefs in the apse, something resembling gilded barnacles in the overturned hull of a boat. He was glad Malecki was talking to him. He needed to hear the unexcited tone of a human voice, whatever the words were.

At his return from the field, Retz had laughed off his irritation at finding that his bedroom had been slept in.

"It isn't like it's *your* room, Bora! You use it when you're in Cracow, that's all. Ewa and I had a little get-together with friends, and there was need for some extra sleeping space. You wouldn't even have noticed hadn't the stupid cleaning woman decided to air out the mattress."

So he had argued with Retz. It had been long in coming, and, all considered, he'd brought up everything with less anger than might have weakened his arguments. Retz had actually listened at first.

"Therefore," Malecki was saying in his steady voice, "the image of Christ as bringer of illumination would be particularly significant to one whose spiritual convictions revolved around divine grace." The priest had been speaking with his eyes on the devotional booklet by the abbess, and only now realized that Bora was distracted. "You disagree?" He sampled his interest in what was being said.

Bora looked at him. "Do I disagree on what?"

The theatre dressing room was cold. Whatever heat radiated from the coal stove only warmed a small area around it, and the two women sat close to it. Ewa Kowalska had got her feet wet in the slush outside the theatre. Her stockings were hung to dry over the mirror. Bare-footed, she stretched her toes towards the stove while rehearsing her part.

She was not happy with it, Kasia knew. It was a little part and Ewa had hoped against all sense to get the lead. Kasia said, "But darling, you played the Queen in the *Libation Bearers* and in *Agamemnon* before that. It makes sense that you should play her now." Kasia wound her reddish hair around her forefinger, legs tucked under her body on the threadbare rug. "Just think of me, who only get to play the slavewoman or a member of the chorus most of the times."

"You don't have my experience."

"I'm also common-looking. But I have been around the company long enough to deserve better. How did it go the other night after I left?"

"It went fine. Richard argued with his room-mate in the morning."

"Oh? About you?"

"About Richard sending him out when I visit."

Kasia laughed. Her teeth were the only beautiful thing about her, and she'd taught herself to laugh well. "The poor thing. Maybe Richard ought to find him a girlfriend. Maybe that's what the argument was really all about."

"I don't know. Richard hasn't spoken to him in two days. It's funny how callous he can be about people's feelings. He said he'll try to get his room-mate transferred to other lodgings."

"Well! You still have pull, Ewusia. Not every woman in Cracow can get a German officer evicted on her account."

Ewa put away the sheets she'd been reading. She rested her head on the back of the overstuffed, worn armchair. With her extended bare foot she prodded Kasia's back. Eyes closed, she began reciting her part.

"Asleep? What good are you, when you're asleep?"

Kasia laughed with a shiver. "Your feet are cold! Next time you see Richard, why don't you find out if his room-mate is looking for company?"

6

9 December

The young Pole had bruises on his face. The left cheek was swollen. A blood vessel in his eye had ruptured, and the pale-blue iris stood out strangely against the red.

Bora gave him a cigarette, lit it for him and watched the prisoner puff from it with relish.

As one of the partisans flushed out by the SS from a tenement building across the street from the convent, his life wasn't worth much at the moment. According to Salle-Weber, two of his companions had been shot while trying to escape. He'd sprained his ankle jumping out of a low window and the SS had nabbed him on the spot.

What they were getting out of him now was beyond Bora's concern, although he, too, had questions. He began by waving the armed guard out of the room.

Past the barred window panes, the hour of day was imperceptible in the twilight of a dismal inner court. Bora kept his attention on the outside, feeling with his hand how draughts of cold air knifed their way in from around the window frame. He wasn't himself sure whether by turning his back on a prisoner he meant to convey careless self-confidence, or that he was just unafraid. But he did look out into the sad day as he spoke.

"I'm told that you understand German, so this is going to be easy enough. You were on the top floor of the tenement on the morning of 23 October, the day before you were arrested. There were binoculars and weapons in the room you occupied, and right now the weapons interest me less than the binoculars."

No word came from the prisoner. When Bora looked, he was smoking greedily. His battered face conveyed no readable emotions. He had heard, but no questions had been asked, so he stayed quiet.

Bora said, "Did you look into the complex of the convent below on that day, and if so, did you see something out of the ordinary?"

Pinching the stub with his bruised fingers, the prisoner sucked a last drag out of the cigarette. "Can I have another one?"

Bora tossed the pack at him.

"You want to know if I saw the dead nun?"

"Precisely."

"We had nothing to do with it."

"I know. Did you see her?"

Leaning forwards to get his cigarette near to Bora's lighter, the prisoner nodded. "She'd been out there awhile, near the well."

"Was she walking, sitting – was she alone?"

"At one point she was standing. Then she lay down, face down. Praying or something, I wouldn't know. I didn't see anyone else, but there could have been. I didn't look out again for a couple of hours, and when I did she was still lying there. Except that now I knew she was dead. I could see blood around her through the field glasses. That's all I know. I figured one of you had killed her."

Bora replaced the lighter into his breast pocket, and buttoned it. "One of *us*?"

"Who else would kill a nun?"

The point didn't merit arguing over, but Bora was intrigued. "What time was it when you saw her dead?"

"I don't carry a watch. Maybe four thirty, maybe five. Within moments there was a hell of a confusion in the cloister – nuns and two German officers rushing around. One of them crouched down to touch the body, and that's all I know because I didn't want to push my luck and be seen. I went back inside."

Bora, of course, had been the one who had touched the body. So, the abbess was still alive two, two and a half hours before his arrival with Colonel Hofer. "Did you hear a shot?" he asked.

The prisoner spoke with the cigarette in his mouth. "No. All afternoon, we were trying to listen to a radio broadcast inside. The channel was jammed, so we had to pay close attention to make any sense out of it. That was the day tanks came rolling down the street, too." Spewing smoke, he gently massaged his distended left cheek. "We knew the SD could bust us any time, so we kept mostly out of sight."

Bora stared at the wall behind the prisoner, a grimy unpainted wall with pockmarks of nails and scuffs from the backs of chairs. He tried to think back, to reconstruct his own schedule for 23 October.

He and Hofer had worked through the noon hour. From the midday meal until her death, *Matka* Kazimierza had been in the cloister, joined at one time or another by her murderer. At a quarter after sixteen hundred hours, he'd left with Hofer for the convent.

Thinking of the repairmen in the chapel, Bora asked, "Did you see anybody leave the convent?"

"After the killing? No. I told you I went inside."

Jealously, the prisoner stuffed the cigarettes in his pocket when Bora walked to the door, and knocked to be let out.

Who else would kill a nun? Back at Headquarters, the prisoner's question prompted Bora to list Polish personnel who might have had access to Radom guns: police officers, security guards – the military, of course. Collective, anonymous groups. Double-checking on his own schedule for the 23rd, he found that, except for one hour in the morning when Colonel Hofer had excused himself and asked him to man his phone, he'd been as bound to his desk as a dog to its chain. Would that everyone's alibi were so easy to verify.

Standing by the window, Bora found himself staring at the pigeons crowning the church across the street. Unless the killer was an inmate of the convent (it could be, it *could* be), someone, somehow, had entered it undetected, worked his way to the cloister and left unseen after killing the abbess. Sombrely Bora recalled that in this very office Colonel Hofer had stood by him, holding back ill-concealed tears. Visit after visit, what had Mother Kazimierza prophesied to him that would cause him to weep? Poor man. *Poor all of us*, Bora thought, *if we're curious about the future. Better not ask, especially if you're a soldier.*

"Remember, we set off early in the morning!" Colonel Schenck stalked into the office, tossing a handful of forms on Bora's desk and stalking out again.

That evening, when Bora found Helenka sitting with Retz in the living room, he scarcely paid any attention to them.

10 December

Father Malecki woke up with a sore throat. He wasn't one to get ill often or nurse himself once he did, but this morning he had to force himself to get up. The room was extremely cold. He touched the radiator and felt cold metal. On the dry sink, the blue-and-white wash basin he'd filled last night had a thin layer of ice on the surface.

When he went downstairs for breakfast, *Pana* Klara told him the furnace had gone off during the night.

"Can it be repaired?"

"I'm afraid we ran out of coal, Father, and there's none to be had just now. You don't look well. Why don't you at least stay in bed? I'll get you another quilt."

"On Sunday? You know I'm due for early mass at the convent."

After waiting for more than fifteen minutes at the streetcar stop, Malecki had to conclude that there'd be no transportation today. So he walked the windy streets at daybreak in growing discomfort, and had a full-blown cold by the time he reached the convent's sacristy.

It was still dark outside and Helenka couldn't tell whether Bora was awake, but a strip of light filtered from under his door when she left Retz snoring in bed. Lovemaking had been good once Retz slept off his drinks – not long, just good. Now she felt a warm, pleasurable laziness that no longer called for lying down.

She went to the kitchen. Bora had already had coffee, and there was enough left for her to fill a cup. Helenka looked around. The counter was tidy, the whole kitchen well equipped with china cabinets, double sink, large gas stove, an ice box typical of men who don't do their own cooking: there was nothing in it except for some butter, milk and white wine. A forgotten box of kosher salt sat in the pantry. Cups had been left out for the cleaning woman to wash. Helenka finished her coffee and rinsed her cup.

She could hear small noises from Bora's room when she stepped back into the hallway. A drawer being pulled out and pushed in, stepping around in boots. Next door, Retz's heavy breathing rose and fell in regular waves.

132

The bathroom was spotless, especially considering two men lived there. Washing her face, she thought military training might be accountable for the orderliness. Towels were folded neatly, the soap sat dry in its dish. She was curious about who used the aftershave. From the pungent scent from the uncorked bottle, she recognized it as Retz's.

She wondered why Bora was up so early on Sunday morning. Did he work on Sunday? Retz slept in. He wouldn't drive her to the room she shared with a girlfriend until after breakfast.

She sighed, looking at herself in the mirror. After breakfast. She was finding out that food was an important part of going out with Germans. Being fed decently, having breakfast, real coffee. How mercenary, in the end.

She liked Retz, his gruffness and shameless want of her. It made her feel a little unclean but she liked him. She even cared for him, a little.

Bora was opening the window in his room. On tiptoe, Helenka stole to the library and turned on the light.

So, this panelled, book-lined space was where Malev had written some of his works. She admiringly walked around the shelves, read some of the titles. His plays in Polish and German formed an incomplete leaning row, since most of those in Yiddish had been removed.

On a round table by the armchair lay an open book with a photograph as a marker in it. Helenka looked at the photo. It was a blond young woman on horseback; the dedication read in German, *"To Martin, from his favourite horsewoman Benedikta."* It was dated a year ago exactly. The young woman looked healthy, haughty, sure of herself.

"Good morning."

Bora's voice revealed no surprise at finding her in the library. Greatcoat on his arm, he was dressed in a simple field uniform and was obviously about to leave the house.

Helenka nodded her head. "Good morning." She felt awkward for having his book in her lap. Bora didn't seem irritated by the fact. He stared at the book, however, and Helenka put it away. "I didn't mean to pry. I thought maybe Jacob Malev had left it out."

Bora half-turned towards the bookshelf. He wasn't angry at her. Rather, he felt a kind of impatient sorrow for her embarrassment. "I'm looking for a dictionary." He chose to justify his presence here. In fact, he had meant to look up the word *Lumen* before leaving. Now he reached for the Latin book and decided to take it along on his drive east.

Huddled on the armchair where he'd sat to read until late last night, Helenka was embracing her retracted knees.

Bora sensed an odd affinity with her for being here and having shared that chair, and although he wasn't attracted to her he grew close to arousal, just because she was a woman and it was early in the morning and they were alone in the room. *The rustle of her skirt,* Garcia Lorca had written, *was like knives slicing the air.*

She said, "I hope Richard told you yesterday that I'd spend the night. I didn't mean to inconvenience you."

It was a strange apology, which made him angry at Retz for creating these situations. For all his haste, Bora didn't want to leave the room before saying so. "It's difficult for me not to think of the reason why you come." It was a confusing, accusatory statement, and he sought to correct it, aghast at what he actually said next. "I miss my wife very much."

"She's beautiful," Helenka said, glancing at the photograph. "I can see why you miss her."

Bora looked away. He hadn't meant to reveal himself. The thought that she had just made love turned him suddenly insecure and shy and desirous: not of her necessarily, but of the act itself, because she'd been entered by a man, and he was looking at her and sensed the unspoken, troubling essence of that intimacy.

"I must go now."

He was perspiring when he reached the street below, and it was a relief to plunge into the frigid snowy air of the morning. He had just enough time to drive by the convent before his appointment with Colonel Schenck.

At Bora's coming into the sacristy, Father Malecki sneezed into his plaid handkerchief.

"*Gesundheit.*" Bora said. "The sisters told me I'd find you still here." He was rummaging in his pocket, took out a flat box of mint drops, and presented them on his open palm. "My mother sends me Altoids wherever I go. It's her way to keep me well, I think. You may have them."

Malecki looked miserable. He put a mint drop in his mouth, but would not accept a ride back to his apartment in the German staff car.

"As you like," Bora said amiably. "The streetcars are scheduled to start running again at nine. You won't have to walk. How did you catch such a bad cold, anyway? Surely the weather isn't any better than this in Chicago!"

"No, but there's less chance for furnaces to stop running in Chicago. If you're here for mass, you're late."

"Oh, I don't go to church these days. I've only come to say that I'll be busy and won't be seeing you for a few days. You'll kindly let me know of any developments at my return."

No sooner had Bora left the sacristy than Malecki went to open the closet where vestments were kept.

"All right, come out." Vexedly, he looked inside after the man obeyed. "Look what you've done with those damn muddy boots." He took out the stained vestments, with a critical eye checking the hems for tears in the cloth.

Now that he saw him in the full light, Malecki was sure this was the same man he'd spoken with on the stairs of his house.

"Look, I told you before. I have no intention of dragging the sisters or the American government into whatever you're doing. The convent is off-limits to arms and armed people, and you'll have to avoid coming to see me at the house as well. Why are you here, anyway?"

Kneading his cap with both hands, the man was bleary-eyed, with the look of one whom constant tension has made into a mask of strain.

"If the convent's off-limits to armed people, what's the German after? *He* comes around!"

Suffering from his cold, Malecki didn't like to be confronted. He briskly stepped past the man to get his scarf from the coat stand. "It has nothing to do with politics. Look, I have to go, and I'm not leaving you behind. Tell me your business, and let's be done with it."

Having heard what the business was, he had to lean against the door of the sacristy, unwittingly swallowing the powerful mint Bora had given him. It went down his sore throat with a chilly burn.

"A relic?" He coughed.

"Yes."

Malecki snorted through his aching and congested nose. "No new relics are acknowledged unless by authorization of the local bishop. I can't give you anything of hers, even if I had anything to give."

"But she's a saint."

"Miracles have to be approved all the same. Besides, 'nothing new, or that previously has not been usual in the Church' may be resolved on without consulting the Holy See."

"A saint's a saint, *Ojciec.*"

The man's insistence was testy, Malecki saw well that he wouldn't get rid of him easily. He put on his coat and edged the man out of the sacristy. "You seem to know more than I do."

"She's worked miracles."

Malecki stopped where he was, on the threshold of the room. He was familiar with the tales that had risen about Mother Kazimierza in the last six months, had investigated some and found them unsound when not ludicrous. The abbess herself had dismissed them angrily.

He said, "Miracles are something else that need proving."

He didn't expect the rude pressure of a gun barrel up his ribcage, and grew stiff with anger for it.

"You had better give us a relic of *Matka* Kazimierza, *Ojciec.*"

Malecki slapped the gun away. "I haven't grown up in Chicago to be pushed around in a Cracow sacristy. You will give me one piece of information, and then go. When God wants to make a saint out of the abbess, he'll let both of us know."

But afterwards he did give the man a framed photograph of Mother Kazimierza that hung just outside his door.

When he left headquarters with Bora, Schenck had the face of a bridegroom. His happiness for going out in the field after weeks behind a desk was contagious, and Bora didn't need much to be exhilarated those days.

They would ride to the Russian sector under the escort of an armed patrol; at the demarcation line they'd be met by a Red Army convoy and continue to Lvov for a round of talks with Soviet Intelligence.

"Given that the Wehrmacht had made it to Lemberg first." Schenck sneered, bent on using the German name of Lvov. "It's too bad we had to relinquish it."

"Borders are reversible," Bora said.

The staff car passed people going to church, grey bundled people who didn't so much as look up. At the end of nearly every other street, churches rose against the sky like prows, or gigantic theatre props left over from forgotten performances. They had come to the cemetery by the rail junction before Schenck laughed in a delayed response to Bora's words, "It's true, they are." And soon the staff car was speeding down the state route to Tarnów.

Once they left the city, no traffic – military or civilian – slowed their progress to the east.

Bora said, reading, "There are at least ten related but different meanings for the word. *Light, torch, source of light, light of the eye, daylight…*"

"Really?" Schenck threw an amused look at the cumbersome dictionary Bora held up. "I do think it was a good idea to get you into Intelligence business. You like to dig. You're likely to dig up bones if you keep at it."

They had passed the first line of hills east of Cracow, slung diagonally as fingers extending from the distant heights of the Carpathians. The weather forecast called for a clearing at midday, and already some widening wells of blue opened in the clouds.

Fastidiously, Schenck removed his gloves. "Bora, after your request I went over Salle-Weber's head, and we stand a good chance of getting our hands on the *Lumen* file. Salle-Weber will know the pressure came from you, but tell him you had nothing to do with it, that it was my idea. Captains can pull punches with captains, but not so well with colonels." Schenck let the ripple of a smile cross his lips. "To think I almost joined the SS, some years back. It was the wholesale quality of their eugenics program that left me unconvinced."

Bora waited until Schenck finished talking before looking into the dictionary again. Examples were given of the use of the word, in the singular and plural form; none of them seemed to apply in the least. He was beginning to think that Father Malecki was right. Attaching too much importance to a sentence only kept him from seeking out *real* reasons. He said, unthinkingly, "Colonel, would we eliminate someone like Mother Kazimierza?"

Schenck didn't move a muscle of his leathery face. "Yes." He said then, "Of course we would. If we found it useful to our cause or to security, we most assuredly would."

"Have we?"

Again, Schenck's face was motionless. He waited some time before answering. "I've seen perfectly good dogs go digging in the wrong places, Captain Bora. You have to refine your sense of scent before you end up wasting a lot of energy, and come up with a fat rock in your teeth instead of a bone. The answer is no."

Bora tried not to feel embarrassed. Cheerfully, Schenck looked out of the window, to the fields that ran past the car. Tarnów had been left behind. Frequency of hills intensified ahead and only after turning due south before Lvov would the land grow flat again. "I suggest you also sharpen your sense of diplomacy before you ask the SS the same question."

The first thing Father Malecki noticed upon entering *Pana* Klara's house was the lack of cold dampness that had enveloped him each time he'd started up the stairs in days past.

When he opened the door to his room, his impression was that he must be running a fever, because he felt warm. He freed himself of coat and scarf before noticing that the water in his wash basin had lost its veil of ice. Stretching one hand towards the radiator, he felt heat rising from it.

"*Pana* Klara!" he called out hoarsely. "What's happened with the furnace?"

The landlady came up the stairs wiping her hands in a dish towel. "Things one wouldn't believe, Father Malecki. An hour ago the coal truck came and the men knocked on my door to tell me there was a delivery for the tenement, and asked whether I was going to show them where to dump it, and sign a receipt for it. I told them I wasn't about to sign anything because I hadn't called them to begin with and I didn't know what the bill was going to be. They told me there was no bill."

Father Malecki sneezed into his cupped hands. "Well, what do you make of it?"

Pana Klara took a card out of her apron's pocket. "Instead of the bill, they handed me this. 'For the priest,' they said."

The card was blank on one side. On the other one, in English, Malecki read, "*You should have accepted a ride.*"

As for Major Retz, he dropped Helenka at the corner of her street and watched her walk up the sidewalk towards home.

She was worth it, he told himself. She was worth the little agonies of lovesickness and his argument with Bora – he'd get Bora to leave the apartment sooner or later. There she went, little feet, thin waist. The way she held her head high like her mother. The quick strut that gave life to her small hips.

Helenka disappeared inside the gloomy front door of the dingy tenement. Retz put the car in reverse, turned direction and headed for the Old Theatre.

The smell of inexpensive perfume and women's sweat welcomed him to the narrow hallway that led to the dressing room. Retz sniffed it, nostrils dilating. It reminded him of the last war, although it wasn't the same theatre and it wasn't even the same city. Women's odours excited him.

He heard Ewa's voice rehearsing her part from behind the closed door.

"I go, because of you, stripped of my honour —"
Retz knocked on the door.

It happened half an hour east of Debica, and too quickly for either Schenck or Bora to realize what had hit them. It came as a loud crash and whipping sound, with a spray of blood and glass that flew at them from the front seat.

The staff car lost control and careened before jumping the shoulder and sideswiping a low stone wall. A hand grenade thrown in their direction missed the car and went on to raise a column of snow, earth and twigs past the wall. Behind them, another explosion blasted the sidewalk, sending metal and chunks of asphalt flying.

Rapid fire cracked down at the convoy from an incline to the right of the road. At once, by reflex, Bora and Schenck left the car and stood in the open in a firing stance, side by side. Rifle fire and bursts of machine-gun fire converged against them, as if the brushwood had a life of its own, hostile and determined to keep them from getting past. The escort truck was already pouring men out in a sequence of burnished helmets, and nothing short of a battle followed on the stretch of solitary road. A furious and wordless, largely mindless shooting back and forth, with men who crawled and ran for cover or out of it to shoot.

When it was over, Schenck was recriminating over the dead driver and a ruined windshield. He barely paid attention when Bora came back from the incline where the attackers had been hiding. He hadn't even noticed Bora was gone.

"It seems they were all killed, Colonel. Six men, no uniforms, one empty machine gun, three carbines and five handguns retrieved."

Schenck disregarded the news. "Damn, I'm not meeting the Russians with a totalled windshield. I wouldn't give them the benefit of knowing we've been shot at." He struck Bora's shoulder with the companionable rap of a closed fist. "Let's you and I drive to the next post and get ourselves another staff vehicle."

Bora only had time to order the removal of the dead driver before Schenck methodically took to breaking with the butt of his Walther what remained of the smashed windshield. "At least we can see where we're going," he said. And when the job didn't proceed quickly enough for his impatience, he vaulted on the hood and kicked the rest of the glass in.

As for Bora, he was glad Hannes had not been the driver today. With a rag he wiped blood and glass from the front seat and the dashboard as best he could, turned the key in the ignition and backed the car up into the road.

Still cursing under his breath, Schenck took his place alongside him.

"The colonel should consider riding in the back," Bora said.

"Get this thing going. The colonel rides where he goddamn well pleases."

Retz and Ewa had breakfast at the *Pod Latarnie* restaurant.

"Aren't you hungry?" she asked.

They were sitting in the middle of the room, and Ewa could see from where she sat the sparse population of midmorning on Sunday. There were some well-fed German soldiers, ethnic German civilians with narrow, bony faces; two women wearing ratty furs around their necks sat at the table where the soldiers drank and laughed. Looking over her shoulder, she glimpsed at the recess of the window where she had sat with Bora. There was no one at that table now. She brought to mind Bora's stern attention, unflattering to her.

Retz, who'd breakfasted with Helenka at the apartment, simply said, "I guess I'm not hungry. Do you want more coffee?"

Ewa held out her cup.

"Richard, do you dye your hair?"

Her question came so entirely out of context, Retz was confused by it despite his ability to joke about it. He spilled some coffee. "Why, does it look like I dye my hair?"

"Yes." Ewa put a crumb in her mouth. "It didn't look this colour twenty-one years ago."

"You have a good memory."

"I think you'd look more distinguished with grey hair. Was it turning very much grey?"

Retz grumblingly said something about having started to turn grey at thirty. "I don't see why I should look older than my age."

Ewa pushed her shoulders back. She had her hair up and liked the way she looked this morning, so she could afford this little cruelty. "We don't look a day older than we are, Richard." Out of the pack he had laid by his plate she extracted a cigarette. She placed it in her mouth, and when she took it out again to remove a speck of tobacco from her lips, rouge had drawn a bright circle around it. "I stopped menstruating this spring."

Retz's lighter was aluminium, with a brass regimental crest. He held the steady small flame for Ewa to take a first drag of the cigarette. Some good humour had returned to him. "Well, it makes it safer for us, eh?"

*

143

While they waited for a car to be driven for them from Rzeszów, Schenck and Bora went to sit on a bench in the yard of the small field *Kommandantur*. Slim birch woods bristled the land down the way, pencilled white against the ground. It was not cold, and a jay whistled sharp. Most of the snow fallen among the trees had melted or formed clean blue patches in their shade. A glory of sunlight filtered through the woods.

The accident, if anything, had made the two of them euphoric. To Bora, being alive had been downright heady to him until moments ago, like on the day the armed man had jumped out of the haystack, which was the same day he'd seen for the first time the photograph of Mother Kazimierza.

Schenck seemed to read his mind. "These sudden jolts are good for a man's nerves. They're like a tonic. Danger gets the adrenaline flowing, with all that follows I did some reading about it. Adrenaline at first raises your pressure, dilates the bronchi, increases production of saliva. It stimulates the seminal vesicles, I'm sure you've noticed."

Bora had noticed. He wondered whether Colonel Schenck ever thought of anything else.

More and more, as a reaction to the drop in stress, he sat entirely relaxed, smelling the odour of wood burning in the stove of the building behind them.

Schenck kept his arms crossed tightly against his wiry self. "Take today. You and I could have been killed. You could be dead now, or worse." He caught Bora's rise in curiosity, although no questions followed. "You could be mutilated. In Spain I saw a man whom a grenade had castrated. Took both testicles clear off. What do you say about that? Luckily the man – he was a Basque from Santander – had produced children prior to his accident."

The mention brought Bora back to the sight of mangled bodies in the Jewish schoolhouse, with an unexpected rise of disgust. He guarded it, but euphoria and relaxation had gone. He felt reminded of mortality and very insecure.

Schenck smiled his bony, mean smile at him. "I hope you don't mind my interference, Captain, but I wired General Sickingen to bring your wife along to Cracow."

Bora said something disciplined, he was sure, though a wild urge to whoop risked breaking out of him all the way to Przemyśl.

There, the Russians were leery, not unfriendly. Rosy-faced, stuffed in uniforms with the peculiar peasant shirt pattern, they resembled overgrown gnomes. They insisted that Schenck and Bora be shown at once a display of captured Polish equipment and insignia. A Red Army photographer took snapshots of the Germans listening to the explanations of a tow-headed, bespectacled commissar. Vodka was brought out. Lunch, they were told, awaited in Lvov.

"As if I came to eat with the Russians." Schenck grumbled to Bora, and then, "Tell them we look forward to lunch."

In Cracow, Father Malecki said he doubted it would help, which didn't keep *Pana* Klara from presenting him a demi-tasse of strong coffee with brandy.

"It's the old-fashioned recipe, Father. Gulp it down when it's hottest."

At half-past noon, while at the border Bora translated for Colonel Schenck the third toast of the Russian post commander, Malecki was about to fall asleep in the parlour. The combination of head cold, drink and comfortable temperature would have succeeded except for the landlady's call from the hallway.

"Father, there's someone from the American consulate to see you."

Immediately behind her, towering over her small stature, a youthful foreign-service officer in a white trench coat greeted the priest. Malecki recognized him from his visits to the consulate. His name was Logan, and he'd graduated from Notre Dame some five years back.

"Father Malecki, I hope I'm not intruding."

"You're not intruding. You'll probably just catch a cold from me."

Logan removed his hat but not his coat. "I'm not going to stay long. I really didn't come officially. The consul told me to stop by."

"Well, sit down."

"No, thank you. Father, the consul is aware that you were instructed by the Holy See not to leave Cracow, even though the reason for your visit terminated with the death of the abbess at Our Lady of Sorrows. We also understand that German authorities have taken over the investigation of her death." Logan made a meaningful pause. When he saw that Malecki didn't encourage him to continue, he cleared his throat. "The consul feels very strongly that soon the violent cause of the abbess's death will become known, whoever was behind the killing. Due to her popularity among the Catholic population —"

"You speak as if you weren't Catholic yourself," Malecki interrupted. "Come, come. What are you trying to say?"

"The consul feels you might want to consider leaving Poland."

Malecki rested his hands on the crocheted doilies *Pana* Klara pinned to all the arms of the overstuffed chairs there were in the house.

"Why?"

Logan cleared his throat once more. The bulge of the Adam's apple on his neck rose and fell above the line of his collar.

"The consul fears there might be violence in the streets when the news breaks out."

"And?... Does the consul think I'd get involved in the riots? Or does he think that in their blind anger the Poles will attack a Polish-American priest? That's nonsense."

In the silence that followed, the hollow ticking of a mantel clock made itself conspicuous. Malecki sneezed. Logan was about to start another sentence, but was prevented.

"See here, Mister Logan. I appreciate your motoring here on your day off to tell me what the consul thinks – except that it isn't what the consul thinks." Malecki held up his hand to avoid recriminations. "What the consul really thinks, if I'm allowed to speculate, is that I shouldn't continue to visit the convent while the investigation proceeds. Has His Eminence the archbishop called at the consulate, by any chance?"

Logan fingered the rim of his floppy hat. "It makes little difference what lies behind our concern for an American national. The concern is real. We understand there has been some violence against your person already."

Now Malecki knew the archbishop was behind this. He decided to take his time before replying. He loudly blew his nose, opened the box of mints and rested one on his tongue. Logan watched him expectantly. Malecki offered him a mint.

"To tell the whole story, I struck first."

Logan needed a few seconds to recuperate. He swallowed the mint without even tasting it. "Father, if the consul were informed – do you realize to what risk any action against a German places you?"

"From one Midwesterner to another, Mister Logan, I'd much rather if you didn't take it upon yourself to inform the consul on this any further. I will speak when and if I see fit."

"You cannot ask me to ignore the fact that you're in danger!"

Malecki shook his head. "With a war in the offing, I wouldn't lose sleep over the danger any of us run in Cracow." He rose from the armchair. "You know, I have this nasty cold which I would like to sleep off. Be kind, Mister Logan. Go and tell the consul that I'm obliged to him. I have no wish to leave Cracow and I don't think you or the consul can make me. My church work here isn't done, and I promise I'll deal with the Germans more wisely than in the past. As usual, they're their own worst enemies."

Two hundred and fifty kilometres to the east, Colonel Schenck told Bora that one more toast was all he'd accept from the Russian commander. "The last thing we need is to get to Lvov stone drunk."

Bora held liquor well, but felt an increasing level of giddy merriment at the thought of what alcohol might be doing to the colonel's seminal vesicles. He hardly worried about his own, now that the perspective of Dikta's coming was sure to set him on an edge of perpetual urges for the next three weeks.

The Russians were installed in the Hotel *Patria* at Lvov. The hotel was within walking distance from the museum on the four-fountained Market Square, which the Germans were made to visit for a last-minute aperitif.

"*Dobro pozhalovat!*" A dapper colonel in steel-grey tunic welcomed the guests in the venerable carpeted lobby. Inevitably he was flanked by a commissar, identifiable by the red star on his sleeve. Bora couldn't help comparing these to the shabby uniforms of the privates outside, standing under their long-eared cloth helmets.

Schenck frowned. "Tell him I'd like to start the talks right after lunch, Bora. I don't want to be stuck with another tour of the city or propaganda sales talk."

Bora translated throughout the reception. The commissar was seated across the table from him, and observed him closely. He said at one point, "You speak Russian well. How is it that you studied it so zealously?"

Bora answered with some polite generality. What Schenck had whispered to him on the way to the table was probably closer to the truth. "Mark my words, Bora, we're going to take back this town. We surely haven't entered Poland to leave half of it to the Reds."

In the afternoon, the church of the Dominicans in Lvov reminded Bora of the church of Our Lady of Seven Sorrows in Cracow. The same Roman baroque volumes multiplied into cupolas and side chapels, although the open square gave this building more relevance than the convent had along the narrow street in Cracow.

Schenck had succeeded in obtaining a first round of talks immediately after lunch, primarily matters of common intelligence, the preliminary draft of an agreement to collaborate against local resistance by open exchange of communiqués and issues of border protocol.

The Russians took their revenge by dragging the visitors through a sight-seeing tour of the city. Benignantly, the commissar turned to Bora. "You see how adversary propaganda has done Marxism wrong, Captain. The churches are intact, open and useable."

Bora had been glancing at the street signs in the Cyrillic alphabet, aware that they carried the same signs of temporariness of the German ones in the west.

"Yes," he spoke back, and smiling came easy. "But there's a nursery rhyme in English that goes, 'Here's the church / and here's the steeple…' Today is Sunday, and I wonder where all the people might be."

*

With news about Helenka in mind, Kasia almost forgot she was carrying a small piece of margarine in her pocket. When she pulled out a coin for the streetcar, her fingers met with the paper wrapper. Luckily it was cold enough for the margarine to stay solid. She stood through the short ride, holding on to the hand strap with an anxious eye to the names of the streets.

This was the stop for Święty Krzyża. Kasia got off in the slushy remnant of snow at the edge of the sidewalk, careless of wetting her shoes. Her toes were soaked in the time it took her to go from the corner of the street to Ewa's door.

"I'm a friend of *Pana* Kowalska," she explained to the porter. Ewa had told her the house management was strict, and the war had made it even more suspicious. It was easy to see, Kasia told herself while the porter kept her waiting, why Ewa didn't take Richard Retz home.

"What is your name?"

Kasia answered.

"Why are you in such a hurry, young lady? What is the matter?"

A malicious desire to gossip about Helenka and to see Ewa's reactions nearly caused her to snap back at the porter, but still Kasia controlled her temper. An idea came to her. "I have urgent need to see Ewa Kowalska," she said, all the while unwrapping the margarine and pushing it into the narrow window of the porter's cubbyhole. "Will you let me go up?"

The porter reached for the margarine, sniffed it and gave it back. "She lives on the fourth floor, first door to the right. 'Going up' is just what you'll have to do: the elevator's out of order."

It was nearly five o'clock in the evening when Father Malecki awoke from his nap in the parlour's armchair.

He'd slept soundly, and could not remember his dreams except for the last one, which was bizarre enough to stick in his memory.

He'd dreamed that he was getting ready for mass. From the wardrobe where his vestments were kept, the bleary-eyed, moustached man who wanted the relics leaped out, holding hands with one of the nuns.

The nun's face was nondescript, no one that Malecki could identify. She was wearing an oversized portrait of Mother Kazimierza around her neck. It looked like an ancient medallion with the abbess's profile at the centre, surrounded by the letters *L.C.A.N.* From the depth of the wardrobe, a bright light came forth like a beacon.

"What's that light?" Malecki remembered asking the nun in his dream.

"Why, Father, don't you know? It's what killed the abbess, and what made her a saint."

Shielding his eyes from the light, Malecki had reached for his surplice, unable to see it but feeling for it by touch. There was a spray of bloodstains at the cuffs, on the side and at the lower hem.

"Now you too have a relic, *Ojciec!*" the moustached man had shouted, skipping out of the sacristy with the nun. "Just make sure you tell the German that you know where the repairmen went!"

Mister Logan had come out of the wardrobe last, clearing his throat. "The consul thinks you should return the relic of the surplice, Father Malecki. It's against American policy for you to become a saint outside of the country."

This is what happens when one has a bad cold and receives foreign-service officers, Malecki told himself. Sneezing into his plaid handkerchief, he left the parlour and climbed the stairs to his room.

7

"She's a dear girl," Sister Irenka asserted, hands clasped in her ample sleeves as in a muff. "Her dreams may be no more than that, but then perhaps they're worth your enquiring about them."

Father Malecki savoured the mint drop as its coolness coated his tongue and began to rise to his nostrils. He was regaining some of his sense of smell. The odour of onions frying in the convent kitchen floated, though faintly, to his nose. He said, "How long has she been at the convent?"

"She took her vows two years ago on Easter Sunday. She's originally from Biała, south of here. She's also a convert from a very strict Jewish family, which says much for her."

"Was she close to the abbess?"

Sister Irenka wrinkled her nose like a spiteful girl. "I associated with the abbess more than anyone else in the convent, as I'm sure you noticed. Not even *I* was close to the abbess. However, Sister Barbara entered this order because of Mother Kazimierza. She was converted on Easter Sunday seven years ago after a bout with infantile paralysis." Father Malecki now remembered the pudgy young nun with a stoop. "A medal from Mother Kazimierza is credited with her conversion and, according to Sister Barbara, with her healing as well."

Had he not dreamed of the nun wearing a medallion? Malecki thought so, but made nothing of the coincidence at this point.

"Would it be better for me to speak to Sister Barbara in confession?"

"It will be up to you, Father. Why don't you meet her meanwhile? She's been unwell since the abbess's death. The doctor thinks it's nerves, but the doctor doesn't truly understand women *or* nuns."

Sister Barbara worked in the kitchen. She came to meet the priest in the waiting room with high windows, cold and spotless and under the sad watch of the crucifix.

"Praised be Jesus Christ," she greeted him.

"Always, Sister."

"Sister Irenka told me I should meet you."

Unlike the other nuns, she was very dark of features. Sister Irenka had bluntly said that she knew the first time she'd set eyes on her that she must be a gypsy or a Jewess. Malecki had seen Spanish and Italian nuns in Chicago looking like her, with mournful black eyes that seemed to well up from the soul.

Her skin had no colour. Although she was no more than thirty, flesh hung about her cheeks as in one who has lost a lot of weight too quickly. A veil-like onion skin hung from the hem of her sleeve, and her nearness still smelled of onions.

Malecki had planned a direct approach, but now it didn't seem easy to say anything to her. She kept an expectant, quiet defensiveness, which he might have to circumvent before trying to enter.

"Sister Barbara, you're aware of my months of study here in relation to the abbess. Given Mother Kazimierza's role in your life choice, I wonder if you'd care to tell me about your conversion."

"I will, Father."

To Malecki, ever since the abbess's death, the convent was as though under a spell of silence. Even Sister Barbara's voice – a deep monotone, a teacher's voice – seemed unable to break the spell, and sounded dull, muted.

She was saying, "It's always like the first dream. There are some variations, some details that reflect things that happened during the day, but the essence is the same." Holding a black rosary in her hands, mechanically she rolled each bead of the chain. "I am in my father's house at Biała. There is *tsholnt* on the table, so I think maybe it's Friday, because that's when that dish is prepared. My father is outside. I can hear him chopping through meat with his cleaver. It seems to me that every time the blade goes down, a voice next to me is saying, 'Body of Christ. Body of Christ.'"

"Whose voice is it?"

"I don't know. A man's voice, but then I know it's Mother Kazimierza's voice, too. I feel that I have to get out of the house, but won't be able to do so until my father leaves. My mother is in the back of the house, reciting the Kaddish for some relative who has died. I call out to her and ask who is it that died, and she says, 'You, *Bubele.* How can you not know I'm reciting it for you?'" Sister Barbara glanced up, as if fearful of having said too much already. "Sometimes the dream stops here, but most often it goes on to the end."

Malecki was interested in the end, of course, but didn't pressure her. He sat with his right elbow on the knee, resting his aching forehead in the open hand. His cold was not gone, by any means. It throbbed in his sinuses and made him less alert than he needed to be.

The nun let out a small sigh. "When the dream continues, I have somehow got out of the house. My father seems to be very distant. I am standing on a brick platform and Mother Kazimierza is with me. She has her arms outstretched." Sister Barbara's eyes stole to the crucifix on the wall. "Like *Him.* Blood drips from her hands and feet, but she is smiling. She asks me if I would like to come with her. My legs feel bound, and I tell her that I would love to follow her, but I don't think I'm worthy or even able. She simply takes my hand and starts walking. I had a dream similar to this part seven years ago, which is when I became well again. We walk and walk and walk. The platform follows us wherever we go. At one point Mother Kazimierza asks me if I want to be a saint. I say, yes, and she says that if I want to be like Christ they will come to take me away as they did with Christ. 'Will you come also?' I ask her. She opens her arms again and lies down on the platform. The same voice I heard in my father's house I hear now, saying, 'No one but my name.'"

From the nun's silence, Malecki understood she had finished her story. "'No one but my name,' Sister." He opened his eyes. "What does that mean?"

"I don't know. I wake up in tears every time, not because of what happens in the dream but because I am reminded that she is dead, and even though I know I should rejoice that she is with Christ, it is so difficult to accept her absence."

Two days into her stay in Retz's apartment, Ewa felt triumphant.

Brushing her hair in front of the sink, she watched him bathing in the tub. His fleshy knees rose from the suds, bald as his chest was shaggy, with tufts of wet hair that clustered and curled like blond shavings of wood. He'd been lounging in the bath for the past ten minutes, now and then adding hot water to the tub.

She said, "What happened to your wedding ring?"

Retz opened his eyes.

"I took it off."

"I can see that. Why?"

Retz smiled. He liked looking at her nakedness. "I didn't feel like wearing it any more." Ewa was big-breasted, though her breasts were still quite pert for her age. Only the once-perfect line of her buttocks had changed noticeably; her arms had always been rounded, dimpled at the elbows. Now that she reached for the back of her head with the brush, the yellow sprig of hair under her right arm showed. The right breast rose with the motion. "Doesn't it tell you the ring means nothing to me, Ewusia?"

"Well, then give it to me, for old times' sake."

Water splashed in the tub as Retz sat up in it. "I couldn't do that, Ewusia. What am I going to tell my wife if I don't bring it back?"

"Who cares?" Vigorously, Ewa brushed through her hair. "She's a sow."

Retz tried to laugh. "Ewa..."

"Tell me she's a sow."

"She's just an old girl."

"You know she's a sow. Tell me."

Retz sank back into the water, this time nearly to his chin. "She's a sow. All women are sows compared to you." His head went under for a moment, and emerged again. "Is that all right?"

Ewa laughed. She grabbed the wide bath towel and tossed it at him. "That's better." When he began to stand up, the water-soaked heavy cloth clung around him and he fell back in the tub, laughing also. He struggled to get free from the towel, hands and feet splashing soapy water around the bathroom.

Ewa was sitting on the side of the tub when his head came out of the dripping cloth.

"Does being married to a sow make me a swine?" He stepped out of the water and reached for her.

She pulled away, slapping his hand. "You know it does."

*

The woods started just off the road. From where Bora stood at Schenck's side, the darkness of firs ate some of the luminosity of the sky. For two hours officers of the Russian 17th Rifle Corps had shown them more equipment taken from the defeated Polish army, bicycles and horse-drawn vehicles, heaps of cavalry harnesses. Among the other vehicles Bora noticed two convertible Polski-Fiat staff cars. He remembered the Polish cavalry officer had told him some of his colleagues had been dragged off to be shot after riding in their cars to surrender.

Schenck was anxious to read the Russian proposal for collaboration in Intelligence matters, especially as related to partisan activity. He champed at the bit while viewing more trophies. Where the woods opened into a snow-patched dirt expanse, a camp was set up, complete with table, chairs and bottles of liquor.

With the commissar constantly keeping pace with him, Bora found it difficult to have a private word with the colonel, and gave up the attempt of using the field latrine for the purpose when the commissar showed that he was headed in the same direction.

Colonel Schenck did not show half the anger Bora knew him to feel. Still, "Go ahead," he said after a time, "tell these shit-headed Ivans that we have no reports that Polish nationals manhandled Ukrainian settlers in our sector. Make them understand that if we had such reports we would have followed up on them. Tell them I reject the insinuation that we have ignored reports."

The discussion had been degenerating for the past quarter-hour, primarily on issues of communiqué-sharing and joint anti-partisan activities. The thin veneer of the occasional alliance began to wear down as soon as generalities were forsaken in favour of details. Schenck and the Red Army colonel made as unlikely a pair of bedfellows as Bora could envision, saving perhaps himself and the commissar. He translated accurately, feeling the tension of the job every time a word lent itself to misunderstanding or multiple meanings.

They were sitting at a long dining-room table incongruously placed in the middle of a clearing, fringed with fir trees and lined with Russian army tents. Everyday vodka, straw-coloured vodka from Georgia, the overwhelming dark one they called "huntsman's vodka" sat before him. Bora decided he would not drink past the fourth glass, and chose his words, certain that he would ever more associate the resinous scent of firs with a sense of unease. Matters grew worse when a veiled accusation was brought up that German troops had fired on Red Army units, not only during the confusion of the first days, but as late as a week past. Schenck demanded a clarification, which came back as a naked indictment. In a rigid fury, he ordered Bora to counter with accusations of the opposite. "Give them dates, places, the whole of it. Show them pictures of damage to our equipment."

Bora complied. The photographs were at once snatched from his hands by the commissar, before the Russian colonel had a chance to view them. An animated exchange ensued, during which Schenck grew irate enough to charge the Red Army with wholesale execution of Polish prisoners of war.

"Get to the point, Bora. Ask them how they would like for us to make an international issue out of *that*."

Brusquely, the Russian colonel left the table in a flash of steel-grey cloth. Vodka danced in the bottle and the glasses tinkled at his hasty departure. The commissar at first engaged in a silent staring match with Bora, and then rose from his chair and went to retrieve the colonel.

"Shit." Schenck let himself go to frustration. "I didn't mean to bring up the damn story of the Polack prisoners. What did you exactly tell him?"

"I kept it vague, but they still took it badly."

"I can see that." Schenck looked beyond Bora, at the tent in front of which their counterparts thickly discussed this turn of events among themselves. He reached for the bottle and poured himself a dose of dark vodka, which he swallowed in a gulp. "When they come back, let's pay some lip-service. Tell them you didn't translate correctly, that it was your mistake."

"They'll know it isn't true, Colonel."

"Make it credible. You're young enough and low-ranking enough to take the blame."

13 December

The afternoon was sunny and cold in Cracow. Helenka's voice through the telephone made Retz lusty and hopeful at first.

"No, Richard. I can't. I'm not even done preparing the part, and dress rehearsals begin pretty soon. It's my first important role, and I can't foul it up. We can see one another again after the first night, depending on how it goes."

Retz groaned. "Do you mean we don't get to spend any time together between now and then?"

"We can see each other for lunch or something like that. I just don't feel I should be using time at night this way, that's when I study the part best."

"Well, people don't make love only at night."

"I don't like hotels – I mean, for that kind of thing."

"I'll tell you what, *luby*. I'll compromise. I'll leave you alone for three days, and then I'll call you and see if you want to get away for a couple of hours. Study hard those three days." Retz flipped through the pages of his appointment book on the desk, looking for Ewa's number. "I love you, too."

There was only one telephone in the tenement where Ewa lived, so he had to wait until the porter went to check if *Pana* Kowalska was home, four storeys worth of slow climbing and descending steps again. It was one more disappointment to hear that Ewa was out. Pages flipped forwards in the appointment book.

"Yes, hello? I'm looking for *Panienka* Basia Plutinska – Yes, please put her on."

After liberally partaking of vodka over a satisfactory agreement in the woods, the appeased Russian and German representatives had adjourned with the prospect of more sight-seeing and dinner at Lvov. By mid-afternoon on the 13th, though, Schenck had had enough of the meeting. He waited until he and Bora sat alone in the car, while their Russian driver filled the tank from an aluminium can. Then, "Screw them all," he spat out. "I'm going back tomorrow, Bora. Stay behind to supervise details, and meet me at the border. From there we travel to Tarnów and there we part ways. I expect you to resume your routine interrogation of Polacks before you return to headquarters."

But neither Schenck nor Bora could avoid one more dinner with the Russians. Fish served raw, salted, in vinegar, opened the way to grouse swimming in cream, and to thick ham slices lying on beds of caviar and boiled eggs. Watching him eat, from the moment he sat down beside him, the commissar seemed to take perverse pleasure in challenging Bora with complex sentences and verb forms. Bora did well but was troubled, and he didn't know why. Over a dessert of *mazurek* he finally understood.

"Tell me," the commissar was saying, "how could a fluent speaker as yourself make such a patent mistake during our talks? I don't believe there was a mistake at all, Captain."

Bora took a discreet belly breath. Sedately, he put down the fork on his plate. From a bowl in front of him, he selected a small cake, whose thin paper wrapping he undid. "You call these 'chocolate bears', do you not?" He smiled. "I hope you're not accusing me of lying."

"No. Mistakes are more acceptable."

Cracow was frigid, but the temperature in the Curia was drowsily pleasant, and it wasn't easy to rouse the archbishop's attention. If Father Malecki hadn't felt compelled by the need to discuss Sister Barbara before Bora's return, he'd have given up the effort. As it was, he allowed himself to insist.

"Your Eminence, she runs a high risk," he said. "Her family has repudiated her since she converted. After all, her father was *shochet* in their hometown. From his perspective, it was a terrible humiliation for him that his only daughter should forsake her people's ways. One of the requirements for the position of ritual animal slaughterer is that the man be of unsullied character, and he voluntarily resigned after the scandal broke."

"What did you say the community was?"

"Biała."

"Hm." The archbishop frowned as he controlled a yawn. "I know the town. The Jews account for less than twenty per cent of the population there."

Malecki fixed his eyes on the window behind the archbishop's head. Snow twirled furiously beyond the panes, a wet snow that wouldn't last. He found it odd that the number of Jews in Biała should concern the archbishop more than his story.

"Not that her family could help her now, Your Eminence. I hear that the Biała Jews are being resettled."

Obliviously the archbishop folded his elegant hands in his lap. "It is a glory for the Church that someone from such a background would be called into the fold."

"Well, the Germans are requiring that all Jewish women attach the name 'Sarah' to their given name. I don't think I should be telling Captain Bora about her, just in case."

"Will you keep the dream from him also?"

"Yes." Malecki blew his nose moderately. "Making the Germans aware of Sister Barbara's presence would be a worse sin than withholding information about a dream. I doubt Captain Bora could do much with it anyway."

The archbishop read through Malecki's intentions plainly enough. Still, he asked, "Have you come to share with me the meaningless recurrent dream of a distressed nun, or is there another motive?"

"I was hoping we could devise a way to protect Sister Barbara, in case her background were investigated."

"Father Malecki, the superior of that religious community has been assassinated in the seclusion of the cloister. What makes you think that any measure we might take would protect any of her nuns? Jews have the unfortunate inheritance of their guilt for condemning Our Lord to the cross. Converted or not, I'm afraid the blood price follows them wherever they are."

Malecki found the argument sickening, although out of respect he kept silent while the archbishop dismissed him.

Bora's room at the Hotel *Patria* in Lvov was old-fashioned but comfortable. Through a door that was now open, it communicated with Colonel Schenck's room. Schenck was in his pyjamas, but hadn't relinquished the starchiness of his demeanour. Bora stood up from his chair when the colonel appeared on the threshold.

"Do you have anything to read, Bora? I find it hard to fall asleep in a new bed if I don't have something to read."

"I doubt that the colonel would want to read the Latin dictionary. It's quite dreary."

Schenck stepped into the room. "You're still reading that silly thing? How many more meanings do you think you'll dredge out? No, I don't want to read the dictionary, and as sure as hell I don't want to reread the documents we worked on. You don't happen to have brought along a magazine or something, do you?"

He watched Bora swing the overnight bag onto his bed and open it. There was a change of clothing in it, neatly rolled socks and linen underwear. From an inner pocket he pulled out a middle-sized black book. "I'm embarrassed to say this is all I have, Colonel. I had been doing some research on the word *Lumen* in it."

Schenck took the book in hand. "*The New Testament?*" He opened it with a sneer, leafing through the Latin-German text. "Oh, well." He started back for his room. "It's the last kind of reading I'd do, but it beats army documents and the dictionary. Good night."

Less than a minute later he opened the door again. "Are you a very religious man, Captain?"

"Not at the moment."

"Good. One never knows with Catholics."

14 December

While Father Malecki did his morning weight-lifting in front of a prudently closed window, Richard Retz accompanied the woman home.

Basia wasn't Retz's kind. He didn't like redheads and didn't like women who shaved their legs and armpits. He also didn't like prostitutes, because they didn't make him feel as though he'd gained something challenging. Basia filled the void, that was all. She was available and pleasant and didn't ask questions.

When he'd got an unexpected, agitated call from Ewa early this morning, Basia had shown no interest as to who it might be; she'd gone to wash up leaving him a chance to chat. Although she'd heard him agree to a meeting "tonight or tomorrow", she'd quietly pocketed her money from the bedstand and put her galoshes on.

At eleven o'clock Bora was met at the border by the staff car and escort truck. Taking advantage of the fact that Colonel Schenck was not in sight, the commissar accompanied him all the way and saw him into the car.

"Have a good trip, Captain."

"Have a good stay."

The commissar's long teeth were bared in a short smile. "You don't mean that."

"You probably don't mean for me to have a good trip, either."

As he prepared to close Bora's door, the commissar made a face of ironic puzzlement. "Germans and Russians – can it work?"

"Poland's map is the living proof of it, Commissar."

"Not so much a *living* proof, but you're right."

Schenck had been using a telephone inside the improvised checkpoint hut. He'd seen the commissar from the window and chose to remain indoors until he was gone.

"He's a despicable man," he said as he joined Bora in the staff car. "What did he have to say?"

"He reminded me that they trust us and like us in the measure we trust and like them."

"I never associated trust and liking with the Reds." The book of Scriptures emerged from Schenck's briefcase. "Thanks for this. Not my idea of stirring literature, but I did fall asleep reading it. Ah, look here." The colonel took out of his blouse and unfolded a large map, printed in sepia on pale yellow paper. Bora read *ХАРЬКОВ*, and, below, *Voyenno-topograficheskaya Karta Yevropeyskoy Rossii* 1:126000.

"What is it, Colonel?"

Schenck had a singularly ugly grin, which briefly made him look like the Phantom of the Opera. "He, he. Swiped it from the Reds while they weren't looking. The map of Kharkov. Ukraine, Ukraine, of course. What do you think? We might as well get familiar with the next theatre of operations. What does it say here?"

"Train Station Osnova."

"Isn't it the railroad that goes straight through Russia, all the way to Rostov?"

Bora was calculating the scale of the map, translating to himself the Russian measures into metres. "It is," he said. Every centimetre indicated a kilometre, and the car in which they presently sat was one thousand five hundred kilometres away from Kharkov.

"Keep it, Bora, one of these days it'll come in handy for you."

The weather stayed clear but grew increasingly cold. When they reached the hill country, it quickly clouded over, with high masses of pearly clouds racing north from the Carpathians. Through the haze covering that part of the sky not yet overrun by clouds, the sun was a round and splendourless disk, like a communion wafer.

Bora thought of that dimmed glare as *Lumen*, although he'd concluded last night that in a late sense the word also meant cleverness and insight. No matter how much he tried to disregard the vague lead, he found himself returning to it by instinct. Soon a speckled multitude of flakes infinitesimally small and bright like fireflies began to drift from the south against the paling circle of the sun.

Schenck said, "Your stepfather will stay in Cracow only two days. Do you think you can make something of two days if your wife comes along with him?"

"I'd be most grateful to see my wife even for an hour, Colonel. I realize it is a privilege."

Schenck only half-smiled. "I'm not doing you a favour. I'm just thinking practically. Be sure you keep yourself perfectly sober and clean and at peak performance level in these three weeks. I suggest you give up any hard liquor and smoke, if you smoke."

"I don't smoke or drink much."

"Good meals, hard work and lengthy walks is what you need. Your wife must sleep long hours and not exhaust herself in any way. Both of you must absolutely refrain from alcohol in the week previous to conception. I will give you a copy of a scientific pamphlet on how to ensure production of male offspring. The mistake I made the first time around with my wife was having sherry after dinner. That's how she bore a daughter. You've seen me accept vodka from the Reds: I never would have accepted it had I been planning for conception. Of course your wife has never been pregnant, so it is impossible to say whether there might be some impediment on her part. Are her menstruations regular?"

"I believe so."

"Don't be embarrassed, Captain. These are perfectly natural subjects for responsible men to discuss. Try rather to remember when her last period was. Hopefully it will not happen to recur at the time of her coming. It'd be a waste of intercourse."

Bora wondered with an aching worry what he'd do with himself at the end of these two weeks if Dikta wasn't allowed to travel to Poland after all.

15 December

The presence of German vehicles by the convent gate made Father Malecki's thinning hair stand on end. They were not Wehrmacht trucks, and the staff car wasn't Bora's. He threw a glance down the street, where the Jesuit church also was flanked by SS vehicles.

He stopped a passer-by in the street. "What's happening, do you know?"

The man hurried off without answering. The few other civilians were also scattering at a rapid pace, seeking side streets and doorways.

Malecki stood alone. He knew there was a telephone at the corner and his first impulse was to try to reach the Curia to inform the archbishop. At that moment a truck pulled out from an alley and parked sideways across the street, barring his way to the corner.

So Malecki remained on the sidewalk, hands nervously fingering keys and coins in his pockets. More trucks seemed to be moving in to the right, beyond the Jesuit church, towards Stradom and in the direction of the ghetto.

Mister Logan's words of prudence floated past him as he stepped off the sidewalk, across the street and up to the grim, gun-toting guards by the convent's gate.

16 December

"Was this necessary?"

Bora found that he wasn't outraged or even angry: only irritated by the stupidity of the action. One of his goals for the week had been to investigate this small Ukrainian settlement at the eastern end of the Cracow province. Since leaving Schenck at Tarnów, he'd been rejoined by Hannes and they had driven down towards the mountains. Finding the SD in the village ahead of himself was vexing enough, and seeing an army unit in tow caused him to stalk to the officer and ask about the combined operation.

The SD man looked him up and down. "Yes, it was necessary. What's that to you, have you never seen people hanged?"

In fact, Bora hadn't. He removed his eyes from the limp, barefoot bodies dangling from a tree in slow circles.

"We had precedence in this sector. Why wasn't Intelligence informed, and who is responsible for providing army troops to you?"

The SD turned his back on Bora, bound for his car. "You're just sore because you've got here late. We can question these animals as well as you can, and our methods go a long way in convincing the wives to talk."

"You haven't answered me."

"Look, Captain. Why don't you go home and inform your commander? Have him submit a request for the information you want, and proceed through routine channels."

"I think I'll just ask your NCOs." Rashly, Bora started towards the group of soldiers, only to be checked by a rude pull on his sleeve.

"I wouldn't do it if I were you," the SD officer was saying.

Coldly, Bora pried the fingers off his arm. "Do me the favour."

Within minutes, parked within sight of the hangings, he wrote his incident report in the car. "*The two Polish nationals were executed without trial in a farm community three kilometres north of Ciężkowice in the Tarnów area. They were not 'hanged', as the SD major on location reported, since there were no facilities for carrying out a regular hanging. Inasmuch as there was no apparent breakage of the neck vertebrae, pending a medical report the method for the execution seems rather to have been strangulation. No information of value was extracted either from the men before their death or from their wives, who have since my arrival been removed by the SD for further interrogation. The non-commissioned officer leading the Wehrmacht platoon was unable to provide me with clear information as to how the combined operation originated."*

Helenka expected Retz's visit after rehearsal, but he didn't come. She was again disappointed when she called from the theatre and didn't find him home. While the telephone rang uselessly, Kasia waited behind her, with one of her scribbled numbers in hand. She said, "Good job today, Helenka. You'll pull through it fine."

"Thank you."

"Your mother did a good job too. Don't you think?"

Helenka forced herself to continue facing Kasia, because she knew how close she was to her mother, how much she confided in her. "Ewa is an old hand at it," she replied when the gall in her throat mellowed enough to say the words with a smile. "Of course she did a good job."

"She's also looking good. I mean, like she's happy. In love, or something. Are you going out tonight?"

"I don't know." Because she was annoyed, Helenka assumed a petulant, young woman's voice. "Are you?"

Kasia shrugged. "Me? It depends. If I can get this phone call through and find enough warm water to wash my hair, I guess so."

In the springlike temperature of the Curia, the perennial frown on the archbishop's face was smoothed out by an expression of blank surprise. "Arrested? Is that what you said?"

Unwilling to repeat the word, the secretary nodded his head.

"Well, then: has the American consulate been contacted? Have the appropriate steps been taken?"

"We only heard about his arrest because one of the sisters came ten minutes ago to report it. Does Your Eminence wish to see her?"

"No, no. You take care of it. There's nothing she can say to me that can't be explained to you."

"Of course, arrest and detention are not the same thing. I have at once placed a telephone call to Father Malecki's residence. Since he isn't expected home until later this evening, we cannot simply assume that he is indeed being detained by the Germans. I will attempt to reach him again after seven p.m."

"Still, the American consul ought to be made aware."

The secretary's long, skirted figure swayed a little. "I'm not sure it is what Father Malecki would want. Premature intervention by the American authorities might complicate his chances of remaining in Poland. Your Eminence recalls how the Holy See specifically instructed him to stay through the investigation."

"But might the Germans not expel him from Poland when they find out he's an American?"

"In that case, Your Eminence, it will be out of Your Eminence's purview to keep him here. Father Malecki's departure, I believe, was one of Your Eminence's priorities."

The archbishop settled himself more comfortably in his chair. He passed a ring-laden finger over his furrowed brow. "What was the cause for German trespassing on Church property today? *That*, I will respond to at once."

"They were searching for Jews, Your Eminence. It was rumoured that some of the inhabitants of the Kazimierz ghetto found refuge in religious institutions after last night's SD raid on Jewish businesses."

"Is it true?"

"We're trying to ascertain that. True or false, the Germans took it upon themselves to enter a number of convents and other Church property. Here is a preliminary list of those that have come to our attention. Fortunately, no refugees were found. Those who interfered with the operation, however, were arrested. Father Malecki is one of seven such clergymen. I have their names here."

The archbishop's finger rubbed his worried forehead. "If there is any more bad news, I'd like to hear it all at once."

A cheaply printed leaflet appeared in the secretary's hand.

"Several of these were found pasted on walls overnight. As you see, news that Mother Kazimierza's death was not due to natural causes has reached enough ears to justify this response."

"For the love of God, it accuses the Germans directly!"

"I took the liberty of organizing an effort to remove as many as we can before a reprisal."

The archbishop agreed it was a necessary first step. "Now get in touch with the Intelligence officer who is conducting the murder investigation, and state our position in reference to the leaflets."

"We disclaim them, Your Eminence?"

"We disclaim them."

Within minutes the secretary was back in the archbishop's office to say that Captain Bora was not available, and not expected back until the morning. By nine o'clock in the evening, the secretary also reported that Father Malecki's landlady had confirmed his absence.

"He hasn't gone home for dinner, and she's worried. I deemed it best not to inform her. What we have to confront now is this, Your Eminence."

A terse communiqué from Governor General Hans Frank threatened measures against the Church in Cracow, unless the identity of the person or persons who had leaked information on the murder case was promptly made available to German authorities.

The archbishop groaned. "How am I expected to sleep at night with these blows constantly directed at us?"

Bora spent the night in a small village at the foothill of the mountains, where a reconnaissance detachment had also halted.

A wind had risen, and although the snow had tapered off, it was exceedingly cold. A full moon sailed above stringy clouds of a sickly colour. The colour and curdled texture of sour milk, Bora thought. Before retiring, he took a walk down the rutted central street to be alone and think, to free his mind from the scenes of the day. Against the ragged grey sky, like a sharp-angled herd, the army half-tracks were stationed at one end. Few houses had lights in them, visible as flickering lines around windows and under doors.

As on the day he had identified his dead companions in the schoolhouse, a sudden sense of surprise for finding himself here caught him, like an awakening. Everything outside this moment had the quality of a dream. Colonel Schenck and Father Malecki were ever so briefly like phantoms to his mind. He had to ask himself if he had really seen a dead nun in the cloister, if he had really punched a priest and quibbled with a Red Army commissar.

The moon seemed to roll swiftly on, past the stringy sour-milk clouds. Odourless, cutting, the wind pushed the moon ahead of itself.

Bora turned at the end of the road and walked back. Another grey, ragged horizon, with the shaggy back of thatched houses to limit it. One thing he could count on: having to put up with Major Retz, who in a few weeks had become an unpleasant inevitability in his life.

Well, he'd go directly to work in the morning, and at least avoid running into one or the other of the major's women visitors.

18 December

On Monday, Bora stopped halfway through the removal of his greatcoat, one hand still clasping the button. "The major is *what?*"

"Dead, sir." The orderly lifted from under the desk a box with a few personal items Bora recognized as belonging to Retz.

"When?"

"Sunday morning, sir. He was found dead at home. Colonel Schenck thought you might want to take these along."

Bora lowered his eyes to the box. He had a hard time connecting the orderly's words to Retz, and whatever other questions pressed him – how, why – he didn't ask now, but automatically took the box and brought it to his office.

A colleague was sharpening a pencil when he walked in, and said at once, "You'd never expect he'd kill himself, would you?"

"Is that what happened?"

"He put his head in the stove and breathed in. It's a miracle the whole building didn't blow sky-high. The cleaning woman smelled gas from under your apartment door and had the good sense of calling for help. It had saturated the place, and all it would have taken was for her to go in and flip the light switch on."

"But why? Did he leave a note, or something?"

"Nothing that I heard of. Salle-Weber would know, maybe. He was looking for you yesterday." The pencil came out of the sharpener with a long clean point, which Bora's colleague licked with his tongue. "You roomed with Retz, don't *you* have a clue?"

Bora went to see Salle-Weber. Patently unimpressed or uninterested in the news, the SS looked conciliatory for a change.

"Of all the officers in Cracow, Bora, you're the one who spent the most after-hours time with Retz. You're an observant fellow. Did Retz tell you anything that might hint at private trouble? Did he behave in an out-of-the-ordinary way just before you left?"

"Why, no. Not at all. The only thing is – on weekends he always drank a bit."

"He drank *a lot*." Salle-Weber corrected him. "But drunks usually kill themselves by the bottle. No, I mean women trouble, affairs, matters of money. *Political* things."

Bora wondered if he should speak of Ewa Kowalska, but Salle-Weber was ahead of him. "We know he had a girlfriend or two he liked above the rest." He glanced at the file on the desk. "One Ewa Kowalska, one Basia Plutinska and there was also a younger woman, Helena or Helenka Sokora. He took those home, so you must have seen them if nothing else."

"Yes, I've seen them. And nothing else."

Salle-Weber smirked at the answer. "So, he got along with all of them?"

"He seemed to."

"Well, I don't know why I even ask. We routinely checked the women out, and they all looked distressed, especially the Sokora girl. He'd been 'nice' to all of them, according to their depositions, and I had the feeling they'll miss their sugar daddy. We have to look elsewhere, just for the satisfaction of figuring it out. All I'm interested in is making sure there was no politics involved."

"I don't think politics was the major's weakness. He was completely orthodox. Two of his brothers are in the SS, you know."

Salle-Weber closed the folder and put it away. "Has Colonel Schenck contacted you about writing a letter home to Retz's wife?"

"Yes." Bora knew that Salle-Weber wanted to instruct him in reference to that, so he added, "I'm at a loss as to what I should say."

"You should say that Major Retz died in an accident during the execution of his military duties."

"Very well."

The conversation continued for nearly an hour. When Bora was about to leave, he had a curiosity of his own. "What did you tell the captain's women?"

"That it was an accident, but I'm sure they found out the truth from the cleaning woman or the house scuttlebutt." Salle-Weber gave Bora a perceptive, amused stare. "In case you decide to pick up with one of them where your roommate left off, stick to the accident theory."

"The girl you called Sokora – I thought Kowalska was her name."

"Sokora is the name she uses on stage. I guess she doesn't want to be confused with the other one."

It was snowing hard when Bora came out into the street after talking to Salle-Weber. Straight ahead, the Wawel and the Old City resembled a Christmas-like sketch of themselves, cold, conventional and graceful. It would be dark soon. Spires and walls and buildings old and new would be swallowed up by night and other images would take their place, mind-born and less graceful.

Bora was due out in the field early in the morning, but tonight he had to go home.

As soon as he entered he expected to smell gas, but of course the apartment had been totally aired out. Nothing seemed different at all. Bora stepped from the vestibule to the living room, to the hallway and from there he found that he was in fact ambling his way towards the kitchen, because he had to see the kitchen.

He looked at the stove as if seeing it for the first time, and as if it bore little resemblance to what it was, because it had served another purpose. It didn't disgust him, it just seemed alien and sinister.

Retz's bedroom had been "thoroughly gone through", in Salle-Weber's words. Now all was back in place. Uniforms hung, magazines stacked, his toiletry in order on the dresser. Bora realized he'd never entered the room before. He'd come to the threshold of it once or twice, chatting, but – well, he'd heard plenty of what had happened in this room at night.

Bora's eyes sought the bed with a little envy and much expectation. When Dikta would come, if she should come. He'd do what Retz had done with his women, only more, harder. Better. Longer. Then he caught himself, blushing: it seemed somehow sacrilegious to think of his wife here. He walked out and closed the door.

The perspective of sleeping in a house where a man had killed himself wasn't disturbing, though Bora did feel guilty for not mourning Retz. After uselessly trying to read for nearly an hour, he admitted that he wouldn't fall asleep any time soon.

Close to midnight, when he finally went to brush his teeth before going to bed, he glanced at Retz's little bottles of salve and hair dye with a new eye. How things never meant to survive their owner manage to do so. Toothpaste, nail clippers, security razor. Retz's absence amounted to those, and whatever beer and wine he'd left untouched in the refrigerator.

What would his own absence amount to?

In the mirror, his face was new in some ways, too. He saw himself serious and younger than he felt. Ewa Kowalska must have thought him immature because of the lack of hard-edged wear in his features. Maybe he *was* immature.

Strange that Retz had left the blade in the razor. Is that what men do before committing suicide – breaking their own little rules, like never leaving a wet blade in the razor?

At dawn, before leaving for the field, Bora divided the objects to be shipped to Retz's widow from the useless ones. These he threw away, bottles and cigarettes and prophylactics and vitamin tablets. Retz's razor, he forgot in the glass.

8

The girl's breasts pressed against the cloth of her faded blouse, small like gathered fingertips. She was still a child, really, and Bora looked away, at the round-faced infant astride her hip. The baby had wetted her, and she didn't seem to notice.

At Bora's prompting, Hannes continued to ask questions in a monotone. The farmers listened and now and then answered, wide-eyed with worry. Despite the season they were all barefoot; crusts of snowy mud coated the heels of the women, who had been surprised at their wash.

By their looks, Bora had a sense for the relationship among them. There were two elders and an aged woman – the parent group – and three sons with their wives, the girl and the infant. Two steps away stood a small woman of undetermined age, snub-nosed and pale. She drooled from an open mouth and had since Bora's arrival been picking furiously at the back of her left hand, where the skin was covered with sores.

"Hannes, make them understand that all I want to find out is which way the armed men went. Tell them I know they're not hiding Polish soldiers here."

Again Hannes spoke. The men did all the answering this time. Bora caught a few words that resembled Russian, and the name of a nearby hamlet, Skalny Pagórek.

"They say they were going towards Skalny Pagórek the last time they saw them, Herr Hauptmann."

"And when was this?"

The men consulted one another. Leaning on a knotty staff, the oldest among them posed questions, listened, nodded. Bora, too, listened, without understanding, staring at the archaic profile in shoulder-length hair, plaited in wiry grey braids down the sides of the elder's face. Next to him, daughter or in-law, Bora recognized the young girl's mother by the clearness of her eyes. A stout, fair woman, she'd stepped ahead of the others to greet him by kissing his hand, in peasant deference for the uniform. He'd drawn back and now he knew he should not have done so, out of respect for the same uniform. The sores on the snub-nosed woman's hand began to bleed.

Dates, directions, bits of information trickled in. Bora and Hannes were almost through, when two SD vehicles came bouncing up the dishevelled country path. Bora expected them to drive by, but the staff car turned instead into the snow-rimmed track that led to the farm. It stopped by the wooden covered well, and so did the truck. Several soldiers alighted from it, checked the well for ice and filled their canteens.

An officer emerged from the car. He made no attempt to draw closer to the threshing floor, where Bora had gathered the farmers. He remained by the car, thirty or so paces away, consulting a folded map.

Bora said, "Wrap things up, Hannes."

By the time he reached the well, the SD officer had finished reading the map, and was now replacing it in its case.

"Are you done, Captain?"

Bora took a short, irritable breath. "This is army-controlled territory. We have jurisdiction over it."

"Well, we're on a slightly different errand from yours, so don't you worry about a duplication of tasks."

The soldiers, Bora saw, stood in the cold, blue shadow of the truck. They had stacked weapons to one side – machine guns, carbines – and were beginning to eat their rations. It was too early in the morning for lunch, so they might have travelled overnight. Their boots were covered with dry mud, and their uniforms looked slept in.

"What's your errand?" he asked the officer.

"We're getting provisions for another week in the field."

"There's nothing left on this farm. We came through during the invasion, they've been hit hard."

"We'll do our own asking, Captain. Have a good trip."

Bora checked his watch. He'd spent more time here than expected. He still had a long list of tasks in the field before making it back for a staff meeting at three in the afternoon, and Schenck didn't tolerate lateness. Waiting for Hannes to bring the car, Bora debated whether he should stay until the SD carried out their search.

They didn't seem to be in a hurry, any of them. The soldiers munched on their food or sat in the truck smoking.

Their officer dipped a canteen in the pail to fill it. He drank from it, rinsed his mouth and spat the water back in the well. "You can wait around, Captain, but I'm sure you have better things to do."

Bora would for ever regret the lack of foresight that made him get in the car then, and drive off.

They'd come about a kilometre from the farm, past a double line of gaunt trees that sheltered it from the north wind, before they had to slow down to a creeping pace to negotiate a ford. It was a steep, muddy incline they'd had difficulty crossing on their way here. The mud was beginning to ice over and was slippery. The car reached the bottom, which was a frigid mixture of rocks, loam and water, and began straining.

A high wind carried sparse clouds coasting from the south. After sunrise it had turned comfortable enough, and now Bora kept his window rolled down. Against Schenck's advice to sobriety, he lit himself a cigarette, and watched the smoke escape from the car in capering blue curls. Skalny Pagórek. Skalny Pagórek came next. Spread across his knees, the map showed a criss-crossing of country paths and Slavic place names.

"Hannes," he began to say. And then, over the low grind of the straining engine, Bora heard a sound that made his back harden against the seat.

Machine-gun fire. Not so distant, machine-gun fire was breaking out from behind the line of gaunt trees. Hannes' nervous look met him in the rear-view mirror.

Bora put the map away. A void seemed to open at the pit of his stomach, a sudden sharp ache. But he could not have made such an error: he couldn't have misread the men's intentions to that extent, it was impossible. He was prejudiced against the Security Service. He always thought the worst. What he should think was – what he should think was that the SD had met with the Polish army stragglers.

"Go back, quickly!"

They were at the middle point of the ford. Hannes put the car in reverse and caked mud spun from the tires before he was able to back up the incline and turn around. They roared past the trees in a storm of reddish pine needles, and devoured the flat space that separated them from the farm.

All Bora could make out from afar was a handful of soldiers leaving the barn.

The truck was empty. The staff car was empty. There was no one on the threshing floor.

Bora ran from the car, crossing the expanse of snow trampled over the muddy dirt. He halted on the doorstep of the barn.

The void in his stomach caved in.

"What have you *done?*"

The SD officer shouldered past Bora to get out of the barn, and stopped with him on the threshold.

All around the building, soldiers were bringing gasoline cans, and pouring a consistent trickle of fuel on its foundations. Stubble and hay were thrown on it by the handful. Bora smelled the gasoline and heard the soldiers move about, but paid no heed to them. His eyes were riveted on the dirt floor of the barn.

"For God's sake, they're not even dead!"

"Your job here was done when we came, Captain. Don't you get involved in ours."

Bora stepped forwards to enter, unlatching the holster.

The SD gripped his wrist. "I'm warning you," and when Bora freed his hand with a twist of his arm, he pushed him hard against the door frame. "Don't meddle."

Bora pushed back. He took his gun out. The SD came chest to chest with him, shoving him, and Bora elbowed him back. Grimly they confronted each other by stance and hardness of muscles, vying for control of the doorway.

"I want your name, Captain."

"And I want yours."

Fire flared up next to them when it caught a tall bundle of straw and engulfed it in red, in a surge of suffocating smoke. The SD backed off, waving with contempt, and Bora walked into the barn.

Smoke was already starting to seep from under the disconnected planks all around the building. Bora's boots pasted blood into the dirt floor as he drew close to the centre of the barn. The bodies were heaped there. First he saw the girl. Face up, she'd been shot through the forehead. Her left hand twitched frantically in the blood, where her mother's arm pinned her down. The back of her mother's head had been blown off. Bora stumbled over a man's bloody bulk to reach the girl. Straddling her body, he finished her off. Then he turned to the others, one by one firing point-blank into them. When he was out of shots, he changed clips and kept firing.

"Herr Hauptmann, Herr Hauptmann!" Hannes called to him from the threshing floor. "The roof is giving way!"

Bora kept firing.

When he walked out, the SD vehicles had already left. Turning his head towards the well, he saw their wake braiding a storm of ice crystals on the dirt road that headed east. His eyes burned and ached with smoke, and he wouldn't wipe them for fear of appearing moved, because he wasn't.

Hannes stood by the car, his slight field-grey figure looking insignificant against the immense background of rolling pastures. His face was pale and averted.

Bora was not moved. Only conscious of an unbearable weight at the end of his arm. Morning sounds came from the fields. Very far, it seemed. The crispness of morning lovingly brought them to him, once he turned away from the crackling and smell of the flames.

Many times afterwards he would think of this day, and feel the drain of standing there with the bulk of the Walther weighing his hand, his arm down. There was a heaviness in the gun that wanted to drag him low, and sink him.

He found out after Hannes had driven halfway down the street, by the shop signs and shop fronts, that he'd instructed him to go the wrong way, past the Cracow Botanical Garden, nowhere near Headquarters.

At Headquarters, Colonel Schenck was not interested. He was not unamiable, but showed no interest in intervening. He said he understood.

"If you start feeling sorry so early on, Bora, you're screwed. What should you care? We have our orders and the SD have theirs. It was only an accident that you didn't happen to have similar orders. And these Polack farmers – they aren't even *people*, they're not even worth reproducing. I can see you're perturbed, but believe me, don't start caring." Bora said something, and Schenck interrupted. "We're *all* in it. If it's guilt, we're all guilty. This is the way it is."

"I cannot accept this is the way it is, Colonel. We also have laws."

"So early on, and you're already talking about laws? You yourself have come tearing down through Polish villages like a cyclone in your first days here. What laws? Leave things very well alone. First you report to me about the hanged Ukrainians, and now it's Polack farmers. Harden your heart, as the advice was given to us at the beginning of this campaign. It'll do you good in life. You're just a young captain with scruples, not a relevant or even useful position at all." Schenck patted his shoulder. "Go to your office and get ready for the staff meeting."

Bora felt as though he'd been dropped from a stunning height. For the next few minutes he fingered through papers on his desk, without even seeing them.

Schenck checked on him from the doorway. "By the by, Bora, I'm expecting a phone call from Germany. My wife is in labour. Should the telephone ring while I'm chairing the meeting, I want you to answer and pass it to me at once if it is from the hospital. And another thing – I got word from Salle-Weber that your American priest is in the slammer for obstructing search operations. You have my permission to get him out after you're done here."

Without questions, Father Malecki followed Bora out. They had hardly exchanged any words at all since Bora had shown up in the cramped detention room with an SD guard in tow. They now sat side by side in Bora's car under a dim evening sky.

"Should I take you home? I know where you live."

"No, thank you."

"I see. To the American consulate, then?"

"Absolutely not."

Bora didn't feel like playing guessing games. "Where do you want to go, Father Malecki?"

"Let's go have a drink."

The back room of the *Pod Latarnie* was a cosy tavern.

Malecki's American clerical garb, with trousers instead of a cassock, didn't make him immediately identifiable as a priest. Bora chose a private table to the side, but could tell by the way Malecki slipped the scarf off his neck that he didn't mind showing his Roman collar.

"I'll have a *Żubrówka*," Malecki told the waiter.

"Yes, *Ojciec*."

"What'll you have, Captain Bora?"

"I'll have the same."

Malecki hadn't been a priest for thirty years without having gained a good insight into men. He observed Bora distractedly play with the car keys, rigid in excess of his profession. It was the kind of rigidity that counters the need to slump.

"Do you know what you ordered?" he asked him.

"No."

"It's the best flavoured vodka, with forest herbs from Białowieża."

Bora lifted his eyes to the priest. Whatever troubled him – Malecki doubted it had anything to do with his being arrested – he wouldn't voluntarily speak of it. He decided by the sullen bent of Bora's lips that it was best not asking him at this time.

The waiter brought the drinks.

"Here you go, *Ojciec.*"

Bora felt a little better after the drink. He pulled back on the padded leather seat. "I'm sorry you were detained, Father Malecki."

"It wasn't so bad after I convinced them that I wasn't Polish."

"I would have thought the American consulate would obtain your release."

"They don't even know I was arrested, I think."

"Didn't you tell the SS?"

"I told them I was a British subject."

"You *didn't.*"

"I did, and it wasn't a very bad sin. It wouldn't have been so easy after tonight, since the answer from the British Embassy in Warsaw was expected in the morning. But thanks to you I don't have to worry about that."

Bora shook his head. "You're very unorthodox, for a man of God."

"There are times when one must defy orthodoxy."

Bora was struck by the words. He knew they were not aimed at him, yet they sank in with the ease of a blade.

"What times are those, Father Malecki?"

It was the first evening since Retz's death that Ewa had returned to rehearsal. The play opened the following day.

Kasia caught up with her in the dark outside the theatre, and together they walked to catch the last streetcar until morning. At the corners the wind was so chilly, they had to wrap their coats about themselves and bury their faces in the collars.

"Don't ask anything, Kasia."

"Who's asking anything? I'm just walking."

As soon as she arrived home, Ewa Kowalska removed her stockings, careful to handle them with wet fingertips, so that cuticles would not cause runs or snags. After putting on a pair of worn slippers, she stepped to the telephone at her bedside and dialled a number she knew by heart. Smoking, she waited to lower the receiver until it was clear that Bora was not home.

Her head ached. She had smoked too much in the past few days and now her throat felt dry; she worried her voice might give way tomorrow. She kept vinegar-and-water on her bedtable, and having poured a tablespoon of vinegar in a half-glass of water, she gargled until tears ran down her face.

Some irritating radio tune, sung by a shrill female voice, came floating from the kitchen through her bedroom door. *Nur du, nur du, nur du-u-u.* Ewa went to turn the radio off. She turned the light off. Seated on the bed, she closed her eyes. She couldn't sleep. She was tired and couldn't sleep. It ached in and out, this anger and loneliness.

She needed to talk to a man, and found that she was angry at Bora for not being home.

At the *Pod Latarnie,* Malecki said, "How did you come to the conclusion that by 'her name' the abbess might have meant *Lumen?*"

Bora closely observed his small empty glass as if it were anything but a plain small glass. "I'm not at liberty to say. It's not a conclusion, Father, only a viable possibility. If the abbess meant that she would die 'through her name', and the name is *Lumen,* by understanding what is meant by it I might discover who killed her. The Latin dictionary was helpful, but I can't connect any of the meanings given with a cause of death. I remembered that in philosophy we refer to *lumen naturale* as the cognitive powers of the human mind, unaided by the grace of God."

Malecki nodded. "The *lumen gratiae.*"

"Yes. On the other hand, *lumen* might represent a physical entity. The word also means 'window' and 'opening'. Should we think she was shot through a window?" Bora glanced at the waiter and shook his head when asked whether he wanted another drink. Father Malecki did the same. "Now, admitting that the abbess was right in her prophecy and that I'm right in pursuing this lead, does it mean that *lumen* is the *cause* or the *agent* of her death?"

Malecki dabbed his nose with the handkerchief. "Do we even have a firm motive for her death?"

"So far, only the political overtone of her utterances."

"She was more apocalyptic than political, Captain."

"Maybe."

"Well, do we have suspects?"

"Only faceless and nameless ones." Bora moved the glass away. "I did consider the possibility of someone – even from my army – finding his way into the convent some time before the colonel and I got there. Someone who could have killed the abbess, and with the confusion of the times, could be far from here by now."

Malecki appreciated Bora's discomfort at the supposition. "But how would a stranger enter the convent without being seen?"

"I don't know. Whoever placed the bag of guns on the roof managed to enter." With his forefinger, slowly, Bora followed the edge of the table. Malecki thought this might be a good time to say that he knew where at least one of the workmen could be found. But Bora was already thinking of something else. "Father," he asked, "what percentage of the abbess's prophecies have come true?"

"It's difficult to judge. Most of them haven't yet come to pass. Of those referring to the events in the recent past, perhaps six out of ten."

"Would you call it a remarkable percentage?"

"I would call it indicative. The theological view of prophecy is bound to the instances we encounter in the Old and New Testament. St John of the Cross said that God makes use of different means to transmit supernatural knowledge: at times words, at other images and symbols, or any combination of those. Mother Kazimierza was highly literate, so words and puns constellate her prophecies. I would expect *Lumen* to imply some sort of double entendre – if that's the right expression. To return to her quota of successes, in some cases she was patently wrong. When I first arrived, she informed me that an older woman close to me would die within six months. Young or old, the only woman in my life happens to be my mother, and by the grace of God she's alive and well to this day."

"Unless the abbess meant a contingent closeness, and considered herself the woman in question. After all, the word *nun* originally meant 'old lady'."

Malecki shrugged. "You know, I spoke to Mother Kazimierza two or three times a week for six months. Still, I can't say that I knew her. My impression was of a well-schooled, opinionated, conservative, controlled and controlling woman."

"The last kind of person you'd identify as a mystic."

"Precisely. The archbishop asked the Holy See to begin an investigation because of the unofficial cult beginning to accrue around her in her own lifetime. She very much resented my presence at first. It was only after a direct order from the archbishop that I was allowed to visit regularly. No doubt she was an intense believer. Her relationship to God was exclusive, jealous, deeply felt. You read some of her meditations."

Bora offered a cigarette to the priest. "I did. I found them sometimes banal, sometimes unintelligible. Her descriptions of the 'penetration of God's light into the cleft of the soul' I found frankly erotic." With deceptive nonchalance, Bora busied looking for his lighter. "Father Malecki," he said then, "was she involved with the underground?"

Malecki took the blow like a boxer. He'd expected the question would come at some point, but not now. It was too soon, and he was unprepared. He put his cigarette near to the flame, nervously sensing Bora's alertness to an untruth, how he would perhaps understand the reason for his lying but take measures nonetheless.

Across the table from him, Bora put away the lighter with a weary gesture. In truth, he was beginning to feel the weight of the day upon him. Like a load of stones being suddenly tied to his neck and shoulders, he physically ached with the strain of the day. Colonel Schenck had made things worse by saying, "You administered the coup de grace; technically it was you who killed them."

Father Malecki said, "Whatever I answer, Captain Bora, you will either disbelieve or follow up on it."

"Absolutely."

"Then my answer is not really relevant."

"But your silence is."

"Only by default."

Bora tightened his lips. He tried not to show it, but was vexed in excess of disappointment. "I though we had agreed to collaborate."

"Not politically."

"No? I could have left you in jail, Father Malecki."

"You have me in jail right now, just by asking me questions I can't answer."

When Bora stood, obviously about to leave, Malecki made a mild gesture to detain him, no more than a raising of his open hand. "You'll find the contractor who worked in the convent at this address, Captain." And his hand lowered again, to extract a folded piece of paper from his breast pocket.

The telephone rang shortly after Bora had returned from driving Malecki home.

He recognized Ewa's voice even before she identified herself. His first reaction was to put down the receiver.

She said, preventing him, "I'm not going to take much of your time, Captain. I realize how late it is."

21 December

There were no signs of concern in Schenck's countenance the following morning, when he mentioned, "Man the phone for me, Bora: my wife is still in the delivery room. It seems to be a breech birth this time around."

"I'm sorry to hear it," Bora said for the sake of saying something.

"Why? That's the function of woman, Captain. A man risks his life in war, a woman in childbirth. I have an interview with the Governor General, but you can call me at this number if any news comes through. Did you get the priest out? Good." Schenck took the Iron Cross from his pocket and hung it by the ribbon around his neck. "I see you recovered in a hurry from your mercy tangent. It was most unbecoming."

At midday, when Bora finally phoned Schenck with the news of his latest paternity, Father Malecki was speaking to the nuns gathered in the refectory. He told them there was suspicion among the Germans that the abbess might have had contacts with the underground, and watched their reactions. Most of them seemed surprised by the possibility. Sister Irenka and Sister Barbara denied the allegation because "it couldn't be". Sister Jadwiga brooded and kept silent.

Eyes planted on her, Malecki addressed the group. "If any one of you has knowledge of such contacts or any other political issues, I'll be listening to confessions this afternoon. The safety of this entire community might depend on the information."

Schenck's satisfaction at having fathered a fourth son resulted in an afternoon off for Bora, the first since the invasion.

Now Ewa looked at Bora sitting across from her, with a blade of cold sunshine falling on him through the café's window. Under the light, his jaw was smooth and as if scraped clean: it had the texture of a boy's skin. Stern, unblemished. It was an impression of great tidiness, attractive yet intimidating to her. She recognized in him the pitiless prejudice of youth.

"I'm glad you asked that we meet," she said.

"Why?"

She had a narrow smile. Twirling the spoon in her cup, she said, "Don't look at me that way, Captain. Mondays aren't my best time of the week, and I've been through a lot lately. 'Why,' you ask? I'm glad you think I might have something more to say about Richard. Something to explain things."

"What is there to explain?"

"The fact that he killed himself. I heard it, like everyone else, from the cleaning woman."

Salle-Weber was right, Bora thought. The news had travelled. He sat back on the metal chair, stretching the lean uniformed length of his body. "Well, Frau Kowalska, what can you tell me that you didn't tell the SS?"

"It depends on your reasons for asking."

"They're eminently private. I didn't like Major Retz, frankly, but a brother officer is a brother officer. I was his room-mate, I want to understand."

With the crook of her finger in the handle, Ewa turned the cup on the saucer so that the handle was at her right. "I went to see him Saturday evening. He'd told me you wouldn't be there, so I went. I had to talk to him." She sipped from the cup, leaving the mark of her lipstick on the rim. "You might or might not know that Richard and I had been acquainted a long time. Since the last war, in fact."

Bora said he knew.

"We'd have got married then, had there been more time. Maybe. It's not important any more. What's important is that I found myself pregnant and with an acting career just beginning to show promise. Luckily there was someone else in the company who'd always 'cared', and I fell back on his offer. It's a fairly trite story so far, and it would have remained a trite wartime romance for ever if Richard hadn't been what he was. Unable to keep to one woman."

"Did you know that he had a wife in Germany this time around?"

"Oh, yes. That wouldn't have changed things. And then, how can I put it – I still felt I had some precedence over any other woman." When she looked over the cup, Ewa saw that Bora's face was averted and slightly hostile. "There is a young actress in my company, Helenka is her name."

"Helenka Sokora?"

Ewa's mouth hardened at the edges, though she was quick to relax again. "I see you know her."

"I know *of* her. She's your daughter."

Ewa put more milk in her tea, and for the next minute seemed absorbed in stirring it. Only when the rustle came of Bora crossing his legs, with the faint tinkle of his spurs, did she speak again. "It wasn't that I resented Richard seeing other women. That's the way he was. But Helenka – I couldn't let him carry on with her."

The instability of her hand was at once obvious to Bora, by the way the cup knocked against the saucer when she tried to lift it. Though his body stayed relaxed, he became very intent.

"Helenka was his, Captain." Again she tried to lift the cup, and failed. "Richard didn't know. My ex-husband suspected it, but didn't actually know. Helenka has no idea of it and must never find out. It's true that she and I don't see eye to eye. We don't like each other, we're very similar yet very different. We live apart, we avoid each other everywhere except on stage. We dance very complicated dances to stay away from each other. When I heard through the theatre grapevine that she was going out with him, I was frantic, because Richard wasn't a man to stop at polite niceties. I had no way of knowing if the irreparable had happened, but I hoped not."

Bora's face stayed still. He knew she wanted to know if Retz and Helenka had made love, and decided not to volunteer the information.

"So, you went to tell him?"

"What else could I do?" She rummaged in her purse and took out some papers that she handed to Bora. "I showed him her birth certificate, to prove to him that at the time he left I was already pregnant. I was frantic. I told him he couldn't – that he couldn't do this or plan to do this with his own daughter."

Bora swallowed. "And how did he respond?"

"How did he respond?" Ewa shook her head. "He fell apart, Captain. He didn't grow angry, or excited, nothing. He collapsed within himself, that's all. I even felt sorry for him. I asked him before leaving if he'd be all right. He told me to leave him alone."

Bora was not brazenly taking notes, but Ewa had the strongest feeling that he was carefully storing the information inside. The sullen boyish face remained downcast, though he looked her way.

"This is the fabric lurid myths are made of, Captain. How would *you* feel, if you were told that your lover is also your mother?"

"I wouldn't have a lover so much older than myself."

The words came out of him before he could stop them, and Bora was embarrassed by the empty arrogance of them.

Ewa looked away, and then at him again. "But I wager you've slept with women quite a bit older than yourself," she said mildly.

"It's true, I have."

"Richard was your age when I met him. *I* was your age. It's a wonderful time of life if one is wise. If one gives oneself wisely."

Bora sat up, at once undoing the relaxation of his body.

"So, were you surprised to hear that he had taken his own life?"

"No. I was sad. I was sad and distressed, but not surprised."

Even through the metal grid of the confessional, Father Malecki could tell that the nun on the other side of it was Sister Jadwiga.

She whispered some excuse about her worry after the bag of guns had been turned over to the Germans.

"I should have spoken up earlier, Father, but who was to know how the Germans would take it? On the morning *Matka* Kazimierza died, the colonel was here alone."

195

Not since his cold had Malecki felt such a clammy sweat bead up on his forehead. Bora's suspicions came back to him and he fought not to pressure the nun with the questions screaming inside him. "Yes?..." was all he said.

"I happened to be watching the door that day, because I knew the workers would be coming any minute to fix the roof. Instead, at ten or so, here comes the German colonel. He wanted to come in and see the abbess. I told him she'd be meditating until the afternoon, that no one was allowed to interrupt her meditations. He said he'd got a call from his family and that it was most urgent. He almost had tears in his eyes, you know. Still, I couldn't help him. Then all of a sudden he asked me if I would at least go and fetch him one of the abbess's books we have for sale."

Malecki held his breath. "Yes, Sister. Yes. What else?"

"I didn't see anything wrong in his request, so I left him in the doorway and went in the next room where I keep the extra copies and the cash box. When I came back, he took ten marks out of his wallet – that's twenty times the price of the book, you know – paid and left."

The irrelevance of the narrative came close to infuriating Father Malecki.

"Is that all?"

Sister Jadwiga lowered her voice to a hiss which the priest could barely make out, straining his ear against the grid. "No. The key to the door that separates the convent from the church hangs from a nail in the vestibule. When the workers showed up an hour later and I went to get the key to the inner chapel, I realized that the other key was gone. It was there before the colonel came, Father, and no one entered the vestibule between his visit and the workers'. What I think is —"

"Speak up a little, Sister."

"What I think is, that he took the key, went into the church from the street, climbed up to the organ balcony and let himself into the convent from there."

"Where's the key now?"

"Back in its place. On the evening of the abbess's death, one of the sisters found it in the hallway. You see, Father, I didn't say anything because I thought maybe our mother superior was working with the Germans, which was a terrible thing for me to think. Now she's dead and the colonel's gone, and I don't know what good it'll do to anyone to let this be known."

Malecki slouched back on the uncomfortable seat of the confessional, trying to check his anxiety. He was grateful to see, by the blurring of the silhouette past the grid, that Sister Jadwiga was leaving. He closed the little window then, and in the semi-darkness fumbled in the pocket of his cassock for Bora's phone number at work.

Helenka did not expect to find Bora waiting in the square outside the theatre. She acted as though she knew she could not ignore him, but she gave him a quick nod and then began walking down the sidewalk.

From a few steps away, Bora said, "It's better if you enter my car and we drive somewhere than if I walk with you on the public street."

She stopped, without turning, shoulders squared in her flimsy coat. "I don't feel like speaking to anyone right now, Captain Bora."

"I think you should. I met with your mother this afternoon."

Helenka was wearing the yellow pumps Retz had bought for her. When she turned, the soles of her new heels squeaked on the icy sidewalk. Her face was exceedingly pale, so that the rouge on her lips stood out like a gash on a chalky mask.

Bora let her in first, and then sat behind the wheel.

They'd driven out of the city to the mound of the Kościuszko Memorial before Helenka even opened her mouth.

"There's nothing to say. I don't know why he killed himself, and I've nothing to say. I don't want to talk about him. There's nothing more I can tell you. Why do you want to know?"

"Because I was his colleague."

"Well, what did my mother tell you? I'm sure it was rich, whatever it was."

"She thinks you were just *seeing* the major."

Helenka had been crying, and now laughed bitterly, with a trembling lip. "It goes to prove you can still fool your parents." Her profile against the waning light of evening was hard.

She reminded him of Retz in her mannerisms, and Bora wondered how such things are determined, that she would act like the father she had never known as a child. "What gets me is that she and I were rehearsing all morning, from nine to half-past one, and while we were spouting absolutely useless theatrical diatribe to each other, Richard was killing himself. Why? I don't know why. I don't think I'd tell you if I knew."

Bora spoke the next words without looking at her. "He was very fond of you. More than of anyone else."

He felt Helenka's eyes on him. The day was getting dark rapidly, and he'd have to find an excuse for driving a Polish national in his car when they returned to Cracow. The hump of the mound stood before them like a big breast of dirt, less and less visible against the sky.

"He told me I reminded him of her." Her voice came to him through the small space of the car. "But I didn't weary him the way she did. I found it exciting to take my mother's lover, for a change. You probably understand none of this. Men aren't clever enough, or deep enough."

"I'm not stupid."

By the way her voice sounded, she might be smiling, but not out of friendliness. "Richard told me he fully expected you to show up and join in sooner or later, and he even left the bedroom door unlocked once."

"It's not my idea of entertainment."

"I'm sure you have your own."

"Was he happy with you?"

Helenka reached for Bora's hand, and met with his startled resistance.

"I just want you to feel the ring around my finger. It's too dark to show it to you. It's his wife's wedding band. He used to wear it around his neck with his identification disk. He gave it to me Friday night, and told me he might give me one of my own next. He was very happy with me."

The touch rankled him. Bora could feel the sensation of it all through his limbs, unpleasantly or uncomfortably, he didn't know which. It felt like a spot of fire travelling from his hand to the rest of his body. He resented being touched as an intrusion in the mesh of his self-control. Touch opened him up, and he didn't want to be opened.

Helenka's nearness had a scent of violets. Bora could smell it in the dark, faint and grateful to his nostrils. "Let's go," he said, unkindly, and started the car.

9

The sound of footsteps echoed in the church as if the vaulted space were being slapped, brief sharp sounds as Bora and Malecki climbed the steps to the organ. The organ was set on a balcony of the left nave. A door beside it offered the only communication between the church – and the street on which the church opened – and the interior of the convent.

"See, Captain, the sisters insist that the door is always closed. For a time the lock was only workable from within, but after a small fire two years ago it was modified so that you can enter from here." Malecki placed the key in the lock and turned it twice.

The well-lit fugue of a narrow corridor appeared behind the door, with the prescribed plaster-of-Paris saint guarding the corner ahead. Bora checked a sketch he had drawn from the original plan of the convent.

"So, this leads eventually to the upper balcony of the cloister, in a roundabout way that avoids the inhabited sections of the convent. How would Colonel Hofer know about it?"

Malecki stepped over the threshold, and invited Bora to do the same. Once they were in the corridor, he locked the door again. There were latches that he pulled shut. "It was not a secret. What is more interesting, if in fact he entered this way, is that he found the door unlatched. I believe you were told by Sister Irenka that this door is never left unlatched."

"Which is why I didn't pursue the possibility of someone coming this way."

Malecki preceded Bora down the corridor. "That day the door was unlatched because the repairmen were also expected to do some work on the stucco frame behind the organ, which had come loose. I showed you where. This brings me to another thing. Please do not ask how I know, but the worker who absented himself from the chapel didn't go to kill the abbess."

"Really." Bora's off-handedness caused the priest to turn around. "You believe he had a mind to recover the guns, I'm sure. In that he did not succeed, so I will ask no more about it. Still, the contractor whose address you gave me suspected him from the start: he knew nothing about tools, and even less about roof repair. The crew thought him at first a German plant." Bora stood motionless in the corridor, as Malecki also was. "Imagine that."

"It doesn't mean —"

"On the contrary. Your white-livered contractor, whether he just wanted to keep me happy or not, seems to think the interloper did in fact kill the abbess. It means a great deal."

Malecki avoided Bora's stare.

"I heard – actually, I did hear he fled to the country."

"No, Father Malecki. No, no. Your sources have been shamelessly misleading you. He fled, all right, but not out of Cracow. He's in town, somewhere. And you know that we'll find him." Coolly Bora gestured for the priest to resume walking. "No need to be embarrassed, Father. The truth is, whether Colonel Hofer came to visit in the morning or not, it really doesn't make any difference. The abbess had been recently killed when he and I saw her in the afternoon. I will find the man who did it, and that's all there is to it. Tell me this, rather. Do you think my commander actually hoped she would miraculously cure his son?"

Malecki swallowed hard, but did not answer.

"I am in earnest, Father."

"Well, Captain Bora, so was Colonel Hofer. He swore that if faith is what it takes for miracles to happen, his son would be well as soon as the abbess's prayers reached God."

Bora recalled the first time Hofer had spoken about mysticism, staring into the street from the window of his office. "And did you support his opinion?"

"He didn't ask for my opinion. I doubt he wanted to hear anything that might crack his belief in the abbess or in supernatural aid."

They had come to a stairway that led to the ground floor, and by a series of crooked corridors found themselves eventually in the waiting room. Malecki nodded his head to the crucifix as if it were an acquaintance.

"The hallway behind that door, Captain, is where the key was eventually found."

Bora ignored the comment. Hands driven into his breeches' pockets, he paced the length of the waiting room. "You know I was raised Catholic and all that. Still, I can't help seeing Hofer's trust in the abbess as a weakness. I'm not ready to jeer at it as Colonel Schenck does, but it bothers me nonetheless."

"Does it bother you from a theological standpoint or because you just don't believe it?" Malecki sought the lion-footed bench near the crucifix, and sat down. "Perhaps you have never been desperate."

"I was taught by the Church that despair is a mortal sin."

"Yes, and so is pride, but men are prone to both when their circumstances are extreme, for the worst or the best.

It seems that when the colonel came that morning, he was distraught about a call he'd received from his family."

"He'd learned that his son's condition had worsened." Bora kept walking, restlessly. "Which explains why he came to see the abbess twice in the same day."

Malecki could tell what was on Bora's mind. It made him queasy, but as there was nothing he could do to restore his credibility, he simply sat, watching the boots measure the floor.

In the end, from the far side of the waiting room, Bora said, "I'm not angry. It's likely to get me into trouble later, Father Malecki, but for now you're the last person who seems to rankle me."

Colonel Schenck had been complimented by Hans Frank on the performance of Intelligence units in the region. His wiry body exuded more confidence than ever. During the lunch hour, when few people were around at headquarters, he came to Bora's office and took a look at the maps covering the walls. Each map was marked and colour-coded to indicate the range of interrogations, interviews, sightings of stragglers, weapons caches and incidents.

Landing a handful of files on Bora's desk, he said, "Well done. Now you can dispose of them."

Bora looked at the files. "Dispose of them? Colonel, we just opened them!"

"It was your duty to open them. Their maintenance isn't your concern. See that they're burned."

There was scarcely any need for Bora to leaf through the files. He knew they included his reports on SD and Army brutality. "But I already sent copies of these to other offices —"

"I'm sure they'll find their resting places there as well."

Suddenly Bora had the same certainty, and there wasn't enough saliva in his mouth for him to gulp it down. "It's a most irregular order, Colonel Schenck."

"You're not paid to insure the regularity of the commands issued to you." Schenck pointed at the fat stove in the corner. "Let's see you stoke the fire."

Bora's unwillingness was so transparent, Schenck stepped towards him in a rage. "Damn you, go to the stove and burn these files in my presence!" He watched Bora open the fiery belly of the stove and morosely put in the reports, one by one. "Their folders, also."

An odour of singed cardboard rose from the stove, soon smothered by the closing of the metal door. Schenck walked to the closest map on the wall and began pulling markers from some locations. "I want these maps cleaned up before thirteen hundred hours, and the originals of your notes. Where's your log?"

Bora surrendered all things in silence. Under his eyes, Schenck ripped pages from the log, crumpled them and tossed them in the wastebasket. When he finished, the wastebasket was handed to him. "Empty it into the stove."

Bora did so.

"You see that stoves serve purposes other than cutting short the lives of womanizers," Schenck said with a smirk. "Come, come, it's done. Don't be so scrupulous. Let's go to lunch, my treat. We're in for a unit citation! You're the first officer to whom I say this."

At the restaurant, few tables were occupied, and the waiters vied to attend to the officers as soon as they entered. Schenck ordered for the two of them, and engagingly poured mineral water into Bora's glass.

"Take your colleague, Bora, a man who had no children. His legacy is nothing. He squandered his germ plasma on the idle pursuit of racially doubtful women. It's a good and rightful thing that an individual should eliminate himself when he has such little respect for the preciousness of life."

Bora ate slowly. He found Schenck's friendliness repugnant at this time. He had to force himself to keep down the food he chewed. Curling eddies of bright-red blood lined the sauce on his plate each time he cut through the meat.

"What instructions does the colonel have for me as regards tomorrow?"

"Oh, tomorrow is easy. You're due to gather complaints about the Biała Jews: do just that."

"There are no Jews left in Biała."

"But the damage is there. I want accurate details of their money-lending and usury, of course any reports of political intrigue and racial defilement, keeping in mind that dating and work association between Jews and non-Jews are also to be entered as racial defilement. Eat, Bora. Liver is good for you, especially when it's rare. Make sure you eat the sauce. In your eating practices like in everything else, follow my example and you'll be happy you did."

"It didn't go well at all!" In the humid chill of her dressing room, Ewa undid her towering hairdo before the mirror, with a furious jerk removing the postiche braid of blond hair from the top of her head. "I wish you wouldn't open your mouth and give it wind when you know I messed it up and the public noticed!"

"You're making a big deal out of nothing, Ewa. No one noticed but yourself. The director, maybe. People clapped all the same."

"*I made a mistake!*" Hairpins and costume jewellery rained on the dressing table. "I have a fucking small part and managed to miss a whole line in it!"

Kasia shrugged. She was still in her costume, complete with dishevelled grey wig and bloody tears. "What difference does it make? It was just a matinée. The theatre was half-empty."

"*You* didn't make a mistake!" Ewa dropped in her chair and covered her face so as not to look at herself in the mirror. Her shoulders trembled.

"Ewa —"

"Shut up."

"Ewa, darling, it's not your fault. You just miss Richard – that's what it is."

Ewa began to sob into her cupped hands.

"We are ever so pleased to see that you are once more free to pursue your interests in Cracow, Father Malecki."

The archbishop might or might not be as pleased as he said. Malecki had no interest in ascertaining if he were pleased or not. Prudence suggested that he keep everything about the investigation to himself, and he did so. Bora had promised he would stay in touch regarding the contractor, which was as much as he could hope for now.

"Your Eminence, I heard that posters were circulated concerning Mother Kazimierza's violent death. What has been the outcome of that?"

The archbishop waved a fine hand. "Luckily nothing of major proportions. We ensured the removal of most of them. Some students staged a protest, but we managed to make them disperse before the Germans intervened. It is vital that the Church avoid taking a position for or against the posters' contents at this hour. From the pulpit, Father Malecki, make sure that you do not suggest any encouragement of seditious behaviour: you're walking proof of what can happen to those who oppose authority."

"Still, Your Eminence, where would the Church be today if the martyrs had been so lukewarm?"

The archbishop's frown cleared when he smiled. "Between you and me, Father, and with due respect to Tertullian, the seed of the Church has probably sprouted from the Christians who kept their mouths shut and stayed alive more than from the blood of those who went to their deaths. There are enough Jesuit martyrs not to wish for more, don't you think?"

Later that evening, after Ember Friday vespers, Father Malecki had given up hope of meeting Bora and was about to leave the church when he caught sight of the uniform in the twilight of the back row.

It was Bora, bareheaded at the side of the baptismal font.

"How long have you been there, Captain?"

"Only a few minutes. I have to talk to you."

"I'll be out in a moment."

Bora walked up the aisle and approached the priest. "I would like to talk here." Because Malecki was about to say something about closing the church for the night, he added quickly, "May I be assured of your confidentiality?"

"As a priest or as a non-German?"

"Both."

"You have my word on both counts."

Bora dropped his head in the army way of respectful acknowledgement. "Thank you. I'd like for you to listen to my confession."

Snow fell heavily during the night.

For the first time since learning of his death, Bora missed Retz's presence in the apartment. It was true that he had disliked him, that they'd been as different as two people who belong to the opposite ends of the social scale could be, but the house was poorer because of his death.

Bora went to the library and sat there. It seemed to him that at any time Retz's crude vitality would make itself heard or visible. The silence was so complete in the snowfall, the ticking of his watch became faintly noticeable to his ears.

Neither Schenck nor Salle-Weber cared to explore the reasons for a suicide at Army Headquarters. It was bad form, and as long as political orthodoxy was not at stake, an officer's suicide was forgotten as quickly as it was denied. Retz's colleagues hadn't even asked about him. He had obviously related better to women than to men, which meant Bora was as close as Retz had come to anyone in the army.

Strange how the insects in the glass case, beetles and dragonflies, caught every variance of light on their shells and brittle wings if he moved his head. Fictitious life seemed to derive from the flickers in their long-dead, dried-up forms.

Bora had spent some time sorting out his feelings about the suicide after Ewa's revelation, not so much because the idea of incest revolted him – he was naive enough to find it obscure, even curious – but because Retz's reaction to it made him wonder. Admittedly, he didn't know much about him, other than he had betrayed his wife and even the women he slept with. If Retz had had depth of spirit, he hadn't displayed it. But in the end, he must have despaired of life in order to do what he'd done. The *despair* Father Malecki had spoken of seemed as alien from Retz as Bora could think.

In a skinny symmetry of death, the insects flickered under glass when Bora's arm reached out to the lamp to turn it off.

There'd be ice on the roads tomorrow.

"Do you see the dark-haired German officer sitting with the priest? That's Richard's room-mate." Ewa had stopped to adjust her hat in the reflection of the *Pod Latarnie*'s front window, and now Kasia crowded her.

"Where?"

"They're sitting in the middle of the room, looking at papers. There. Don't be obvious."

Kasia peered inside. The men in question were busy scanning what seemed to be notebooks and loose sheets of paper; the German wrote on a small pad what the priest was reading to him.

"He is *so* good-looking! How old is he; what does he do?"

Ewa pulled her away. "He's married and works in Intelligence."

"So – he's not interested, or it's me who shouldn't be interested?"

Ewa took her firmly by the arm. "You can't trust Germans."

"Germans? You can't trust men in general! Who's talking about trust? So, he's the man whose bed I slept in after Richard's party." Kasia laughed, holding on to her cap in the wind. "I'd have fantasized better things had I known what he looked like. If I'm a good girl, will you introduce me some time?"

"No."

"I suppose you wouldn't lend me the key to his place, either."

They had come to the streetcar stop, and Ewa was signalling to the approaching car.

"No."

Kasia pouted. "I guess you and Helenka want to hog all the fun."

Under the stares of the crowd in the streetcar, Ewa's woollen glove was the only buffer between the hard landing of her palm and Kasia's astonished face.

Inside the restaurant, Malecki shook his head. "It'll take you for ever. There are seventy-five instances of her use of the word *Lumen* in the meditations the abbess wrote in the past two years. She obviously had an excellent knowledge of Latin."

Bora agreed. He reread his notes. "Most of the time the word merely translates as 'light' or 'splendour', but she uses it twice in the plural for 'eyes', in seven instances as 'intellect' and a handful of times as 'opening, cleft'. One of these meanings must hint at the way she died."

"But if your hunch is wrong, we're wasting a lot of time chasing a word game." Malecki noticed how Bora checked his wristwatch and swept up his briefcase from under the table. Bora was always in a hurry. Whether they met in or outside the convent, he was always rushing from somewhere to somewhere else. "Aren't you going to have lunch?"

"There's no time, Father, I have to be back at work. I'll call you if something develops."

Bora meant he expected to hear more details from Colonel Hofer, whom he'd traced back to Regimental Headquarters in Germany. His son had apparently died, and Hofer had been on medical leave for the past two weeks.

Malecki came to his feet. "I'll walk you out to the car. Waiter, hold my place."

Mirrored by the snow, the sun was blinding outside. Today was the first time that Malecki had met Bora since he'd come to see him in church after vespers two nights ago. He felt in the German a new wall of reserve, unspoken, and perhaps fear of having divested himself of authority. Bora no longer engaged personally.

After the staff car left the kerb, a puddle of melted snow remained, where the reflection of the sun struggled like a captive fish. Malecki stood blinking in the sun for a minute more. He savoured the privilege and the responsibility of knowing men's hearts, which often kept men from being friends to him.

24 December

The commander-in-chief of the occupation army, General Blaskowitz, would have been a handsome man had he had a stronger chin. Openness and nobility of forehead and the upper part of his face lost energy in the lower half. His eyes were clear and striking, however, and they looked at Bora somewhat disdainfully.

"Should you be here, Captain, when your immediate superior found your concerns irrelevant?"

The words had an immediate effect on the officer facing him. Not nervous but tense to the extreme, he seemed to be like one about to take an extended leap whose outcome is all but certain. The tendons on his neck were hard. There was a small mirror on the wall behind him, and the rigidity of his neck was reflected in it.

"I must be here, General. There's no one else in the *General-gouvernement* I may speak to and hope to be heard."

Blaskowitz didn't sit back in his chair. He continued to stand behind his desk with that judgemental look in his eyes.

Bora found enough moisture under his tongue to swallow. It seemed that all the general was really debating at this point was whether to dismiss him altogether or allow him to stay and be reproached.

"What have you there?"

211

Bora took one step forwards. His arm stretched out to give a manilla envelope to Blaskowitz, who indicated to him to place it on the desk. He didn't lower his attention to it, but continued to look at Bora inquisitively.

"Sir, it is a report of police and army actions I have witnessed in Galicia during the past two months."

"Who instructed you to write a report?"

"No one, General."

"What authority have you then to take it upon yourself to write a report?"

Bora was struggling to keep his eyes on Blaskowitz, while he wanted to look down, or elsewhere. "I have no authority, General. But I feel I have the duty."

Blaskowitz reached with his right hand to the manilla envelope, and tossed it to one side of his massive desk.

"Where did you attend military school?"

"At the Infantry School in Dresden, and then the Cavalry School in Hannover. I was attending a course for regimental close-support gun-platoon commanders in Doeberitz when the war began."

"And how long have you held your present position?"

"Two months."

Blaskowitz sat down. His eyes were now on the manilla envelope, as if Bora's presence were somehow accessory to it.

For a good minute he said nothing at all. A hum came to Bora's ears from the right, from an electric clock on the desk. Bora realized how his head still ached on that side. It throbbed and sent stabs of pain down his neck.

Blaskowitz held the envelope up to him. "Your career is in this envelope. I give you the option of taking it back and leaving my office."

"Sir, my career isn't worth what is in this envelope."

Blaskowitz nailed him with a hard, reproving stare. "Your career ought to be worth everything to you. Didn't they teach you that in military school?"

Bora spoke against his own despair, dourly. "If the general doesn't wish to accept my report, I must let the general know that I will take it higher."

"Higher?"

It seemed to Bora that Blaskowitz had a passing flicker of amusement in his eyes, something which he judged quite impossible. However, Blaskowitz unsealed the envelope, and for the next several minutes read the contents of it.

Two entire nights Bora had spent piecing together from memory and a few scraps of notes the information from the destroyed files. Now Blaskowitz read, and no change came on his face. He read with care, thinking as he read. Halfway through the reading, he asked, "What other schooling did you receive?"

"The University of Leipzig, Herr General."

"Yes." Blaskowitz continued to read. "You don't write like a soldier. You write too well for a soldier." He pointed to a high-backed chair. "Sit down."

Sister Irenka was not one to show her emotions. Her anguish could be perceived only by the way her lips tightened in a peristaltic pucker. Father Malecki was alerted at once, and even before entering the convent he prepared himself for bad news.

"Father, they've taken Sister Barbara."

Malecki pushed the heavy door closed behind him. "Who was it, when? Has the archbishop been informed?"

"We were hoping you'd go to His Eminence for us. We're afraid of sending any of the sisters out after this morning. It was the same group that came searching last week, only this time they went straight for the kitchen. They didn't even give her time to take off her apron. I tried to talk to them, but it did no good. I ran outside after them and asked where they'd take her, and they wouldn't answer, they wouldn't look back. They put her in the truck and left. And on Christmas Eve, Father Malecki!"

Malecki had to breathe short fast breaths to control his passions. He didn't know why he'd mentioned the archbishop: he expected no support from that side, not if it concerned a converted Jewess. Bora came to mind, of course, but Bora might not be at the office or might decide not to receive him.

"How long ago did it happen, Sister?"

"An hour ago, maybe. We were so much hoping you'd stop this way! Please try to see what can be done."

Malecki sighed a furious sigh. "They've already arrested me once, Sister Irenka. This time they'll kick me out of the country if I don't think of a better way than going to the Germans myself."

He left without plans, having agreed to a vague promise that he'd act as quickly as possible. He didn't have Bora's telephone number on him, so it was impossible to get in touch with him without physically going to headquarters. He started heading that way with the premonition that neither the archbishop nor the American consulate would approve.

Captain Bora was out, and not expected back soon. Malecki began to leave, trailed by the searching stare of orderly and armed guards, when rapid footsteps down the stairs caused him to turn. A non-commissioned officer strode to him across the carpeted floor of the lobby.

"You are Father Malecki, yes?" he enquired in thickly accented English.

"I am."

"Captain Bora's commander wishes to see you. Please follow."

Colonel Schenck's second-floor office had the spareness of a monk's cell. Nothing personal cluttered his desk – no family photos, no name plaque, no paperweights or cigarettes. The walls were completely bare.

Schenck barged in with his usual energy after Malecki had been waiting for five minutes or so alongside the starchy non-commissioned officer. "So." He came to his desk and half-sat on the corner of it. "You're Captain Bora's priest!"

Malecki would have answered something witty had he not come to ask for consideration. He nodded, and that was all.

"I understand English better than I speak it," Schenck asserted. "Do you understand German, yes?"

Malecki said he'd studied it in school and all but forgotten it. He was trying to decide whether Schenck was approachable, whether he could bring up Sister Barbara's plight and not make things worse. Bora never spoke of his fellow officers, so he had no clues.

Hands clasped on his knee, Schenck observed him with detached humour. "Has Captain Bora told you to come see him?"

"No, I came on my own."

"*Ach so.* You found the nun's killer?"

"Unfortunately not."

"Why are you here, then?"

Malecki plunged in. "I thought the captain could help the convent resolve an urgent question. One of the sisters has been arrested by the SS."

Schenck's leathery face betrayed no hostile reaction to the news.

"Why come to us? Are you afraid of the SS?"

"Not for myself."

With a mischievous simper Schenck walked around his desk and reached for the telephone. He spoke to someone for perhaps a minute, keeping his eyes on Malecki the entire time. Malecki understood he was being referred to as *der Amerikaner*, but the rest of the conversation eluded him. At the end of it, Schenck resumed his place on the corner of the desk.

"It seems that you were mistaken." He chose the past tense carefully. "It was not a nun they took, but a Jewess."

"She *used to be* Jewish, Colonel. Now she is a convert and a Roman Catholic nun!"

Schenck started laughing. "If a Negro puts my uniform on, is he less of a Negro? Of course not. He stays a Negro. And I know how you treat Negroes in America, Father Malecki." A gruff command brought the non-commissioned officer back into the office. "The sergeant will show you out. And please leave Captain Bora be, these are not things for Captain Bora's interest."

The cleaning woman wore a white kerchief, tightly bound around her forehead. She was raw-boned and red-cheeked, like many a farm woman Bora had met in the countryside. When Bora reached the landing in front of his door, she bowed to him, hands clasped, elbows at an angle, as if praying. He irritably thought at first she meant to thank him for the Christmas bonus, but her face was too pained for that.

In the accented German of a Sudete, "It isn't much, *panie kapitanie*," she said, "but I am responsible for it if it isn't found."

Bora hadn't really been paying attention. He'd come up the stairs two steps at a time, anxious to change from his two days in the field before meeting Father Malecki. He'd found a note from the priest and surmised from it that something was amiss. So he had no wish to listen to the cleaning woman on the stairs. "What are you talking about?" he asked. "What 'isn't much'?"

"The hand towel, *panie kapitanie.*"

Bora impatiently turned the key in the lock. "I don't know what you mean. Explain yourself, I'm in a hurry."

"One of the hand towels is missing, and I thought maybe the captain knows where it is."

Bora pushed the leaf of the door inwards, but did not step in.

"There were five bath towels for each officer, *panie kapitanie.* Five hand towels and five face cloths. I'm to take them down for washing every Sunday and Wednesday. One of the hand towels is missing, and I was told I have to pay for it if it isn't found."

Absent-mindedly, Bora entered the apartment and waved her in.

"Show me."

Ten minutes later he was leaving for the convent, and absent-mindedness had turned to concern.

Father Malecki met him in the waiting room, and reported on his visit to Schenck. "I was asked direct questions about Sister Barbara, Captain. There was no time to waste, and your commander seemed an approachable man."

Bora slapped his gloves on his thigh. "That's beside the point. You shouldn't have brought up the issue on two counts: the Army is an organization completely separate from the SS and the Security Service, and by mentioning my name as a possible go-between you now make it impossible for me to become involved."

"I don't see how —"

"Father Malecki, at some point you must start telling me the truth. You knew there was a Jewish convert in this place and you didn't see fit to inform me. Because of it, what could perhaps have been prevented has happened. What else are you keeping from me?"

Grudgingly Malecki reported Sister Barbara's dreams, though Bora didn't seem impressed by the narrative.

"That's the whole story, Captain. Can anything be done for her now?"

"I make no promises."

"The archbishop isn't willing to intercede. You see that you are the only person who can."

Bora looked insulted. "Don't try to convince me by flattering my sense of ethics, Father. I have a career."

One hour later, it was exactly what Salle-Weber reminded him of, after listening with as much good grace as he was about to use with an army colleague.

"You're wasting your time and attaching your name to useless pursuits. The other day I released the priest to you because I trust you know what you're doing. You even wrangled the *Lumen* file from me, and found there was nothing you could use in it. Right now I'm willing not to put this meeting on record if you drop your request. Give it up."

Bora took a moderate breath. "I'm not asking for consideration because she's Jewish-born, you understand. She's of some use to me in relation to the murder case. I'm not as sensitive as you seem to think I am."

"Even so, Bora." Salle-Weber balanced a pencil between his index and forefinger. Slumped in his chair, he didn't seem as massive as he did standing up. "Recognize good advice when you see it." He leaned back on his chair until the back of it creaked faintly. "Are you giving it up?"

"Yes."

It was not physical weariness, but that evening Bora felt as tired as he ever had before. Even the steps leading up to his apartment seemed an obstacle that he wasn't up to confronting.

Seeing Helenka at the top of the stairs only made things worse. He stopped with his hand on the rail, looking up.

"Fräulein Kowalska," he said from where he was, "it's late and I don't wish to speak to you. I don't know who let you into the building, but I urge you to leave right now. I'm not Major Retz, and I don't entertain at home."

Helenka clutched a knitted handbag in her gloveless hands. "I was waiting in the street. It was the porter who let me in."

"I'll talk to the porter in the morning. Please leave."

"Captain, you're rather conceited if you think I'm here to spend the night with you. I don't even like you."

"And I don't want you in my house."

"It's about Richard's death."

Bora came up the stairs, one step at a time. "You said there was nothing you could add to it. Whatever it is, I'm sure it can wait until after tomorrow and in a less compromising setting for both of us. Good night."

The scent of violets was on her. Bora was outraged by the recognition that she countered his weariness and belied it, because bodily he wasn't tired at all. Within seconds he went from contempt to a state of mild arousal. He reached the landing, and as he did, Helenka went past him, starting down the stairs.

Sudden curiosity for what she might say about Retz tempted Bora to call her back. Out of pride he didn't, or perhaps he was not sure of himself enough to let her into his house at night.

26 December

When he phoned the theatre on Monday morning, Helenka hadn't yet arrived for rehearsal. Kasia took the call.

"Is there a message?"

"No."

Clearly the caller was a German. Without a solid reason for it, Kasia was convinced it was the officer Ewa had pointed out to her, Richard's colleague. Here came a chance for her to chat with him, and he didn't speak Polish!

"Helenka usually gets here by nine o'clock," she spelled out for him to understand. "Please call again at nine."

Bora thanked her, and hung up.

From behind, on the door of his office, Schenck expressed his disapproval. "Captain, are you becoming involved with Polish women?"

Bora stood up and turned. "No, sir. It's not a private call. It has to do with Major Retz's death."

"Well, what about it?"

"I'm not sure."

Schenck was unconvinced. "Steer clear of women, whatever the reason. With your wife coming soon, you must at all costs avoid states of mind that might bring about involuntary loss of seminal fluid and weakening of the germ plasma."

"I believe I can control myself, Colonel."

"Don't be so confident." Schenck lifted from Bora's desk the map with the itinerary he would follow in the morning, glimpsed at it and put it back. "Speaking of other matters you're involved in, I want you to conclude the investigation on the nun's death as soon as possible, with a provisional statement and recommendations if no solution is available. Unless you can prove to me that the Polish underground assassinated her, for example, there's no sense in keeping things up in the air. I want a full report two weeks from now."

Bora showed none of the disappointment Schenck's words gave him. "May I be candid in my report?"

"Naturally. But remember that I have a stove in my office, too."

10

The place was identified on the map as Święty Bór. It did not figure as a stop in his itinerary and Bora would have gone past it, if a mounted army patrol hadn't halted his car down the road from where the forest began.

"I'm in a hurry," he rolled down his window to say. "What is the matter?"

He recognized the lieutenant leading the platoon from one of his previous errands in this wooded region. A plump young man, he approached the staff car and greeted Bora with an unusual strain in his behaviour. "Please, Captain Bora." He leaned towards the window, whispering, "I urgently need a word with you."

Bora looked at his watch. "About what? Be quick, I have to be in Wiślica by noon."

The lieutenant's eyes stole past Bora to Hannes. "In private, sir."

Bora told Hannes to park at the side of the road, where the platoon mounts were also gathered, and left the car door open to signify his haste. "What is it, Lieutenant?"

"This way, please."

The growth of fir trees reached very close to the road at this point. The lieutenant led Bora in that direction. By the hoofprints in the snow, Bora could tell the platoon had come through the woods.

The lieutenant straddled a bush, still whispering. "It's a miracle you should be coming this way now. There's

221

something going on beyond the woods. I think you should take a look. The men called my attention to it."

Bora followed in the tangled brushwood. His greatcoat became caught in low branches here and there, and he intolerantly freed himself. "What's *something*, Lieutenant? A military operation? This had better be justified." But he was already uneasy, angry at his uneasiness.

The lieutenant turned around to bid him silence. The terrain climbed after a while, where the trees grew closest and tall. Soon the road seemed lost behind the curtain of other trees behind them, and very far. More and more uneasily Bora trod on, removing the sweeping branches of the firs from his way.

"There's a clearing ahead." The lieutenant spoke with his hands mostly. By the angle of his advance, Bora understood they were following a wide half-circle to their destination. No snow had penetrated the woods, and the earth lay strewn with crunchy fir needles, broken twigs that snapped under one's steps. The horses' hoofmarks were only visible where the animals had slipped on the vegetation carpet, or the bare soil was clayish and still warm enough to receive the imprints. Larches began further up, on a steep, rocky incline.

The lieutenant halted short of the incline.

"Listen."

Bora stood still. Now that his movements no longer awakened a rustle underfoot, silence followed. Straight ahead, deadened by trees and the rise in the land, the staccato sound of single gunshots marred the silence.

He climbed alone, hands and feet finding anchor on exposed roots and tangled brushwood. From below, the lieutenant watched him anxiously. "You'll need these." He stretched his field glasses up to Bora.

Bora ignored the offer. He had reached the shrubby crest of the incline, where he crouched to look. His shoulders braced and hardened into a vigilant and then aghast immobility. Field glasses in hand, the lieutenant clambered to his side. "Here, take them," he insisted. "I don't care to see any more." And he dropped down again.

When Bora returned to Cracow that evening, a red afterglow made the bristling skyline of steeples resemble its own eerie forest. Pointed as firs, shaggy with crosses and spires, the churches punctured the red sky, and it seemed to Bora that the sky should burst and sag upon them.

As always, Hannes had taken Florianska to bring him home through the Old City.

"Take a right here." Bora caused him to slow down and turn the steering wheel at a sharp angle. "Go to Karmelicka."

The house where Father Malecki lived was tall and not unlike the other tall buildings which darkness was overcoming from the ground floor up. "Leave the car," Bora dismissed Hannes.

He looked up at the façade before ringing the bell. The eaves were the only part of it that still held a flesh-coloured tinge, while the sky all around had grown sickly grey. Father Malecki's window, who knows, might be the one where a light shone through the glass.

Two clumsy steps backwards were all that *Pana* Klara could think of to disguise her distress at the visit. She improved on it by continuing to step back as if to invite Bora in.

"Which floor?" Bora asked in Polish.

She lifted three fingers. When she started up the stairs after him, Bora made her a sign to stay. "*Dziękuję,*" he thanked her, and went up alone.

Father Malecki was reading a week-old copy of the *Chicago Tribune* Logan had set aside for him at the consulate.

"Come in, *Pana* Klara," he replied to the knock on the door. "It's open."

Bora was the last person he expected here. Malecki stared at the visitor's distraught paleness over the top of the newspaper, very casually, he thought, given his surprise. Bora spoke a few formal words of apology for coming without notice.

"Well, won't you sit down?"

Bora removed his cap, which he rigidly held under his arm. "No, thank you. I have come to tell you that I cannot help Sister Barbara."

"I see." Malecki doubted this was the only reason for Bora's ashen-faced presence. "I'm grieved to hear it. I was hoping you might assist us."

"Yes." Bora suddenly found he had to steady his breathing. Having kept control all day, his muscles began to tremble with the first inopportune release of tension, an unexpected and painful process. Stiffening his spine didn't help the pain but stopped the chills at once. The priest's avoidance of direct eye contact allowed him to think himself less obvious. "I have also come to say I received orders to conclude the investigation."

It was closer to the truth than the first statement, but this wasn't the reason for the visit or the distress. Malecki felt it.

"It's a shame, Captain. Do we have any time left?"

"Two weeks."

"God might lend us a hand between now and then."

"Maybe. You know God better than I."

Malecki folded and put away the newspaper. "I wish you'd sit down a moment. Must you rush off?"

Bora had hoped for the invitation. Impulsively, he sat facing the priest, tight-lipped, holding the cap on his knees.

What he needed to say, he could not say. He could not. It was forbidden. With all the prudence and repression of his upbringing, he swallowed back a gut-wrenching need to cry out to Malecki what he'd witnessed that morning. Words clashed and rammed inside him until by habit of self-control, wearily, he was able to keep them down. He skilfully opened a lesser wound in order to bleed his anguish.

"Father Malecki, my room-mate died last week. It troubles me. May I speak of it?"

At the other end of town, Ewa Kowalska found that she couldn't avoid waiting for the same streetcar as her daughter. A few steps away, Helenka kept her face averted, and the cold wind made her eyes water.

"Helenka, look at me."

The young woman only lifted her collar.

"Will you look at me, Helenka? I have to talk to you."

Helenka wouldn't turn. She held on to her purse, face in the bitter evening wind. Ewa reached for her arm.

"I told you I have to talk to you."

Unexpectedly, Helenka wheeled around and shook herself free of the hold. There wasn't enough light left for them to see clearly, and as from behind masks each looked at the other's blurred countenance. Helenka felt a venomous desire to hurt the woman facing her.

"Mother, you're old. You're forty-six years old. What can you possibly say that even applies to my life? If it's about Richard, keep from preaching to me, because you did what you wanted at my age. You're just jealous because Richard fell in love with me. Don't even try to talk about him."

Ewa kept her temper by some miraculous effort. "I had no intention to talk about Richard. It's your brother. He's back in Cracow, and I met him this morning."

"So?"

"He wants to know if he can come stay with you for a while."

"Tell him no. I'm sharing the room with someone else. Why can't he stay at your place? You have two bedrooms."

Ewa could weep in frustration. "You know how difficult it is to come and go at my place. For the last two days a German patrol has been stationed at the end of the street. I can't have him there."

"Why not? It's not like it's the first time you had men over."

The temptation to strike back choked her, but Ewa managed again. She said, swallowing her pride, "He says he killed somebody."

The clanking arrival of the tramway under a small shower of sparks kept them from continuing the conversation. Helenka climbed on first. When Ewa followed, she saw that her daughter had chosen the seat closest to the conductor, making it impossible for her to speak in private.

On Karmelicka, *Pana* Klara tiptoed to the hallway at the head of the stairs to listen unseen, just in case Father Malecki was being abused by his German visitor. Through the partly open door, she didn't hear the priest talk. The other voice spoke steadily to him, not in anger, posing earnest questions as it seemed.

Now Malecki was certain that Bora kept from him a much larger issue. Bora's steadiness of voice and composure were not artificial, but layered too accurately not to betray the effort of the process. "So," Malecki said, "your colleague's death troubles you. From all you've told me, I don't gather that you mourn his passing, even though the mode of it should."

Bora stretched his legs in a first sign of relaxation. "The mode of it does, Father. There are some things, some small things – details. They keep me awake at night, when I didn't even care for him. A towel is missing from the house, the blade was left in his razor when he had a fetish against doing so. As you heard tonight, my colleague had as good a reason to be despondent as I can envision, still it troubles me. It's a clear case of suicide, there were no marks of violence on the body, no indication of forced entry into the house. All the women who were involved with him have impeccable alibis. It troubles me, that's all."

Malecki clasped his hands slackly. "Perhaps you resent a lifestyle your education kept you from sharing."

"It's true, I did. I'm ashamed to say there were nights when I envied him."

"What troubles you then may be your own resentment, not your colleague's death. Moral men cannot escape desiring what they deny themselves. I for one am ready to make all kinds of allowances for their disgruntlement."

Bora let go a little more, enough to toss his cap on Malecki's bed. Talking about other things helped somewhat. It numbed the anguish without removing it, which meant it would return later, when he would be alone.

"Even when they're unable to separate the practice of virtue from arrogance? Father, people without moral scruples seem always nicely shorn of pride, while *being good* costs me so much effort, I'm not even pleasant about it." Sorrow wanted out of him and Bora still tried to give some other shape to it, so that the priest wouldn't suspect. "What's the point, Father Malecki? God doesn't give a damn about any of us."

There was no motive for Malecki to feel so sure of himself, but he came around Bora to shut the door of the room behind him.

"Really?"

"Really."

"If you're in the mood to blame God, blame Him in my face. I may not know Him better, but I've known Him longer than you have."

29 December

At seven in the morning, Doctor Nowotny used his foot to close the door, since his hands were busy with cigarette and lighter.

"It's the second time you've trundled into this office so early, Captain. What's Schenck put into your head now?" When Bora handed him a sealed envelope, he stared at it. "And what's this?"

"It's the report of the autopsy performed on Major Retz, Colonel. I wonder if you'd read it for me."

"Retz, Retz – the fellow that cooked his head in the stove? Well, what does it have to do with you? Oh, I see. I didn't realize you quartered together." Nowotny ripped the side of the envelope. "There was no need for my colleague to seal this, it isn't a state secret. What do you want to know?"

"Anything you might find unusual."

Nowotny scanned the report. "It looks pretty straightforward, but give me some time to read it. I'll call you when I have something to say. Is anything wrong?"

"I'm just curious to hear a professional opinion, Colonel."

"That's not what I mean. I mean *you*: what's happened to you?"

Bora evaded Nowotny's scrutiny with a blank army stare. "Nothing has happened to me."

After he left the hospital, the sleepless night threatened to catch up with him, and he spent the first minutes at work with his head under the bathroom faucet. What the cold water didn't do, plenty of black coffee did, so that he looked his usual prim self when Schenck called him in to report.

The events at Święty Bór did not appear in his notes, and although he felt guilty about it he made no mention of them to the colonel. Blaskowitz's words prevented him. "Now that your career is in this envelope, give me something I can use," the general had told him on dismissing him. "Bring me proof."

While Schenck read through the notes, Bora thought of how he could "bring proof" directly to the general's headquarters at Spala. With his schedule, it seemed only dimly possible.

Schenck lifted his live and dead eye from the notes.

"Much improved, Bora. You're developing selective vision."

Bora thanked him. Selective vision? He felt as if the last twenty-four hours had scooped out of him a careless enthusiastic life principle. The zeal that replaced it was severe and exacting and made him new to himself. All actions seemed untried as he took them.

"Colonel," he said. "I wonder if I might be given two days to concentrate on some research." He didn't say which, in order not to lie brazenly. "The report on the abbess's death is due sooner than I can possibly put it together by working after hours."

Schenck gave back the notes. "I expect so. We owe it to old Hofer, don't we? Two days is more than I want to spare you, but I'll give you thirty-six hours starting in the morning."

"I don't think you believe I was in love with him."

Helenka wore her hair pinned tightly at the nape of the neck, and her face seemed bare now that she had no make-up on it. The dressing room was very narrow and poorly lit except for the over-illuminated mirror, in front of which she sat. Like a dead black bird, a wig rested in a cardboard box. Paunchy jars and rouge sticks, hairpins, curls of hair pulled from the comb after disentangling the wig – there was a variety of feminine objects strewn on the dressing table.

Bora recognized Retz's phone number pencilled on the wall by the mirror.

"You see, Captain, it wasn't like it was for Ewa and him. Ours was different. I can't explain it to you."

Bora stood behind her chair with hands in his pockets, following her motions as she opened one jar, then another, and with two fingers began smoothing the mixture on her face.

"I know what being in love is, you don't need to explain it."

She glimpsed at him through the mirror. "But you're married. It's not the same. I know it becomes stale when you're married."

"My marriage isn't quite stale yet."

A new pallor was created on Helenka's face by the salve she daubed on. When she spoke, the inside of her mouth looked bright pink by contrast. "What I meant to tell you last night is I don't believe Richard had any reason to kill himself."

"Perhaps none you knew of."

She ran rouge over her lips, first on the lower lip then on the upper. Small hooked gestures, still controlled. Against the white of the skin, her mouth was turned into a moist red wound across her face. "You don't understand. He loved me too much. Men in love don't kill themselves."

"It depends on whom they're in love with."

"You still don't understand! Even if he had a thousand reasons to commit suicide, Richard would have told me about it. He called me that morning, you know. He was getting ready to come see me after the rehearsal." Her hand trembled too much now for her to apply mascara on her eyelashes, so she waited with the soot-black little brush suspended, quivering. "He looked forward to it, he said. He had bought me a gift. Is that the sort of conversation a man has while he's turning on the gas to suffocate himself?"

"We hardly know what goes through a suicide's mind."

"But I didn't phone him, he called *me*! Wouldn't he have something better to say to me if he was about to die?"

Bora stared at the limp blackness of the wig, which Helenka now lifted and primped in her hands. The gift she mentioned must be the boxed engagement ring he'd found in Retz's bedtable. He'd decided to ship it to the widow, all the more since Retz had given away his wedding band. Helenka tucked the blond fleece on her neck under the wig.

"I need to ask you a few questions," Bora said.

"So, that's why you came after work. What kind of questions?"

"Some of them are personal, but I don't ask them for personal reasons."

Now Helenka seemed another creature, born out of the mirror. Dark and white, with that crimson slash across her face, her clear eyes like glass splinters set in the blackness of painted lashes and brows. She was newly alien, nearly frightening to him.

"Very well. Ask."

Half an hour later, Ewa ran into him in the uncomfortably cold, narrow semi-darkness of the backstage corridor as he came out of Helenka's dressing room. Bora brought his hand to his visor in a salute.

Whatever was in Ewa's mind, she said, "How nice to see you, Captain. Are you staying for the play?"

"I'm sorry, I have no time."

"Pity."

They stopped face to face. Ewa, too, was transformed. Like swatches of night sky, a black dress gathered and fell around her body, making the whiteness of bare shoulders and the deep line of breasts glare from the twilight. Her lead-white face seemed to Bora bloodless like those of dead women he'd seen sprawled on threshing floors and barn floors, a reminder that made him physically cringe. He thought, with sudden shame, of the bloody and torn cotton briefs around the farm girl's knees; her belly was no less white, and like mashed snow with blond grass on it. A queasy need to get out of here overtook him.

The corridor was narrow, and when he moved, their bodies nearly touched.

"I must go."

"Good night, Captain Bora."

Nowotny's phone call arrived two hours later, at half-past ten. Brusque as always, the physician's voice began by asking, "Are you alone?"

"Why, yes, Colonel."

"Good. I read the autopsy report, and I'm coming to see you. No, I don't want to meet at the hospital. I know where you live; I'll be there in ten minutes."

Bora was waiting on the landing when Nowotny arrived. He heard him call from below. "Why in hell didn't you get a place with an elevator?" And then the clump of his boots on the steps. Once in the apartment, the physician headed straight for the hall. "A Blüthner piano! Well, I see why you billet here. Will you play some Schumann?"

"As the colonel wishes."

"Not now. Later." Nowotny found a portly armchair to sit in and for perhaps a minute looked around. His eyes were still taking in the sober decor when he began speaking again. "I couldn't find anything of relevance in the autopsy. It is consistent with the cause of death, the findings are normal for a man of Retz's age and habits. So I gave a call to the colleague who performed the post mortem and decided to ask him directly about any detail he might have observed but not found relevant enough to include in the report."

"I appreciate it."

"Wait to thank me. He told me nothing worthwhile, unless you consider relevant the fact that Retz's face was only partly shaven." Bora's reaction puzzled Nowotny. "Is it?"

"It might. What does it mean, 'partly shaven'?"

"Just what I said. The right cheek was shaven smooth, while chin, upper lip and left cheek had a twenty-four-hour bristle. My colleague said he didn't notice it at first, because of the fairness of the facial hair." Nowotny fished a pack of Muratti's from his pocket. "What does it tell you, and what is this all about anyway? I thought you were trying to figure out who killed the nun."

"I'm just curious, Colonel. Major Retz's death was very sudden."

"Oh, as for that. I had a schoolmate who breezed through medical school, graduated first in his class, was offered an assistantship on the same day and by the next morning had shot himself. A devout Catholic, too." Nowotny tapped his cigarette on the arm of the chair. "If you're so morbid about Retz, why don't you come to the hospital one of these days before work and ask the medics who brought him in?"

Bora said he would do so.

"It's generous of you to have come to tell me this in person, Colonel Nowotny."

"That's not why I came." Curtly, Nowotny gestured towards the piano stool for Bora, who'd been standing, to sit down. "How clever are you?"

Bora didn't expect the question. "I don't like cleverness much."

"Well, do you have common sense, then?"

"I hope so."

"An intelligent man without common sense will never be able to do what you started to do."

Bora didn't mistake what Nowotny was saying. With unspoken alarm he understood the words didn't refer to investigations or military routine. The idea that someone from the outside *knew* of it made him defensive.

"What have I started, Colonel?"

Nowotny reached for an ashtray, which he balanced on his knees. "Don't practice cleverness with me, it's unnecessary; I'm an unimpressionable Prussian swine. And don't worry, I don't read minds. Like General Blaskowitz, I come from Peterswalde: we keep in touch. Now play me some Schumann."

30 December

Father Malecki had his back to Mr Logan of the American consulate, mostly because he didn't wish to grow angry at him, and he was close to his threshold of patience.

Logan spoke in a bureaucratic sing-song. "A single American citizen, you will forgive me, has no business becoming involved in the internal matters of a foreign country, no matter how charitable in appearance. When the consul heard you had been detained, he threw a fit. I had to calm him down before being able to make him even consider there might have been a misunderstanding. You and I, Father Malecki, know there was no misunderstanding at all."

"I did not 'become involved' as an American, but as a Roman Catholic priest."

"You're splitting hairs, Father. If that weren't enough, you've been seen in public places with a German Intelligence officer by the name of Bora. What is your reason for meeting him?"

"It's simpler than you think."

"Explain it to me, then. Simply, so that I can report to the consul without getting my tail chewed."

When Malecki finished the brief exposition, Logan let out a low moan.

"You take much upon yourself, Father. We are anxious that no more incidents should happen to embarrass the United States government, and with all due respect for your habit and connected allegiances, we must ask you to refrain from these extra-clerical activities."

"Now it's the consul talking," Malecki said with scorn.

"No, the consul wanted to repatriate you immediately. This is Logan from Chicago talking, the one who attended Sunday school at Holy Name's. Father, will you at least look at me?"

"I can hear you just fine without looking at you. And, see? Hopefully I'll be done in less than two weeks. Give me until then and I promise I'll settle down and say my beads."

"Much can happen in two weeks."

"A bomb could fall on our heads this very minute, too. Come, Logan. We're not at war with Germany and we're not at war with Poland. Until we decide which side we're going to take, if any, give me a chance to do some good."

"No more exploits, Father."

"I promise."

"Be discreet in your meetings. Avoid contacts with the occupying forces if possible: people talk and are resentful.

Keep from political discussions and say nothing to Bora that could be used by German propaganda. Reveal nothing to him that might be interpreted as personal leanings for or against the Third Reich. Refrain from praise, criticism or comments."

Malecki turned around at long last, with a grin on his face.

"May I at least save his soul?"

When Malecki met with the nuns later that morning, the good cheer he had shown Logan was gone. The nuns listened in complete silence, and then began to weep noiselessly when he told them that his attempt to get help for Sister Barbara had failed.

"I don't know why I even bothered to approach any of the Germans."

Being disappointed in Bora embittered him because it forced him to admit how much he had counted on his help, as if Bora had ever given him reason to depend on him.

Bora was then stopping his car at the edge of Święty Bór, where tracks left in the mud had hardened, and a new snowfall would soon fill them. A light cloud of steam rose from the hood as he walked around the car, camera in hand. He passed the scrubby threshold of the woods and entered a rapidly thickening world of tangled branches and trees growing in clumps.

The bluish pines that gave name to the woods shot up above the underwood, surrounded by a carpet of needles and short cones bristling open. Bora went past them and straight through this time, soon reaching the slippery incline where larches spread rough branches heavy with years and snowfalls. The ground cover of leaves and needles was disturbed on the incline. Some of the branches were broken or bent. A church-like odour of resin came from them when he brushed past.

Beyond the incline the land opened up again, unknown, wider than a clearing and more like a prairie meadow that would bloom wet in the spring. Combed yellow trails in the dead grass revealed the natural network of drainage into and from it, and although it hadn't rained or snowed in days, the soil felt elastic under Bora's steps. He pushed the advance lever of his camera and took the first picture.

The trench was thirty paces long, four paces wide, running across the field in a roughly east-west direction. The fresh dirt covering it had sunk in places and was so soft that when he stepped on it, it collapsed under his foot close to the edge. His boot went down nearly to his calf, and Bora struggled to extricate himself; when he did, he saw that brownish long strands had become tangled on his spur. With his gloved hand, slowly, he cleared the blackish sod in the hole to look in. He adjusted the distance scale to the minimum, and shot two more photographs. He had to walk nearly to the southern rim of the clearing to be able to photograph the entire trench.

Back on the edge of upheaved dirt where he'd seen the SD open fire, he met with handfuls of rifle casings and pistol casings, some of which he gathered into his breeches' pockets. More pictures followed.

Standing on the spot and staring ahead towards a lacy barrier of leafless trees, meagre against the cinder sky, he knew he was looking at the last image seen by those who had been shot along the trench. Bora instinctively looked down, all too vividly imagining the explosion at the base of each victim's skull, followed no doubt by some convulsed jerking motion when one fell over. The sensation went through him with physical clarity, bearing for the first time in this war an unmistakable warning of grief to come.

He continued to take photographs until the film in his camera was exhausted, and then walked back into the woods.

There was a half-track parked by his car at the edge of the road.

Bora discerned it through the screen of rarefying brushwood, and for a crazy instant felt that by taking one more step he might fall headlong into panic. He looked back into the tangle of trees, thinking, checking the speed of his breathing. Hastily, he removed the leather strap from around his neck, and lay the camera behind an exposed root.

It was a small group of men, composed of a redheaded officer and three SD guards armed with rifles. The doors of his car had been yanked wide. Two of the guards were going through the interior even now.

As he stepped out in the open, Bora saw they had found the empty box of camera film on the front seat.

"What were you doing in the woods, Captain?"

Bora critically looked inside his car before slamming the doors shut. "I'm not aware that I have to explain what I'm doing anywhere. This is open country."

"That's not an answer. I asked you what you were doing in the woods."

"I was heeding a physiological call. What else?"

The officer had been holding the empty film box, and now crushed it in his freckled fist.

"I have no difficulty forcing you to drop your breeches and checking if what you say is true. I'd rather not have to do that."

Bora stared down the armed men. "Then you'll have to trust me on my word. Why shouldn't I be here any more than you are?"

At a nod from the officer, those who had searched the car stepped into the brushwood and began rummaging around with their rifles. The third man took his place behind Bora.

"Where's your camera?"

Bora decided not to answer. He was starting to feel an impotent anger at being caught. "Look here..." He took one step forwards.

The crash of the metal-clad rifle stock between his shoulders burst the air out of his lungs. Bora lost his balance and was knocked on his knees by a second swinging blow. His cap flew off and rolled two paces away, where the officer picked it up and read the name on the diamond-shaped tag inside.

"I thought I recognized you. You serve under Colonel Schenck in Cracow."

Bora tried to stand, with an entirely foolish gesture making for the holster on his side. Rifle stock and hob-nailed boot struck together this time. He landed with his face in the cold dirt. Musty-tasting loam crackled under his teeth when the guard's knee weighed him down to take his gun.

"Here's the camera!" The men called from the woods' edge and walked back.

Bora strained to raise his neck and met the cold pressure of the butt plate. He could do nothing but squirm while the officer exposed the film to light.

"Do you take pictures of yourself when you take a shit?"

Bora dug his elbows in the ground in a back-breaking effort to lift himself. He threw the guard off for a moment, and at once it was the muzzle of the rifle that knocked hard against the base of his skull. The soldier was standing on his back, rifle poking until it lodged cold in the shaven hollow of his neck. Bora cringed at the contact. Muscles and bones locked stiff, but he had suddenly no control over his breathing. The officer could see him lose that control.

"Shoot him," he said.

Bora felt a blaze of fear race up his spine at the cocking of the bolt, instantaneous agony and shutting of eyes and absurd, scary hardening in arousal all at once. The bolt locked in place for firing. His teeth clenched to crush the dirt in his mouth.

The rifle clicked empty.

His heart pumped in a seemingly immense gulp of blood, dizzying him so that his eyes were once more open but he could see nothing other than a red pulsating mist.

A lesson, he thought disconnectedly. He was being taught a lesson. Like the weary lifting of a world, weight and pressure were gone from his back The muzzle was pulled back.

Bora drew himself up on his knees.

Amused, the soldiers were walking away from him, with rifles slung on their shoulders. The officer tossed the camera into the half-track.

"Remember that I know who you are, *Freiherr* Hauptmann von Bora."

It was several minutes before Bora even noticed that his tires had been slashed.

He sat in the car, mortified by having to wait for the unwanted, painful reaction of his body to abate.

Now he thought that anger was as misplaced as the other response. Resignedly, he picked up the map from the floor of the car and put it in his coat pocket. He locked the car, as if it would make a difference, and started walking west.

As for Malecki, he expected to meet Bora at the convent in the afternoon.

He remained there until nearly five o'clock, when it became apparent that Bora would not show up. He'd grown as used to Bora's punctuality as he had nearly started to believe that help might come from him. Bora was probably having dinner somewhere in Cracow this very moment, forgetful that only thirteen days were left to conclude the investigation.

Bora was, in fact, negotiating for a ride at a noticeable distance from Cracow.

The Polish farmer was not about to ask questions. He saddled his only riding horse and numbly took in hand the scribbled receipt the German gave him in exchange.

Bora mounted, winding the reins around his wrist. "*Gdzie jest telefon?*" He showed the farmer his map.

The farmer pointed at the closest village of some size, where shortly before nightfall the driver sent by Doctor Nowotny found Bora waiting on horseback at the crossroads like an lonesome monument to the Polish campaign.

At the hospital Nowotny had no trace of amusement on his hardy face.

"You must have been out of your mind. What you did today – out of your mind. You threw away your career, and you're lucky you were left your life for the time being!"

Bora gulped the drink he was handed, and said nothing.

"Look at your uniform! It's scandalous, it all sounds and looks disastrous, how will you face questions if they come, when you shouldn't even have seen what you saw in the first place?" Nowotny seemed angry at Bora's silence. He returned to his chair, sticking a Muratti in his mouth as if to keep more criticism from coming out of it.

Bora sat with shoulders slumped, shaking his head.

Nowotny watched him reach for the mud-encrusted heel chain of his right spur. "What do you mean, 'no'? 'No' to what? If you mean the casings you picked up, they're like casings anywhere."

"I may have no photographic records, but this isn't anything I dreamed."

Disgustedly, Nowotny looked at the thin strands of human hair on his desk. He took them with two fingers and tossed them into his wastebasket. "Spare me, you fool. So much for common sense. What will you tell Schenck and Salle-Weber?"

"If they know, there's nothing I can tell them that will change their opinion."

Nowotny placed a pad on his desk. "I'm going to write a certificate expressing my professional opinion that the recent trauma to your head – you did get a broken skull – might have affected the soundness of your judgement."

"For God's sake, Colonel. I don't need anyone to lie for me."

"Well, you had better learn how to lie yourself, then."

They said nothing to one another for some time, Nowotny furiously smoking and Bora clasping his hands loosely between his knees, head low.

"So, what happened to all your plans? Your wife will be here the day after tomorrow. Don't you want to live to make her pregnant?"

"I don't know. I thought of it when they put the gun to my head. That's exactly what I was thinking of, that I hadn't even made Dikta pregnant yet. And suddenly it seemed so unimportant that I hadn't. As if the dead came first. As if the debt to the dead had precedence over the desires of the living."

"Balderdash."

"On the contrary. I had my face on the ground and the SD said, 'Shoot him,' and I was bodily petrified but not soul-scared, not really afraid inside. The fear was all physical, but the debt to the dead was being paid."

"Enough, enough! You don't even make sense any more. Go home, sleep it off, and see that you forget Święty Bór and what's beyond it!"

"I plan to go back tomorrow."

Only when he reached the lobby of the army hospital did Bora find out that he was interdicted from leaving.

An oversized medic filled the doorway.

"I'm sorry, Captain. Surgeon's orders. You're to spend the night under close medical supervision. Please do not object. Strict orders from the surgeon."

11

1 January 1940

The note was handwritten on a card with her name embossed in blue on it.

Love, you know how hard I have been trying to qualify for the dressage competition, because you helped me train for it. I don't need to tell you how important it is for me, especially now that you're away and there's so little for me to do in Leipzig. Your father tried his best to convince me to come to Poland, but I told him I was sure you wouldn't want me to miss an opportunity to do well at such an important event. All my horse-loving friends and your family friends will attend. I've become especially adept at the piaffe, even though Quartermain still moves a little forwards, but his hind stays low and his neck is well-erected (I remember how you insisted on those)! I'm having Mother run a film of it, which I will send to you later.

Family and friends have heard how well you performed in battle and we're all proud of you. Mother said the last photo you sent makes you look very much like the von Stauffenberg boys, whom she knows well. Surely that is a compliment, because they're considered a very handsome set.

It's a shame that you can't get away and come see me perform. The cheers of old ladies in furs will have to do, and the occasional colonel with an arm in a sling and a monocle. Except for the daughter of Luisa von Bohlen (those on Trachterstrasse), I am the favourite for the dressage prize. I think my pirouette is better than hers, as is my canter in general. Stay well, dear Martin, and take care that your father doesn't express his old-fashioned Germanentum as heartily as he used to do with us.

Love, Dikta.

General Sickingen stood with his massive head against the early morning sun, a square-shouldered, hefty rock of a man in field-grey civilian clothes that – but for the lack of insignia – might as well have been a uniform. He watched his stepson fold the note he had hand-carried from Dikta, attentive to any emotion betrayed by his face.

Bora put the note in his breast pocket. "I'm so glad to see you, Father. I made reservations for you at the *Francuski*. It's the same room you occupied in the last war, but you'll find the comforts much improved."

Sickingen moved in response as much as a rock does: not at all. Faceless against the pale, suffused glare of the sun, he said, "Is that all you have to say about your wife not coming?"

"Dikta had mentioned to me how important the competition was to her."

"More important than seeing her new husband? By God, had I my way, I'd have forced her to telephone you and tell you in person. *You*'d have convinced her to come. But your mother told me to stay out of your marriage, and so I did."

Bora was disheartened enough not to need reminders. "I hope you had a pleasant trip."

"You're too lenient with her." Grumpily, Sickingen bent his monumental figure to enter the staff car. "Horsemanship should have given you some hints." Only after settling himself in the back seat did he notice how self-control was all there really was between Bora and some unmilitary show of grief, so he bottled back whatever else he meant to add. "Tonight we dine together."

They drove the brief distance from the Cracow Glowny station to the northern edge of the park, and left to Pijarska Street. The *Francuski* was a venerable establishment at the elbow of Pijarska, facing the curving façade of the Piarist Fathers' house. In the street, a car with driver was already parked for the general's use.

Bora was so white in the face, Sickingen took one look at him and said, "You can go. I'll see you tonight at seven."

Kasia wiggled away from the embrace. "Sure, sure. Happy New Year to you, too, Ewa. I'm not falling for it."

"But you *have* to do it for me, darling."

"I don't have to do anything for you."

Ewa looked out from the recess of the theatre's main entrance, at the gaunt male figure that seemed glued to the house wall across the square. He waited away from the wind, face turned in this direction.

"Yes, you do." She gently took Kasia's chapped hand between hers. "You will, Kasia."

"He's nothing to me. You wouldn't do it for me."

The hold of Ewa's hands grew tight. Not unfriendly, just too tight for Kasia's fingers to slip out. "Didn't I get you the position in this company, darling? You'd still be doing vaudeville if I hadn't said I knew you had all kinds of acting experience, when you had none. You just have to do it. You have to."

Kasia glanced out. "How do I know he won't get me into trouble?"

"He won't. It's only going to be three or four days, he's trying to slip out into Czechoslovakia."

"Some good it'll do him, the Germans are there just the same." Kasia turned back to Ewa, and Ewa could see she was trying not to weaken. "No, no Forget it. He's your son. Is he in trouble? I bet he's in trouble. Well, you take care of it. I don't want him around. People are going to talk."

Ewa swallowed her pride, enough to use Helenka's own argument. "Darling," the words came out of her mouth, "it isn't as if you haven't had young men stay with you before."

"Boyfriends, not people I don't know!"

"I'll pay you. I'll introduce you to Richard's room-mate *and* pay you."

"No."

Kasia began to leave. The gaunt figure across the square left the wall for a moment, hopeful, then crept back. Ewa grabbed her friend by the elbows. "Please, Kasia! I beg you, take him home."

"Let go of me!"

"How often have you seen me beg, Kasia?"

Kasia groaned. "Shit," she said, "I'm going to regret this," but she stopped fighting. "Only two days, Ewa. You go right over and tell him. T-w-o days, and nothing else. I'm not feeding him, either."

Ewa kissed her on both cheeks, pressing her to her fur-jacketed breast.

Father Malecki said mass in the convent church, and when he turned to read the lesson from Paul's epistle to Titus, he noticed Logan's trench coat among the people.

He began reading, "*The grace of God our Saviour has appeared to all men,*" thinking of a way he could sneak out through the sacristy without having to face the foreign-service officer. Logan might be here only to start the year on the right religious foot, but Malecki didn't want to risk interferences in these last days of the investigation.

His eyes searched the congregation to see if by any chance Bora was here as well. Unlikely that he'd be here at high mass, and anyway, he hadn't shown up in days.

"...in order that, rejecting ungodliness and worldly lusts, we may live temperately and justly and piously in the world."

The private dining room on the second floor of the Hotel *Francuski* had a carpet pattern of large, dimly green roses on magenta background. Bora thought they looked like pale cauliflowers.

In a low voice, his stepfather spoke ruthlessly to him, aware of his harshness and confident in the benefits of it.

"I told you not to marry her, but you were bitched. That's the word, that's the word. Bitched about her as you were about politics, feeling your oats for marriage when you could have found other solutions if you had to – what are you in the army for – and politically should have kept from selling your soul to the Devil. Of course, you were sleeping with her. Those Coennewitz girls, all sluts. Just like their grandmother. Even in 1899, the cadets knew that when everything else failed, they could get one of the Coennewitz sisters. A good Catholic doesn't indulge in premarital sex, and even so, when you did and found out that she wasn't a virgin – don't interrupt, I haven't lived in Leipzig fifty years without knowing what goes on – you should have got a hint. Now your brother wants to marry, just because you did! I was forty years old when I married the first time, and there are days when I think I was too young even then."

Sickingen paused for the time necessary for the waiter to deposit the menu and leave with a bow. "At least I had the good sense of marrying a woman no one had gone into before me. As for your mother, she was widowed, but only one other man had gone into her before I did. Neither one of you was mature enough to marry, especially you. Now you're caught. You're caught because you love her, you dolt. Dikta is flighty and politically fanatic, and that's the best I can say for her. She has money, but you have money.

Your family name is older than hers, better connected – a Bora marrying into a Nazi family! Her father may have got himself an ambassadorship, but he's a lackey for whatever drivel comes out of Berlin."

Bora felt himself flush from the neck up, as if he'd neared a source of great heat. He said, awkward with the obviousness of his reaction, "I think it offends you that she refused to come. It hurts me, but it offends you."

"No red-blooded man ought to let a woman hurt him, no matter what she does. You musn't be hurt. Outraged, angry, yes. It musn't hurt you."

"We're exaggerating the plain fact that Dikta was unable to come."

Sickingen snatched the napkin from the table and flagged it open. "Unable?" He swept the cloth onto his lap. "Unwilling!"

Bora's whole body ached with pains he didn't know he had. He said, unconvincingly, "Well, I have other things to do. Other things to worry about. It'd have been good seeing Dikta, but there's plenty for me to do as is."

"You almost wept, in the car. Whom are you fooling? Is this why I brought you up as if you were my own, favouring you over my own son, even? To see you hurt by one of the Coennewitz girls? You should separate, right now."

"Separate? We're a little ahead of ourselves! Dikta has done nothing but tell me she couldn't see me now."

Sickingen made a sound with his throat, like a growl. "There's nothing more un-German than lack of loyalty, except for misdirected loyalty."

"Benedikta loves me. I should know better than anyone else. You'll love *her* when you have grandchildren."

"If she finds the time to make me some, between steeple-chases. I can see it's useless to try to talk you out of her. It's like trying to stop from firing when your artillery piece is jammed: it keeps going until it's used up all of its damned ammunition. Do what you want. Stay married. One of these days, you'll find out I was correct."

"May we speak of something else?"

Sickingen made a face. He despised smoking, and someone in the next room had just lit a cigar. A ghost of its pungent odour wafted in, still he turned with a condemning glare to the door, so that Bora walked over to close it.

"We may not."

The menu's turn to be swept up came, and Sickingen was as unfriendly to it as he was to everything else tonight. "I let others educate you, Martin, but the old-fashioned basics of male behaviour haven't changed from when my father taught them to me fifty years ago. A man doesn't cry, doesn't lie, doesn't embrace another man; a man knows how to say 'thank you' to a woman he's made love to; if necessary, a man unquestioningly fights to the death for worthwhile causes. These are the basics. Everything else you learned stands in your way, except for the love of God." The old man moved his burly head from side to side in disapproval. "How will you go through tonight?"

"I don't know." Bora stared at the cauliflower roses on the floor. "I'm off to the field early tomorrow. I might not go to bed at all."

They had dinner in nearly unbroken, army-school silence. Sickingen, who was a vegetarian and drank sparingly, was, despite the long trip, perfectly awake afterwards and would have returned to the subject of Dikta if Bora hadn't promptly shifted the conversation towards politics. It worked, but didn't turn out to be a good choice after all.

Sickingen was even more outspoken than the last time Bora had seen him, which had cost him an argument with Dikta.

"This political travesty, I see through it well. You were a part of it no less than the rest. From the start, you took to it like a horse to a saddle, and you've been jumping ever since. This 'New Army'! Why do you think I resigned in '35? Now you've sworn loyalty to *that man* – not to the Country, to *that man* – and you're bound by your oath and God keep you when it comes to making choices between your honour and whatever else is given such name in Germany today. I'm asking you: how long will it be before they order you to do something your conscience as a soldier forbids you to do?"

Bora thought of the files curling up in Schenck's fiery stove.

"I have good commanders," he said nevertheless.

"Ha! And who commands those? You'll either make a bad soldier or a bad Christian. You can't have both. Try to have both, and you'll be a dead man." Calmly, Sickingen knew he had hit the mark. "Choose, Martin. Right now, *right now*. Because your life you may lose regardless, but your immortal soul you'll lose absolutely if you make the wrong choice."

Bora found the room insufferably hot. Out of respect for his stepfather he listened, but the talk exasperated him, and his mind kept burrowing back into the hole of Dikta's refusal to come. He said blankly that he would choose wisely when the time came, as if he hadn't already.

It was only eight o'clock, and the night ahead of him seemed insurmountably long.

By contrast, the back rooms of the theatre were cold and dank, and smelled of women.

Bora knew it was a bad idea to come here. Perhaps the worst idea he could have followed tonight, this smelling of female sweat and perfume in the half-dark. Telling himself that he needed to speak to Ewa Kowalska was useless and in the end untrue. He needed to speak to a woman, and was too insecure to seek Helenka, because he was attracted to Helenka.

Not to Ewa. Ewa was his mother's age exactly. He thought short thoughts, walking down the steps towards the narrow corridor. Half-dark, damp and smelling, like a bowel the corridor enclosed him.

His mother's age. Exactly.

He'd ask about the lost towel, ask if Ewa had been given a key to the apartment, ask about her visit to Retz the night before his death. He'd listen to her answers and leave.

His boots provoked no sound from the cement floor, except for a tinkle of spurs when he walked too close to the wall. There seemed to be no one around on this festive night. In the end, Ewa might not be here either.

Her dressing-room door opened at the very end of the corridor, where another poorly-lit, drab ramp of stairs led to the stage beyond. From the shred of yellow glare spreading on the floor, Bora could tell the light was on inside.

"Come in."

Ewa might have been startled, but didn't seem so. Having answered his rap on the partly open door, at his entrance she only lifted her eyes to him through the mirror.

"Good evening." Again she looked down. She had no make-up on and her paleness was real, unadorned. Old, Bora thought with relief. "May I help you, Captain?"

All the while she was rummaging in a zippered cloth bag for hairpins. The hairpins resembled the short fir needles at Święty Bór. She placed them on the dressing table, which was like Helenka's but more orderly. Above the table, stuck between the mirror and the wall, a hand-tinted postcard of Tosca leaping off the top of Castle

Sant'Angelo and a snapshot of Richard Retz. The Retz of twenty years ago, when he and Ewa were Bora's age. Now she was, he thought again, his mother's age exactly. The hairpins joined their companions in a little row.

"May I help you?" she repeated.

It was too cold for her to be in her slip. Dimly Bora understood that the blouse crumpled over the back of the chair had been worn until a moment ago, until the moment he knocked on the door, but it didn't matter really. He derived elementary, unexpectedly guiltless pleasure out of staring at her breasts, diverging and erect in the cold, sumptuous like Dikta's, whom he should be thinking of if he wasn't.

"I have a few questions."

She continued to busy herself with the hairpins, so Bora kept his eyes on her.

"About Richard, I suppose."

"Yes."

Ewa turned to him while placing the last hairpin on the dressing table The motion caused the cloth bag to fall from her lap. "Oh, dear."

Beads from an unstrung necklace and buttons rolled from the bag in a clicking race, which she could not prevent but tried to stop, leaning from her chair. Bora halted the roll of a bead with his foot. He picked it up, and another came circling. He reached for it and for two more, nearly under the edge of the dressing table, crouching to retrieve those.

Ewa said, "Thank you," when he began to rise to put the beads in her hand. They were large beads, shiny and red against the palm of her hand like apples from infinitesimal Edens. She closed her fist around them, and the red was gone. Bora pulled back to come to his feet, but neither quickly nor prudently enough. He was saying, "No," when she held his neck to kiss him.

A terror seized him as he found that Ewa kissed better than Dikta, better than the women he'd known in Spain. Her tongue was like silk reaching for the moist floor of his mouth, dipping in it and curling back to pour her own wetness in, to arouse the clean edge of his tongue against itself. He began to bristle and harden without kissing back, tasting her, letting her for ever so brief a time into his mouth only because he needed to be bodily wanted beyond his ability to say no. Kneeling by her chair, he saw and felt himself in bed with Dikta, or himself with Ewa, or Helenka, but it was Dikta's muscular belly that he craved, the tight cleft in her blondness, and Dikta's mouth. It was seconds before he forcibly pulled away from Ewa, so that the bony, taut angle of his face was averted from her.

Out of the theatre, he didn't remember walking to the car and starting it. He didn't even know the time or the streets, other than he hopelessly drove a little distance to the dark edge of the park and then he had to stop and try to compose himself, but it was too late for composure. Blood tided and banged in his throat, his veins. He didn't dare touch any part of his body, afraid to precipitate an orgasm. Like fire, with a cresting ache, need made him sweat despite the cold of the car until he was wringing wet beneath his shirt, trying to breathe in and out when his lungs wanted to stop air in his throat.

His jaw set hard. Eyes closed, he pulled back on the seat. Carefully, he thought, but with the motion the cloth of his breeches fretted the skin of knees and thighs up the painful, engorged cluster of his groin. Breathing became short, difficult. Bora kept his hands contracted on the steering wheel. Still, arms and shoulders began bracing, locking stiff each muscle, each joint, so that he trembled with the excess of tension and in the end had to suffer the great craving to break through him. He fought to keep from crying out when it flooded his groin as if life's dam were yawning open to pour out of him in jolts, and after disgorging itself he'd have no life left, a sweet, sweet dying.

It seemed to go on for ever, this thick, long draining into his clothes. Bora's head was driven against the back of the seat, he could hear himself groan and harden again and start to let go, let go and relax in guilty shivers.

His throat unlocked enough for him to swallow, and breathe again. Cold night air filled his chest, but he wouldn't open his eyes to see the night around the car.

His linen and leather-trimmed breeches felt warm, soaked, sticky. Back and shoulders grew numb. Fingers, palms, wrists unlocked, grew numb. Bora would soon go from feeling relieved to feeling filthy, and a crazy want to weep for Dikta filled the interval with unbearable loneliness and sorrow. He loved her, he loved her. His guts and sinews and soul loved her. And he wasn't sure she loved him any more.

Lights off, motor off, a car with an SS plate was parked by the snowy kerb in front of his doorway.

Bora braked behind it, in a sudden alarmed hurry to prepare himself for trouble.

Even before he opened his car door, Salle-Weber's unmistakable silhouette exited the SS vehicle. The street was dark between lamp posts, and his square-shouldered image had an ominous blackness about it. Bora came out.

"A few words with you, Captain."

"Surely." Bora locked his car, keeping his wits about him. "Should we go inside?"

"No. Let's walk."

Bora looked Salle-Weber's way. Not at him, since there wasn't enough light to read the expression on his face.

"Walk? Where?"

"Start walking."

Podzamcze Street ran long and straight at this point, and enough of the snow had been ploughed from the centre of it to allow for slow, somewhat treacherous pacing. Further down, the next lamp post drew a circle of light like a faint moon, and Bora took a step in that direction. Salle-Weber did the same.

"Where were you just now?"

Bora decided to answer the truth, all the more since he might have been seen leaving the theatre. He was horribly self-conscious, and only grateful to be wearing the heavy winter uniform and greatcoat. The moisture was now starting to dry and feel gummy and uncomfortable on his inner thighs. His linen had become glued onto him, because he wouldn't reach for himself even just to rearrange his clothing. The cutting cleanness of the night made the sensation of filth very real.

There must be signs another man could sense, he was sure, but Salle-Weber was not looking at him. Adjusting his pace to Bora's, as soldiers do by habit, Salle-Weber rifted the icy snow with his greased boots, hard-hewn face turned to the dim glare ahead.

"Your conduct is very unbecoming a German officer, Captain Bora."

"Because I went to see an actress?"

"No. Because you have a sow's propensity to grub with your nose in dung."

"I'm sure I don't know what you mean."

"Just keep in mind this is the time of year when swine get butchered and hung."

Bora felt a limp pain across his shoulders when he tried to stiffen again. His muscles were sore. He needed to wash and sleep, and maybe this was not happening at all. He said, testily, "Unfortunately my job seems to bring me back to pigsties daily."

With a brusque reach of the arm, Salle-Weber turned him around. "Be careful, Bora. I don't appreciate humour."

"And I don't understand your metaphor. Put it plainly to me."

Snow crunched under their steps like small squeaky voices, followed by a snapping sound when a frozen puddle or sheet of ice broke through.

When they reached the sallow circle of light drawn by the lamp post on the dirty snow, Salle-Weber halted, and Bora with him. It was starting to snow again. Like frozen moths or wind-blown cinders, flakes entered the circle of light in weary spirals. Salle-Weber removed a nonexistent speck from Bora's coat.

"You know, Bora, I can smell your kind, and it's only because of the energy and good promise you've shown so far that I bother to address you at all. Take heed. *If you live*, there's still time for a hopeful career, with plenty of fighting ahead of us to test it. You have no experience, so don't presume of yourself. Don't spoil the promise. Bury your arrogance, or rest assured, you'll be buried with it."

"Are you threatening me?"

"Threats presuppose an option. I'm informing you."

Bora heard the words escape him, and Dikta's note might have everything or nothing to do with them. He faced Salle-Weber so that the light made him fully visible to the SS, only a step away.

"Well, *Standartenführer*, the street is deserted. We're alone. It seems to me a perfect time to solve your problem."

Salle-Weber might have actually entertained the thought, because the suggestion unsettled him for a moment.

"Not quite," he said afterwards, resuming his walk by stepping out of the circle of light. "When it comes, Bora, it's not going to come so easily. Nor when you're ready."

A subtle, clean spear of light transfixed the room making the dark denser, like liquid pressing around a filament of gold.

Father Malecki lay in bed, emerging from a dreamless, beneficial sleep such as he hadn't enjoyed in months. He admired the spear of light through half-closed lids, how it reached from a fissure in the shutter to the core of darkness.

Mother Kazimierza's favourite words came to his mind: "...but if the light in thee be darkness, how great is that darkness."

The mystery of what *Lumen* meant might very well be a light shining through the dark of unsolved crime and unspoken hostility. Malecki thought that if no solution ever came, he'd learned meanwhile how much more there was to nuns, to saints, to patriots and to German officers.

With less than nine days to the deadline, the Curia was considering acceptance of Sister Irenka as a new abbess at Our Lady of Sorrows. Malecki had heard from the archbishop's secretary that anyone but a mystic was what the convent needed now.

But things were not through with Mother Kazimierza, not quite: the archbishop wanted recommendations about her from him, Malecki. Pressure would begin building soon in the Polish Church to recommend her beatification, and proven miracles would be needed. Malecki would have to express in writing whether the stigmata and fulfilled prophecies qualified for the name.

As the morning sun moved, the spear of light changed angle and began to widen, flatten, fade. Malecki sat up scratching his neck and yawning, with a lazy mind to open the window and do his weight-lifting.

When he went downstairs for breakfast, *Pana* Klara first complained apologetically that there was no milk and the bread was stale, and then pointed out to him a sealed envelope on the lacy tablecloth.

"A German orderly left it an hour ago. You were sleeping so well, Father, I didn't think you should be roused on account of him."

The note was handwritten, and from Bora.

"*We must proceed with the investigation. I'll meet you on Thursday at the convent, eighteen hundred hours sharp.*"

3 January

The group of stray Polish soldiers had been gathered in the next room. Bora had slept poorly, and chain-smoked while he prepared to interrogate them. Salle-Weber's words hadn't left his mind for one moment, but their impact was seemingly not enough to keep him from feeling drowsy now.

So he smoked, and the room began smelling like the apartment after Retz and Ewa had spent the night in it, a stale odour of cigarettes. Bora opened the window to let the hazy air flow out of the office.

If sleeping poorly weren't enough, he'd even dreamed about Retz towards morning. The *mode of his death*, Father Malecki had said. Bora had awakened with the damnable doubt that Retz's death troubled him because he didn't understand it. He wanted to tell more about it to Malecki, and if all went well by Thursday evening he'd have had a chance to speak to the cleaning woman again and to one of the medics who had worked on Retz's body.

His stepfather left late that afternoon. True to form, he insisted on walking to the station from the Francuski, so he and Bora passed under St Florian's gate, where a side altar was carved in the wall, protected by shutters now open. A nun was praying in front of it.

"What should I tell your wife?"

Bora looked at the drab curtain of government buildings lining the other side of the street past the round red-brick ring of the Barbican wall. "I wrote her a letter."

"Did you send it, or shall I hand-carry it?"

"I'd appreciate your giving it to her."

With the envelope, a small package came out of Bora's pocket.

"I sure as hell wouldn't send her gifts," Sickingen blurted out. "You ought to send a gift to your mother instead."

"I have one for her also. Here."

Sickingen wanted to pass by the square where the monument to the victory against the Germans at Grünwald had been dynamited and lay now in a scattered heap of stone blocks. "I want you to take a picture of it and send it to me," he told Bora. "It'll serve me as a reminder of the idiocy of your political choice. You do have a camera, don't you?"

Bora only said that he'd send the photograph.

After seeing the general's train off, he drove to the hospital. Doctor Nowotny was not in, but in the emergency room he found one of the medics who'd retrieved Retz's body.

The medic didn't mind talking. "I remember it well – my first suicide. The major was kneeling on the kitchen floor with his head in the gas oven, slumped forwards. What was he wearing? Uniform breeches, boots and shirt. No tunic. Had there been a towel lying around in the kitchen, I'd have used it, because I smeared my hand on the inside of the oven. There were no towels around, so I ended up using a dishcloth."

"Was anything out of order in the kitchen, that you can tell?"

"I don't know how orderly it usually was, Captain. There was no food out, if that's what the captain means, no drinks, nothing. It really looked as if he just up and put his head into the stove."

4 January

In the morning, Schenck called Bora into his office.

He had an expression of indefinable contempt on his leathery face, and for a stressful moment Bora thought he might have been approached by Salle-Weber.

Schenck said, "Sit down."

Bora sat.

"I understand your wife has not come. What will you do about it?"

Bora checked himself. "There isn't much I can do about it, Colonel."

"Well, you must intend to do something with the germ plasma built up while waiting for her."

Bora didn't want to say that his germ plasma was now being laundered off his clothes.

Schenck added, flint-faced, "There are German women in Cracow."

"I don't think they'd be the proper receptacle."

"And why not?"

"Because I do not love them."

"Love?" Schenck's disdain went to his mouth, turning it downwards in a grimace. "I thought we agreed that love is a bourgeois expression, having nothing to do with propagating the race. Being inherently opposed to the waste of masturbation, I cannot envision anything else for a German man to do in your circumstance but to find a racially compatible female. Clearly your wife has no sense of the demographic needs of the Country." From the top of his desk, Schenck lifted a typewritten sheet which he handed to Bora. "These are the names of racially certified local women. I advise you to select from the list as soon as possible. As open-minded men, we can distinguish between profligacy and sexual health, can't we?"

Bora ran his eyes down the list. Before leaving, his stepfather had struck him a blow from which he was still reeling. "They say," he'd leaned out of the train window to inform him, "that she had an abortion before she met you."

A veiled redness had stretched in front of Bora's eyes then, as when the SS had nearly shot him. "*That's a bold lie!*" he remembered shouting, and how he'd banged the side of the train with his gloved fist. "Take it back at once, it's a bold lie!"

"Don't get hot under the collar," his stepfather had only added. "Nothing about the Coennewitz girls would surprise *me*."

His numbness now was the only thing that kept him from overreacting to Schenck's advice. Bora found himself looking, guiltily, for Ewa's and Helenka's name on the list, but of course they were not there.

Seated next to Bora's army cap on the bench of the waiting room, Father Malecki looked disappointed. "Was that all Frau Hofer had to say to you?"

"Yes." Bora was restless, but realized how irritating it was to watch someone pace back and forth, so he forced himself to stand still. "The phone connection was bad. She said their son has died, and she doesn't wish to remind her husband of Poland at this time. He's been very ill, and stays at a convalescent home. She expects him back in a week, at which time she'll inform him of my call. So I'll call again in a week. Meanwhile we'll keep looking for our missing worker here in Cracow. The contractor supplied us with an accurate description of him, and I'm very hopeful in that regard."

"But what if the colonel has nothing to add, and you don't find the missing worker?"

"Miracles aren't my province, Father. You know perfectly well I don't even have a shell casing to go by. You and I were not in the convent when the abbess died, so it's neither one of us who killed her. Everything else is dreams and half-baked prophecies."

"Hardly what you can report to your commander."

"Unless we're enlightened between now and then, that's exactly what I'll report." Bora reached for his cap on the bench. "Do you have time for dinner at the Wierzynek tonight?" When Malecki hesitated to answer, he couldn't help himself. "That is, if the American consulate lets you."

Malecki actually laughed. "I'll come."

When Bora arrived home to freshen up before dinner, the cleaning woman was washing the floors.

She looked at him, and he knew what was on her mind. "Forget about the towel." He prevented her. "I said I'll pay for it. Tell me something else, instead." He gestured for her to let go of the mop, and come forwards. "Sit." He pointed to a fancy chair, adding to her confusion. "Just tell me in what state was the apartment when you were called in to clean after the major's death. Yes, of course it smelled like gas. What else? Was anything out of place, or was it as always? Think carefully."

The cleaning woman sat uneasily, neck stretched forwards. "It was as always, *panie kapitanie.*"

"All right. What about the bed? Was the bed – did it seem as though the bed had been made love in?"

The woman's alarm grew and abated under Bora's impassive stare. "No, sir."

"What about the bathroom, could you tell if the major had been shaving?"

"He'd taken a bath. The bath towel was still wet."

"Was the sink clean, or did it have shaving soap in it?"

"It was rinsed clean."

"Now tell me about the kitchen. Anything out of place there?"

"No, sir. Only thing is, two drinking glasses had been washed. The major always left plates and glasses in the sink."

Retz had probably had a drink with Ewa the night before, and she'd washed the glasses. Bora found none of the information useful. He dismissed the cleaning woman. Leisurely he shaved, changed, and although it was still early he had Hannes drive him to the fine old restaurant on the square, where he was to meet Father Malecki for dinner. Hannes was talkative, having just run into another veteran of the Spanish campaign. He jabbered about it all the way to the restaurant, and then asked for permission to have the evening off. What a fine land Spain was, and what an adventure! How young we all were! Who knows how many fine memories the captain has brought back, eh? Bora had grown thoughtful at the recollection, and had to be asked twice before dismissing him.

At the table, Malecki let him talk at length about Retz. So much so, in fact, that Bora caught himself, clumsily. "Am I not boring you, Father?"

"No, no. Keep talking."

Behind Bora's head, the large painting of a sun-bathed mountain scene seemed like a window on a remote world. Sipping his wine, Malecki heedfully listened to all Bora had to say – how he'd asked Helenka if she thought she was pregnant by Retz (not so, luckily), but hadn't had time to ask Ewa for all the information he thought she could give him; how it bothered him not to be able to let Retz's death rest. Then he commented, "It's strange."

"What's strange?"

"That you notice details with such clarity, and yet have a blind spot."

Bora said he didn't understand.

"Well, you say that one of the towels disappeared on the day your colleague died. How do you know that it wasn't taken away by the medics?"

"I checked with one of the medics. He told me no towel was found in the kitchen, and they used none. And anyway, why would anyone steal a towel from inside the bathroom shelf when there was one hanging from the rack?" Bora put fork and knife down, impatiently. "Why did you say I have a blind spot?"

"Because in your heart you don't believe that Retz committed suicide, yet something keeps you from going the distance to admit that you think someone killed him."

Bora felt blood rising to his face, as on the night he'd sat across from his stepfather and his stepfather had seen through him.

"After all, Captain, Retz had already quartered in Cracow years ago, and might have had old enemies. Is it such an impossibility?"

Bora wondered where Ewa's first husband could be now. He replied, just for the sake of argument, "The only people I can associate with him with some certainty were busy elsewhere on the morning he died."

"You mean his woman friend and her daughter."

"Yes. They were both rehearsing."

"I see," Malecki said amiably. "And what is the play?"

"Aeschylus' *Eumenides*. Not that it makes a difference."

"And have you gone to see it?"

"No."

"Have you read it, then?"

"No, I haven't."

Malecki nodded to the waiter, who'd come by to refill his glass. "You should."

After dinner, Bora was relieved that Malecki had said he'd walk home, and that Hannes was gone. He wanted to be alone.

Although it was entirely out of his way, he drove in a circuitous manner north of the Old City to Święty Krzyża, where Ewa's lit window on the grey stucco wall distinguished itself from the others by its trim of lacy curtains.

At the corner, he stopped the car. It would take less than a minute to walk to the doorway of her house and tell the porter he was here to see Frau Kowalska. She'd receive him, of course.

His distress resulted from a nearly untenable desire to ask Ewa to kiss him and make love to him, of which he was ashamed but no less desirous for it. In the crude dark, how different would her body be from Dikta's, except that Dikta was younger?

He remembered stripping off his uniform at the foot of the hotel bed on their wedding night, when every button and lacing had been an enemy to his haste. They had made up for it by not bothering to get up on the following day, at the end of which he had to phone his parents to say that he'd got married. Now Ewa would do the same with him, blond like Dikta but wiser, more appreciative of a young man's worth, of how the man she'd kissed in the theatre would perform with a racially compatible female.

Schenck's inane words were a sobering shower to him. Bora cursed as he welcomed them, those political notions of "sexual health" that undid all lovely images like the turning of a kaleidoscope. Half-heartedly he sat for close to an hour, trying to rearrange them even as they ran into a blur of glitter, and it was no use. *No use, Bora.* In a cold anger, he started the car, jerked it into reverse and drove through the narrow streets towards his house under the Wawel.

5 January

The young Pole extended his hand towards the intact cigarette pack that Bora had laid on the table. There were fresh bruises on his face, and his front teeth were missing. Bora observed him insert the cigarette in the bloody-rimmed gap and expectantly stretch his torso for the lighter's flame.

"I hope they're getting something out of you," he said.

"They ain't."

"The way you're going, you'll get shot one of these days."

"I know."

"As long as you know."

The prisoner sucked the smoke in avidly. "These are good cigarettes."

Bora had carelessly removed his gloves but now put them back on. He'd caught himself anxiously fingering the gold band on his left hand lately, and had resolved to break the habit before anyone remarked on it. He said, "Perhaps you should talk. You'd save everyone much trouble."

With visible difficulty, the prisoner attempted a laugh. Smoke came out of the gap between his teeth as he did. "It's not like I'm trying to save you all any trouble." Whether the offer of cigarettes emboldened him or he'd travelled further on the road to hopelessness, he was merrily impudent. "If it was me holding you, Captain, would you talk?"

"You wouldn't hold me." Bora reached for the pack and took it back. Under the Pole's alarmed eyes he held it in the gloved hand as if wondering what to do with it, whether he'd crush it or not. "The other day you told me you saw the nun in the garden. Was she sitting, walking, was she standing still?"

"She was lying on the ground."

"After she was shot, naturally —"

"No, no. She'd been lying there a good part of the morning." On the edge of his chair, the prisoner kept watch on any threat to crush the cigarette pack. "I'm telling you, she was lying there spread-eagle."

"How did you know she was alive, then?"

"I'd seen her do the trick on other days. I didn't pay attention to it any more, except that later I saw the blood. I was just turning around after checking the street through the field glasses: I happened to see the blood and that's that. I can't say if she was lying down when she was shot, because I didn't see it happen."

Bora put a cigarette in his mouth and tossed the pack back on the table. Before leaving, he said, "We're closing in on one of yours. It's all over for the lot of you, so take my advice. Talk."

Kasia crossed the Market Square with her eyes to the squat, long building of the ancient Clothiers' Hall. German army cars parked alongside it behind the trees, and uniformed men could be seen under the archway. She headed for the theatre under an immense overcast sky, quickening her pace.

Ewa waited for her in a doorway at the corner of Święty Anny Street, where the cutting wind could not enter. She seemed about to ask something, but Kasia didn't give her the time.

"He hasn't left!" She took the initiative. "You said he'd be gone by morning, and your son hasn't left."

Ewa's shoulders rose and sank in the old fur. "He will, be sure. He's a prudent young man."

"Sure. It's been a week! If he's so prudent, how come he's got to hide from the Germans, and how come he isn't staying with you?"

"We've been through all this already, Kasia dear. He'd be noticed at my house, and you know how cramped Helenka's quarters are. If he said he'd leave, he'll leave. It's only nine o'clock."

"Well, you owe me big on this one. After he goes his way, I want you to pay me. You pay me and introduce me to Richard's room-mate. Promise."

"Don't you trust me?"

"Promise." Kasia's freckled face, livid with cold, had an unfriendly, peevish pout. "Your son is still at my house, and there are German cars all over the Rynek Glowny. You owe me. You owe me big. If he's gone by the time I go back, I expect you to call Richard's friend tonight and introduce me to him. Why? Because I just want you to, that's why."

Ewa rolled her eyes. "Very well. Are there any messages for me?"

"No. He's slept most of the time, and twice I had to shake him because he snored." Kasia turned away from the door when a German car drove slowly past, tires squelching the mushy snow. "Knowing you, it's better if I don't know what your son's real trouble is, or I'd piss in my pants from the worry."

Bora understood from *Pana* Klara that Father Malecki was at the Curia, and thought better than going to wait for him there.

"*Arkusz papieru, prosze,*" he asked. After the landlady rummaged around to find a blank sheet of paper, he wrote on it.

"*Something today alerted me to a possibility we hadn't yet considered in regard to the abbess's death. Bear with me if I don't discuss it here. I must absolutely meet you tonight or at the latest tomorrow morning.*" Bora signed his name, then jotted down a postscript. "*I believe Mother Kazimierza was right, when she said that the light in us can be darkness.*"

The matinee was half an hour away, but Kasia was good for nothing. "I'm too nervous," she whispered to her understudy. "I think it's my period. I just don't feel well. I don't feel well, I have to go home. You can stand in for me, can't you? Just for today. I've got to go home. Don't tell Ewa I went unless she asks."

It was sleeting outside when she left the theatre and went south to avoid the Market Square. She was still angry at Ewa, and so upset that she couldn't distinguish between her fear and a premonition of danger. What good would it do to go home if something had gone wrong, she couldn't say. All she knew was that this morning the theatre made her sick, and she had to go home.

She prolonged her way home so that her shoes were soaked by the time she came in sight of her house. There were no people and no parked cars in the street. Her doorway stood ajar as always.

Kasia crossed quickly, entered the dark space at the bottom of the stairwell and looked straight ahead into the inner court. Through the low archway, it looked empty and forlorn.

Up the worn cement tiles forming the steps she went, one hand on the shaky iron railing. Everything was quiet. The usual silence, the usual smells. Opening the door she was relieved to notice the key turned twice, as she had locked it. The dank little kitchen was in order, and what bread and milk she had put out for Ewa's son had not been touched.

A twinge of disappointment reminded her that he'd still be in the other room, sleeping. Careful not to step on a squeaky tile, she peered into the parlour, where the sofa had been turned into a bed. The sofa was empty, and the quilt folded neatly at one end of it. Kasia breathed out in relief.

Gone. He was gone. Thank God, and without fuss!

She switched the light on, and kicked the wet shoes off her feet. In slippers she went to place the milk out on the window sill to keep it cold.

Back in the parlour, she turned the radio on, leaving it on even though the broadcast was in German, only to hear the noise.

Well, Ewa's son was gone. Thank God for that. She'd figure out later a better excuse for leaving the performance today. There was no hurry. Suddenly, all she had to worry about was what she'd wear tonight to meet Richard's roommate. She smiled. The key to his apartment jingled in her pocket. Ewa had resisted giving it to her, but in the end she'd handed it over. Whether she'd use it or not, it was a victory over Ewa. How easily one could move from anguish to delight.

Kasia filled a pot of water and placed it on the gas stove to warm it up before washing her hair. A familiar song came on the radio, and humming to the tune of it she went to the bedroom to pick out a dress. *"I know – one day – something so wonderful.."*

The bedroom was dark. *"You and I will meet aga.."* Kasia halted on the threshold with the song in her throat. She didn't remember leaving the shutters folded so tightly.

Spiteful rage grabbed her at the idea that Ewa's son wasn't gone, but had simply moved into her bed for comfort.

"Well, of all the nerve!" She strode across the room to throw the shutters open. "You'll have to get out right now, see? Right this minute!" She turned around, and the words froze in her throat.

Two armed German soldiers were standing at the sides of the bed.

12

In the convent's waiting room, Father Malecki gasped. He rested his back against the wall behind the bench, trying to look less surprised than he was.

"Is that what you think happened?"

"That's what I think happened," Bora said. "I was ready to give up, and to show you just how ready, I'd have been satisfied to say that it was an act of God. Even that, given the amount of gunfire that was still occasionally fired in October, some stray bullet shot in the air had found its way down to the cloister, and killed the abbess as she lay down in her trance. But now I know better. It could be nothing else, and I have been knocking about the whole thing long enough. But unless I get permission from my commander to follow through with a quick trip to Germany, it all remains in the realm of speculation."

"Forgive me, but it's a chilling prospect."

"Yes, and without certain proof, unless I can lay my hands on the gun. You understand that my interpreter's words is what started me thinking about it, so it wasn't a case of particularly clever thinking on my part. Whether I like it or not, the guns found on the convent roof – however they managed to get there – have in fact nothing to do with it." Here Bora looked straight at Malecki. "We arrested the missing worker, Father."

Malecki sustained the stare, coolly enough. "I see. Did he?…"

"All I will tell you is that we know who he is and what he did, which does not concern you. True, he did join the crew. And, true, he did absent himself at four fifteen to retrieve the guns from the roof. But he did not shoot the abbess. Had he done so, the report would have been heard from the chapel, or the church, or the kitchen, especially when fired in an acoustically resonant place like the cloister. The killing happened ten or fifteen minutes later, when the sisters were singing in church, the repairmen back at work, and the tanks made a racket just outside the walls. And if *nothing else but her name* killed the abbess, just as in Sister Barbara's dream, we now know she meant her file name, since, as you just heard, *Lumen* does in a roundabout way connect with this."

Looking elsewhere, Malecki noticed out of the corner of his eye Bora's uncharacteristic slump. "And if you're right?" he asked.

"If I'm right, the truth will be exposed."

It was late in the evening, and Bora sounded tired. Malecki perceived motives for that weariness quite removed from the matter at hand. Personal motives, he suspected, more intimate than Bora cared to share with others, or even justify to himself.

"If it were true, Captain, I doubt the scandal could be kept within the circle of the sisters or the Curia's staff."

"That's not for me to worry about, especially tonight. Remember, no proof for the time being, and I won't be able to see you for a few days. Let's hope to make sense out of the possibility when we meet again." Bora lifted the collar of his coat, readying himself to leave. "May I give you a lift home?"

"I won't say no."

Outside the wind had fallen, and the cold was more bearable.

Bora let the priest in and started the car. Waiting for the motor to warm up, he said, "Your comment about my blind spot, Father Malecki – I can't deny it's been there. I used to think it was because I didn't like my room-mate, but perhaps there are other reasons. More uncomfortable, less honest reasons. I realize I must remove it."

Malecki half-smiled in the dark. "You are hard on yourself, Captain."

"Am I? Maybe. I'd have made a good priest had I not chosen to be a good soldier." The car began to move slowly down the icy street. "Naturally, being a soldier allows for a certain frailty of the flesh, which might account for my choice."

"We're all frail. The breaking point varies, that's all."

While Bora drove the priest to Karmelicka Street, from Kasia's house Ewa reached the theatre in a frenzy. There was hardly anyone there. Helenka and her seamstress heard her call from the corridor and joined her.

"What happened?"

"They took Kasia – the Germans took Kasia!"

Helenka understood at once what the implications were. "When?"

"Some time after she left this morning. They've seen soldiers carrying her off."

Helenka dispatched the seamstress to find a glass of water, and pulled her mother into the dressing room. She closed the door. "What about *him*?"

"I don't know, I don't know. No word about him, I'm sure the Germans took him as well." Ewa was catching her breath, with both hands pushing her disarranged hair back from her face. "Right now we have to think about ourselves, Helenka."

Helenka gave her an amazed look. "You can't be serious! Your son's just been arrested, and —"

"There's nothing we can do for him. Or Kasia."

"No? Well, how like you it is! You never cared for him, and you don't even care for him now!"

Ewa was regaining her control in the measure Helenka had let go of hers. "And what about yourself? You wouldn't hide him in your house any more than I would. Let's be frank, your brother hasn't been in touch in three years, we didn't even hear from him until he got in trouble and came looking for help. I did the best I could, I found him a hiding place."

"Yes, and now Kasia has paid for it! How egotistical can you be?"

Ewa spaced her breathing with the actress's skill, entirely collected. "It's a matter of practicality, Helenka. Do you really think that my going to the Germans would help your brother or Kasia? If Richard were alive —"

"Don't mention him! I don't want you to mention him!"

"If Richard were alive, he might listen to either one of us. There's no one else we can ask."

"Well, Captain Bora has come to see you."

"And you." For a moment they stared, each waiting for the other to lower her eyes, neither of them doing so. Ewa said then, "Captain Bora has no interest in me."

"You could at least try!"

"I'm not going to the Germans, Helenka. Don't ask, because I'm not. Not for your brother, not for Kasia."

Helenka backed up towards her dressing table, throwing up her hands. "I can't believe what you're saying. You're not even willing to try?"

"It's useless."

"Well, I'm going to try."

Instinctively Ewa tried to reach for her, and though Helenka shrank back, Ewa showed no resentment. "Don't be daft. The Germans might not even know that he's your brother, or my son, or that we know Kasia."

"And don't you think Kasia is talking, since it was you who convinced her to get involved? I'm going in the morning, before the Germans come for me."

Bora closed the door of the library as if someone might bother him in the empty house. He walked to the shelf where the classics were kept, looking for plays written in German. From a boxed set of bilingual tragedy texts, Greek and German, he pulled out a book. *The Eumenides* occupied the last seventy pages of it. He began reading, first from one language, then from the other, to fully capture the meaning of the words.

> "*Eyes are like unto light*
> *To the slumbering brain,*
> *But in daylight our future is obscure...*"

The more he read into the play, the sadder he felt, not just because of the contents. Pain and regret rose from the pages, whether the story dredged out of him some participatory grief for Retz's death, or made him feel guilty about his death, or for letting Ewa kiss him.

> "*What of the wife who kills her husband, then?*"

and:

> "*There is a time when fear is good...*"

Afterwards, with the book on his lap, he sat contemplating the morbid rows of dried-up insects in the glass case, their shiny outer skeletons gleaming. A time when fear is good.

Maybe. Things weren't easy any more. September had been the last easy month of his life. He felt trapped and angry for nailing himself to more responsibilities and ill-advised choices, as if he didn't have enough to worry about. Why should he care about the way Retz had died? Retz had died as he had lived.

It made no difference. "I have to," he said under his breath, rising to put the book back. "I have to care."

Father Malecki was right, he was hard on himself, but only because he feared showing any weakness, at any time. There was no glory in it. So he'd make himself care about the way Retz had died, as he'd made himself write to Dikta congratulating her on her horsemanship, wishing her the best in the upcoming competition instead of telling her that he needed her.

He left the library, drew himself a bath and while waiting for the tub to fill he put a fresh blade in Retz's razor and shaved with it, as if a solution ought to come by contagious magic from it, by thinking like Richard Retz for one night.

After the bath, he started for his room but in the hallway he changed his mind. He walked to Retz's door, and without turning on the light he lay on Retz's bed, over the quilts at first and then under them. In the dark there were no blind spots, and biases lost sharpness. Suspicion alone was keen enough to cut shapes in his mind.

Bora knew he could never fall asleep in this bed, and willingly surrendered to the play of logic that from one thought to another, from one possibility to another, like a magic lantern reeled the shapes of suspicion before him.

6 January

Bora had not sipped once from the cup of hot coffee on his office desk. He listened, balancing the chair on its hind legs. In his right hand, a pencil's rubbery end tapped a silent rhythm on the wood of the desk.

"Why didn't your mother come herself?"

Helenka had avoided facing him until now, but finally had to confront him. Bora's appearance was less arrogant than the tone with which he'd said the words, and the motives behind the sentence could be too many for her to untangle now. Bora reached for the cup and brought his lips near to it.

"I don't know," she said. "I decided to come on my own."

Bora nodded at the coming of an orderly, received a file from him and put it aside, where other files formed a neat stack.

"It's interesting that you should be here to plead for your brother, when our reports indicate that both you and your mother refused to harbour him. Aren't you close to him?"

Because Helenka wouldn't say, Bora drank some more coffee, and then hugged the cup between his hands. "It's a good thing you refused, of course. Only strange." He lifted the last file he'd been given, ran his eyes over it and put it back. "Had we thought you or your mother were involved in the attempt to keep him from our authority, you'd be answering very different questions now. This woman Kasia, your mother's friend, said she acted of her own accord. I doubt it, though my doubt doesn't mean much at this point. But I still want to know why your mother didn't come herself."

"Would it help if she did?" Bora stared at her, and Helenka felt unnerved by the stare. "Perhaps she thought you wouldn't be inclined to listen to her."

"I'm listening to you, am I not?"

"But you're not saying if there's anything you can do."

Bora put away the cup, even though he had not emptied it.

"I'd have to be God Almighty to do something for your brother. He's dead."

As expected, he had to wait until Helenka swallowed her tears; he was made uneasy by them but was unwilling to show it. He gave her his handkerchief and stood up to signal the end of the meeting. "There's nothing I can do for the girl either." His voice trailed off. "Tell your mother that I want to see her."

Within minutes after dismissing Helenka, Bora left for two days in the field which would include a visit to General Blaskowitz. He had no memos for the general. Data and whole reports were in his mind, where more and more he was learning to store them, safe from tampering and destruction.

The same could not be said for Father Malecki, who brought to the Curia copious notes on the case of the abbess. And though he kept to himself Bora's latest theory, he mentioned the possibility of a resolution in the next few days.

"If the proof is found," he added.

The Archbishop scanned through the paperwork without reading it, lending an impatient ear. "Yes, yes. It's all well and good, Father. We shall know them by their fruit, that's what I think."

Malecki expected the reaction, but still he found it unjust. "If you're referring to Captain Bora, Your Eminence, he is doing the best he can under difficult circumstances."

"The 'best he can' hardly changes the fact that reports keep pouring from the countryside of dreams and visions of the abbess, and of miraculous healings through her intercession. Whether she is a martyr or not, I envision a new saint for Poland before long. Speaking of which, Father, it's time you turned in your observations to the Holy See, don't you think?"

Malecki bowed his head. "I believe Your Eminence is anxious to see me back in Chicago."

"Or in Rome, Father Malecki. Wouldn't you like to be in Rome for a while?"

Helenka didn't find her mother at home, nor at the theatre. Only the seamstress sat in Ewa's dressing room, stitching the hem of the long gown she wore on stage. The black satin resembled a cascade of dark water on her lap.

"Mother of God, *Panienka*, what has happened to you? You're as pale as a ghost!"

Helenka swallowed, too angry to cry. She was too angry to speak, words were laced and tangled in her mouth. She neared Ewa's dressing table and lowered her eyes to the crowd of objects on it. Cosmetics and boxes, wads of cotton, envelopes, cards, pictures. Coins. Hairpins. Tosca and Richard. Red necklace beads. Embroidered doily. Her frame trembled and swayed, as if she might fall over before being able to sit on her mother's stool.

She didn't fall, nor sit down. With a hooked reach of the right arm, she sent the multitude of objects flying from the table, breaking, rolling off, floating down, back and forth with the open hand she struck until all was thrown off. The seamstress watched her, open-mouthed, needle suspended on the cloth.

Helenka's trembling was giving way to tears. "Tell *Pana* Kowalska that her son is dead. Tell her Kasia is as good as dead." From behind the mirror frame she snatched Retz's old photograph, and crumpling it in hand she blindly ran out of the dressing room.

8 January

Holding the unfolded map in front of him, General Blaskowitz stood facing the window, whose dim light cut Bora's figure out of the winter day.

Bora had nearly finished speaking.

"Yesterday, which is the soonest I could return to Święty Bór, I saw that the entire area has been sealed off by mine-fields and is now under direct SD control."

Despondently, Blaskowitz tossed the map on his desk. It fell on the floor and he prevented Bora from retrieving it with a dry denial. Bora stepped back.

For several difficult minutes the general remained silent, so that only the hum of the electric clock filled the stillness of the office.

In the end, he said, "There was nothing else you could do under the circumstances, Captain, and Colonel Nowotny acted wisely. You're only starting to see what it means to put your career in a manilla envelope. Were you frightened?"

"At the edge of the woods? I was very frightened in my body, General."

"Then the lesson worked."

"It worked on my body, but I'm not ruled by that."

Blaskowitz moved a forefinger from side to side in slow denial of Bora's words.

"Disembodied mind and soul won't serve you much, so you must keep them attached to the flesh like the rest of us. 'Not ruled by your body'? You have to be ruled by mind, soul and body to do what you chose to do, no one quality over the others! Now go back to Cracow. Perform your duties, observe things, take mental notes. Above all, take notes in your heart, because it's there that they belong. For all practical purposes, this portion of the Polish war is over. The time is coming soon enough to reassign what even your strict commander terms a 'promising officer', an excellent interim solution."

It was just as good that Blaskowitz didn't repeat what he'd told Nowotny in private a week earlier: that he wondered how long his own high position in Poland would last.

The first thing Schenck told Bora when he returned to work was, "A Polish woman has been here looking for you. I thought I had given you instructions."

Bora understood it was Ewa Kowalska, but gave up explaining it. "She's racially compatible, sir."

"Is she? Well, she's too old for you."

"I'm not taking her to bed. She's the mother of the fugitive arrested for killing an NCO in Katowice."

Schenck's contempt relented a little. "I see. She'll probably be back this afternoon. Your priest was just here, too. He told me you came up with a pretty inventive theory about the nun's death. Too bad you can't prove it."

"Did Father Malecki leave a message, Colonel?"

"Check with the orderly. It seems he's leaving Poland at the end of the week." Schenck ignored the cloud of frustration that went across Bora's face. "I see you asked to interrogate the woman who sheltered the fugitive. The SS are handling her. We merely supplied manpower to take her in: what's your interest in her?"

Bora began unbuttoning his greatcoat. "Nothing military. I simply haven't given up on trying to understand what happened to Major Retz."

During the lunch hour, Bora travelled to the SS command, where Salle-Weber gave him a look askance but made no opposition to his confronting Kasia

At the convent, Father Malecki was meanwhile guest of honour at the modest reception celebrating Sister Irenka's election as the new abbess.

"We'll have to call you *Matka* now, Sister Irenka," he told her jokingly. "You gained instant motherhood ahead of all of us."

The nun wrinkled her nose. "The reasons for my new office are such as to keep me from unadvisable pride, Father Malecki. I am sure we all would much have rather have kept *Matka* Kazimierza with us. Now that you leave us, also, we may never find out what happened to the best one among us."

"Captain Bora will carry on, surely."

"Not if His Eminence is successful in his request that Church property be made off-limits to military personnel. Considering all we have to gain from keeping the Germans away, even the grief of not solving this sad killing becomes bearable. It will be what the Good Lord wishes."

Malecki didn't know what the Good Lord wished, but as for himself, he saw well that he had to try to meet Bora as soon as he could.

Bora was at that moment leaving the SS command to return to his office on the other side of the Old City.

Ewa Kowalska was waiting for him.

Led in by an orderly, she wore black, and the dress was nicely tight on her when she removed her wrap. Bora watched the way the orderly watched her, and moodily dismissed him.

Ewa sat down. If she had cried in days past, she put up a good show of control. Bora offered her a cigarette, which she refused. He put away pack and lighter.

"I was at the play, last night. You were very good."

"Thank you."

"Did you see me in the audience?"

"No." Sharply contrasting with the black of her dress, a bright-blue scarf draped her neck, and she loosened it now. "I'm afraid I wasn't paying much attention to the public."

"Your daughter was also very good."

"She was fine, yes."

"Especially considering she had a demanding role."

Ewa removed her gloves. The gestures were deliberate, slow, Bora's eyes followed each motion of her wrists and fingers. He sat back as on the day they had met at the café, stretching his legs under his desk. At long last the gloves came off.

"May I ask why you sent for me, Captain?"

"Yes." Sitting up, unwittingly Bora scraped his spur on the floor, with a brief sharp moan of steel. "I would like to know where your ex-husband is."

"Why?"

"Never mind why. Does he live in Cracow?"

"No. He was in Poznań when I last heard of him. We haven't been in touch for a long time."

"Then he might conceivably be in Cracow."

Ewa took a long look at Bora, whose expression was earnest. More than a little admiring, she thought.

"Well, anything can be. He might, why not. He was jealous for quite some time after we parted ways, and followed me around."

Bora turned his notebook towards her. He offered her a fountain pen. "Kindly write his full name down, and his last known address."

After writing, Ewa slipped the bright-blue scarf off her shoulders under Bora's absorbed attention. Because he said nothing else, she brought to the silence a timely question of her own. "The other night, in my dressing room, why did you leave so hastily?"

Bora capped the pen, without immediately putting it away. "I think you know why. Do you want me to say it?"

"Please."

"Because women such as yourself make men such as myself develop a blind spot, and I can't afford not seeing clearly. I have a wife. I am faithful to her."

"Even though she isn't here?"

Carelessly Bora tapped the left breast of his tunic. "She's very much here, Frau Kowalska."

"But you wanted to be kissed."

"I suppose so." When the cracking open of the door was followed by a glimpse of Colonel Schenck's wiry torso, Bora left his desk and joined him on the threshold. Schenck gave him a file to read. His reproachful look into the office prompted Bora to prevent all comments. "I'll be mindful of my germ plasma, Colonel."

10 January

Father Malecki would have lost his patience had there been a better reason to do so.

"We're so pressed for time and you're asking me to get involved in something completely irrelevant to the matter at hand?"

As he had done so many times since they'd known each other, Bora paced the floor of the convent's waiting room. "I only need you to listen. I'm confused, I have to clear up something. As I told you, the play was *The Eumenides* by Aeschylus, the third work in his *Oresteia* trilogy. I studied only the first of the three in school, so I had to look the tragedy up."

Malecki had a fleeting smile. "So did I. The gist of the story is whether it is more grievous to commit a crime against one's mother or one's husband."

"Yes. More precisely, whether killing one's mother because she murdered her unfaithful husband deserves eternal punishment. Now, there are six female roles of some consequence in the play. The three Furies, who turn into benignant spirits at the end; the Prophetess of Apollo, who speaks the opening monologue; Athena, who is the lead female part; and the Ghost of Clytaemestra – that is, the uxoricide murdered in revenge by her son."

"Which roles did the Kowalski women play?"

Bora nodded at the priest's ready understanding. "Helenka was given Athena's part – her first noteworthy classical role – and Ewa, who'd played Clytaemestra in the two previous plays, had to settle for the small role of her Ghost."

"Did you go to the performance?"

"It wouldn't have been necessary after I read the text, but I did. Since it was in Polish, I understood virtually nothing, but the Ghost appears at the beginning to rouse the Furies against her son, and needn't be on stage again until the end of the tragedy, a full hour and a half in this production."

"So you think that someone —"

"Not *someone*, Father Malecki. The Ghost of Clytaemestra. You see, the only one who could have noticed her absence was the woman who plays the Prophetess, but she also doubles as one of the Furies. She has very little time between saying her last line and rushing to wear a mask and lie down with her two sisters as the temple doors are opened. The Furies don't leave the stage until the end. Even on foot it takes no more than fifteen minutes from the theatre to our flat."

Malecki acted unconvinced. "Still – I don't know how big a man the major was – it wouldn't be easy to *talk him* into putting his head in the stove."

"I know."

"And you're positive there were no marks of violence on his body?"

"None. That's where things become garbled." For a moment Bora leaned against the wall by the crucifix, then resumed his pacing. "Could Major Retz be forced? I asked myself a hundred times Clytaemestra's question, 'How could one then bring death to dreadful men / who pretend love?'"

"You didn't make your suspicions obvious, of course."

"To her? No. I only hinted that I wondered about her ex-husband. But he happens to have been a prisoner of war since the first week in September, so he doesn't even appear in the picture."

"Then the victim had to be already unconscious."

Bora stopped in mid-stride. Malecki seemed to look through him with his clear blue eyes.

"Why not, Captain? During the autopsy they were probably only looking for signs of asphyxia."

"I'm sure they checked for traces of drugs in his system."

"Then it seems to me you ought to look for whatever wouldn't leave traces."

It was late in the evening when Bora arrived at the hospital.

Doctor Nowotny was on his way out of the office, so Bora spoke to him as they walked down the phenol-smelling hallway.

Nowotny was gruff. "What are you up to, anyway? Aren't you in enough trouble, that you should ask about poisons?" Still he turned back, let Bora into his office, and made a gesture towards a metal chair opposite the desk. "Seat your damn self down."

"Colonel, please correct me if I'm wrong. When someone is killed by carbon monoxide, the findings include bright colouring of the mucous membranes, as well as a red sediment from a blood solution in the autopsy."

Nowotny placed his crossed arms on the desk. "Well, at least it's nothing political. Yes, there's a slow clouding of the solution, which then gains a pink tinge and eventually produces a reddish precipitate."

"And what else?"

"What else? Laboratory-wise, you mean? It depends. There can be a rise in the number of white cells in the blood and of albumin in the urine." Nowotny studied him. "Are you still brooding about the way your room-mate went?"

"I'm brooding because he *went*, period. Had anyone wished to make him unconscious without being detected, could they have used – say – aconite?"

"I wouldn't. Aconite causes small welts on the lips."

"Antimonium, then?"

"No. It's like arsenic, too obvious."

"What about atropine?"

"Detectable in the urine." Nowotny undid the fold of his arms, amicably leaning forwards. "Wait, wait. Before you recite the entire alphabet of poisons, let's stop at barbiturates. Like carbon monoxide, they bring a slight myosis. A contraction of the pupils, yes. There can be also leucocytosis and albuminuria." He could see Bora's attention turn to excitement, and laughed. "Don't be so righteous. It's difficult to detect barbiturates in blood and urine. If anyone did what you suggest, he was as smart as you are."

"Are they available over the counter?"

"Drugs are always available to those who know where to ask for them, over or under the counter. Veronal is commonly used. Keep in mind that if the subject is drinking at the time, alcohol increases both effect and toxicity. There are all kinds of strong products around. Luminal is another."

"Luminal?"

"Yes. What about it? Do you think Retz gobbled some before doing himself in?"

"I don't know yet. The name just reminded me of something else I meant to ask you: does the word *lumen* have a specific medical meaning?"

Nowotny tapped a tobacco-stained finger on his greying temple. "I'm beginning to think the rock did more damage to your head than I suspected. Generally, we refer to *lumen* as the cavity of a body organ, or the narrow channel of a blood vessel. Why?"

"Just checking on a theory I have. Nothing to do with Retz, it's about the abbess's death. I think I know who killed her."

"Wait, wait – one thing at a time, Bora. Back to your room-mate's untimely end, didn't I prescribe you Veronal when you broke your skull?"

Bora suddenly remembered Nowotny had done so.

The medicine bottle was still on the lower shelf of his bedtable. Bora looked at it against the electric light, but couldn't tell whether the level of the liquid was appreciably different from when he had used it last. He'd only taken it the first three nights, when pain had been severe, and once he'd inadvertently spilled some. He couldn't tell, but Veronal was here, labelled and available.

Oh, good God.

Bora sat on the bed. Closing his eyes, he could see fragmentary images of the mind pass like shreds through him, disconnected images that meant nothing. Women's faces seemed to have more substance, the little gestures of their hands and lips were set in his memory with a kind of timeless perfection. The way Dikta closed her eyes before kissing him, and the light caught the sparkle of her lashes. Ewa's gloves slipping off and off, baring her hands. The transformation Helenka had wrought before the mirror, from fair and youthful into a female god.

He felt dull and inexperienced before all of them. Almost afraid of the things women knew, and understood.

Easily awed, easily undone. Helenka had said, "Men aren't clever enough, or deep enough."

It was true.

11 January

"I, too, have been reassigned, Father, and will be leaving Poland soon."

"To better things, I hope?"

"To different things."

The snow was almost knee-high in the cloister. Shrubs and flowerpots and the ring of the well bore a tall trim of white, lacy at the edges, perfectly gleaming in the sunlight. Bora cut a straight diagonal through the snow as he walked to the well, with Malecki following in the mashed trail. Looking upwards, Bora took in a blue dazzle of winter sky, pure and deep as if the true well were upwards, burrowing to immeasurable distances.

"I think the abbess was shot there." He pointed to the deep shade of the cloister. "By the door, likely, or at a little distance from it. After the bullet struck her, she stumbled all the way here, where I saw her lie. At first I assumed she'd been shot out here because a prisoner told me he'd seen her lie in this spot earlier that day. But no, she was shot point-blank as she faced her murderer. Because of her bulky habit, blood was absorbed by the cloth at first, and did not leave traces as she staggered towards the well. Not that it makes much difference where in the cloister she was shot. Still, had the Cracow Police been allowed to investigate, we might have had all the details we needed to solve this long ago. But with the abbess's body off-limits even to our army surgeon, and only my amateurish observations to guide us, we couldn't even pinpoint the time of death."

Malecki had joined Bora at the centre of the cloister, where the snow entrapping his legs soon made him envy the German's boots. "Well, then, since we're here, please give me the chain of events."

"It's soon done. On the afternoon of the 23rd of October, I drove Colonel Hofer to the convent. Whether or not he'd already met the abbess in the morning, he asked for an interview and was let inside shortly after four thirty. I needn't remind you of the terrible state the colonel was in those days. A terrible state, anything could have made him snap. His sanity hung on what hope the abbess would give him regarding his son, and my suspicion is that she plainly told him he would die soon."

"Which came to pass."

"Yes. The colonel – I'm sure of it, working as closely with him as I did – could not accept such total severance of hope. Surely he would never intentionally kill her. He was in awe of the abbess, and probably afraid of her as well." Shielding his eyes with his gloved hand, Bora looked across the square of dazzling snow. "When he heard her words, he became unhinged. He took his gun out, and either put it to his temple, or in his mouth, clearly about to fire."

"And Mother Kazimierza intervened."

"I don't know. Somehow she doesn't strike me as someone who would leap to wrest a weapon from a suicide. She certainly gestured towards him, imperiously, perhaps, and the gun went off. All I can think, Father Malecki, is that Hofer must have been petrified at the sight of what he'd done." Bora kept his eyes on the steep eaves around the cloister, where icicles caught the sunlight and gave out diamond-like reflections. On the side facing south, entire layers of snow slid down the incline and hung suspended from the edge. Others had fallen off, and the roof steamed gently.

Malecki blew on his cold hands. "So it all happened in a matter of minutes. Seconds, maybe. And of course the tanks were rumbling down the street."

"Yes. The lead tank had trouble turning the corner, so it backed up and revved its engine, while the others ran in idle. I wouldn't have heard a bomb exploding behind me, and the same goes for the porter nun. My ears were still ringing after the road cleared and the colonel ran out of the convent in a panic."

"Why didn't you immediately suspect him, then?"

Bora shook his head. "Because until I stumbled upon the subject with Hannes, I assumed Colonel Hofer carried no weapon. As I'm sure you noticed, we all go about ostensibly armed. He didn't. I believed he'd chosen to show a token of 'respect' towards an occupied country, or great self-assurance."

"I see." Malecki's eyes ran down to Bora's holster. "But what about the bullet? You yourself told me the murder bullet belongs to a Polish gun."

"It's true. It's made for the Vis-35 Radom semi-automatic pistol. Like those that were hidden in this convent, which is why I was so furious when I first saw them. Except that those were still packed with grease, and obviously had never been fired."

"Do you mean to tell me your commander carried an enemy gun?"

"No. I mean to tell you he used enemy cartridges." Quickly, Bora unlatched his holster, showing to Malecki on the gloved palm the burnished bulk of his Walther. "This is not a fussy pistol like the Luger we had until last year, but it still won't take just any cartridge." He extracted the magazine, lined with slender brass-tipped cylinders. "I would not use Radom bullets in it: they're longer, thicker, clunkier than these."

"What, then?"

"Colonel Hofer – like Colonel Schenck, like myself – served in Spain as a volunteer a few years past. On the Church's side, which should be a consolation to you. On the evening you and I dined together in the square, on the way to the restaurant my driver and I were chatting about the Spanish days when he mentioned that Hofer was still using the pistol he'd been issued in Cadiz. I couldn't believe my ears. Right away, I asked whether he knew what make the gun was, and he said, 'Astra,' adding that Hofer carried it in an underarm holster because of its non-standard appearance."

"And the Astra takes Radom cartridges."

"Not only. The Astra 400 is an ugly blow-back pistol, but I fired it with all kinds of 9mm cartridges, from Parabellum to Steyr to Browning and Colt. It was through Hannes that I realized how at the very least, Hofer's gun could have fired the fatal shot. *Astra*, I needn't remind you, is Latin for 'stars' and 'starlight', so *Lumen* fits the bill after all."

"So, Colonel Hofer, whether he planned it or not, made an accident appear like intentional murder by a Polish hand."

"Exactly. Had the colonel really found the abbess lying in her blood, his first instinct as a soldier would have been to take out his gun, because theoretically the murderer could have still been around. I certainly had my gun in hand when I ran to this very spot. After my chat with Hannes, I had to wonder why Colonel Hofer kept his weapon out of sight on that day." After replacing the gun in his holster, Bora looked strangely unaggressive to Malecki. "He had no choice, you see. He simply had no choice. No matter how distraught he was, he had to pull himself together enough to run out and fetch me."

"So, you will prosecute."

"No."

"You promised you would, Captain Bora!"

"I *can't*. When I thought I was being so clever by phoning his wife last week, I put into motion the one thing that would keep me from prosecuting. Even though I was only guessing at that stage, Colonel Hofer assumed I had found him out. Yesterday, when he came home on furlough, his wife informed him of my call, and how I would be calling again. He answered nothing, but walked into his room, locked himself in, and ten minutes later fired a bullet into his mouth. And that's how clever I am, Father Malecki."

"God keep us."

"Yes. There was no abbess to stop him that time."

Malecki had to hide the distaste he had for hearing a dispassionate description of murder and suicide. Still he said, "Did Hofer leave a note behind?"

"Just a scribble, apparently. Something to do with asking God's forgiveness for what he had 'unwittingly done'. The German authorities took it to imply his failure as commander here in Poland, but we know better. I also received confirmation that Radom cartridges were in the colonel's pistol, and one of them was used in his own death."

Malecki chose to look up at Bora's composure. "Well," he said, "I am the last one to want to admit this, but if things went as you say, your commander did not intentionally and maliciously kill the abbess. Could he not have tried to explain matters to all concerned?"

Bora was tempted to laugh, Malecki could tell. Unamusedly, but laughter was what seemed to well up in him at the idea. "Father Malecki, the German Army doesn't take kindly to officers who attempt suicide. Even less to those who embarrass the corps by committing an accidental murder. No. The colonel had no choice, especially if he wanted to live long enough to see his child again. He was racked enough by grief, I'm sure. But by asking me, of all people, to look into the matter, he also made virtually sure I would not suspect him."

"So, what happens after you conclude your investigation?"

"I know why you ask. There's no one left to prosecute, which means that a scandal injurious to German interests in Poland can and will be safely avoided. Privately —"

"*Privately*, you will tell the archbishop the truth."

"With my superiors' permission, yes."

"And the archbishop, in turn?"

"He knows what's good for the Church in Poland. I trust you will advise him accordingly, Father Malecki."

"And to the sisters? What will you tell them?"

"They're better off believing I was unable to solve the mystery of the abbess's death. Perhaps the archbishop will decide to inform Sister Irenka, *privately*."

Visibly troubled, Malecki trundled off through the snow to re-enter the convent. Bora remained outside. He leaned to look into the well, where – far down – a round of hazy blue showed the ice seal on the water.

He was thinking about what else he had to tell Colonel Schenck that afternoon.

When the time came, Schenck had his usual starched look, even though Bora's report was as unexpected as he could envision. He actually didn't interrupt, limiting himself now and then to an involuntary wink of his good eye.

"Well, the son of a bitch," he said. "The snivelling, hysterical son of a bitch managed to make fools of us all. And he's dead, which is how he really fooled us for good."

"We still need to secure the gun, and find out from his widow what he might have confided to her about the matter."

Schenck snatched a stationery sheet from his desk, and uncapped his pen. "How much time do you need?"

"I think three days would suffice, if I take the first train to Germany. Less if I fly out."

A concise emergency leave was handed to Bora. "Here. And I was beginning to think that you'd abandon the trail! But I see you dig until you find your bone! The Governor General will be stunned. There'll be all kind of goings-on if it turns out to be true. Wait till I inform that jackass Salle-Weber!"

Bora took a deep breath and let it out.

"I have another report to make, Colonel."

Unexpectedly Schenck grinned. "Let me guess. You took my advice and made an ethnic German pregnant."

"Hardly. It concerns my room-mate."

A moment later, the grin had been wiped off Schenck's leathery face.

Bora said, "I'm positive about it. It's from her friend, Kasia, that I learned she had a key to the apartment, which Major Retz provided her: a breach in security, to say the least. Whether her decision to kill him originated in his infatuation for her daughter or not, though I think jealousy was the primary factor, I have no doubt that Ewa Kowalska left the Old Theatre shortly after nine hundred hours on Saturday morning, reached our quarters and let herself in. She had no way of knowing that the major had just phoned Helenka to arrange a date." Bora relaxed enough to pace across Schenck's office with hands in his pockets, and Schenck let him. "You and I, Colonel, are aware of how the major was fond of drinking on weekends. I saw him polish off whole bottles of straight cognac or vodka, and down a few shots before breakfast. On Saturday morning, either he had a drink already poured, or Ewa prepared a drink for both of them, adding what for lack of better identification I must simply call a barbiturate, possibly my own Veronal, which she'd certainly noticed during her previous visits to our place. The major gulped his drinks without even tasting them. He must have done the same that morning, whatever conversation he and Ewa were carrying on. I can only speculate at this stage: recrimination, pleading, who knows? If Ewa did in fact bring Helenka up, it's possible that Major Retz showed insufficient remorse or even lack of concern about his incest. Being on duty later that day, he began shaving while she was there, but never had time to finish. When the drug had its effect – depending on the amount, it could be a fairly quick matter according to Colonel Nowotny – all Ewa had to do was drag his groggy or unconscious body to the stove. She put his head in the oven, turned on the gas, washed the glasses, the sink and the razor, unthinkingly leaving the blade in it. So that the detail of his partly shaven face wouldn't be too obvious, she wiped his face clean with one of the towels stored in the bathroom shelf, and took the towel along. Then she returned to the theatre, in time to appear on stage at the end of the rehearsal."

Schenck made a very small movement which might be interpreted as a complacent nod. "Wouldn't the porter be aware that someone had come to see Major Retz?"

"Not necessarily. It's likely that Ewa had been given the key to the front door as well. I have more than once gone by without the porter noticing me."

"And you built all this construction on the unlikely foundation of a misplaced razor blade?"

Bora stopped pacing. "Not only. Also by reading a Greek play, by being tempted by an older woman and through the fortunate enlightenment of a blind spot, thanks to the American priest. It was an instance of seeing the light, Colonel. *Lumen*, if you wish, had its part here as well."

"Well, well." Schenck had a grin so brief, it was a mere baring of teeth. "What will you do now? Arrest the Kowalska woman on this evidence?"

"I think it has to be done."

"Surely not for that scoundrel Retz's sake."

"For justice's sake, then."

"There you go again, with your fixation on upholding the law. Take two men with you."

Bora hesitated. "I thought I might begin by going at it alone."

"No."

The street seemed cut in two by the low winter sun, with an azure line limning on the snowy sidewalk the roofs of the houses across from Ewa's apartment. A blue quilt was airing across the sill of her window.

The army car stopped at the Święty Marka end of it. One armed soldier stationed himself at the corner. The other had already been dropped at the opposite end of the street. Bora alighted last, and was soon past the doorstep of her house.

It didn't take long, nor was it as awkward as Bora had expected.

Ewa slipped a nightgown in the small suitcase, locked it and removed it from the dresser to stand it by the bedroom door. She closed the window, folded the quilt, lifted it over her head to place it on the wardrobe. She couldn't quite reach, so Bora did it for her.

"Thank you," she said. "Do I have time to put some make-up on?"

"I don't think so."

"I'm ready, then."

Bora looked at her and past her, at the framed photograph of a younger Ewa holding Helenka in her arms.

She followed his stare. "You never liked me, did you?"

"On the contrary, I did."

"You didn't act on it." She seemed truly old today, much older than his mother. "Ah, but I forget you're a married man." She bound the blue scarf around her neck. "Though I wager not nearly as happily married as you say."

Bora took her small suitcase. "Let's go."

After they left Święty Krzyża, they found that some of the other streets were blocked. Armoured columns were in transit through the city, so Bora's car was redirected alongside the Vistula in the direction of the bridge. Like an island the massif of the Wawel, castle- and cathedral-crowned, seemed to pivot to their left as they approached the curve of the river.

Ewa did not look out of the window, but Bora did. Her profile against the hill betrayed no emotion, only some weariness. He felt very lonely.

They had nearly come to the curve when the driver had to slow down to a halt. Under the watch of German engineers, workers were unloading heavy equipment from a barge, and two trucks obstructed the sidewalk. One of the trucks was being weighed down with road-constructing machinery even now.

Ewa was layering rouge on her lips, the small round mirror firm in her hand.

Bora's driver turned the engine off. "There's nothing much we can do, sir."

"I can see that." Bora waited for some minutes, then walked out of the car to speak to the engineers overseeing the operation.

They told him all towing had to be done before the river froze. "It's going to be a little while yet, Herr Hauptmann." But they recognized his impatience, and how he'd stay there to make them feel pressured. "We're moving as fast as we can, Herr Hauptmann."

Bora didn't move from where he stood. A brutal wind arose from the riverside and along the shore, making the men tearful and stiff. No matter how he turned his back to the wind, Bora had to give up trying to light a cigarette in the open.

Crates packed in tarpaulin were followed on the trucks by the road-constructing machinery. Jointed steel bodies like gigantic insects, powerful belted gears, grooved chains.

Bora was considering the alternative of driving through the deep icy snow off the side of the road, when not so much a commotion of voices behind him as the reaction of the engineers made him wheel around.

Ewa had broken out of the car and was running away from it, headed for the rise of the land that rimmed the south end of the Old City and the Wawel. Both escort soldiers were also in the open. They'd lifted their rifles and were yelling at her to stop, aiming at her already.

"Don't shoot!" Bora bolted from the disconcerted group of workers. By long strides he made for the direction Ewa had taken through the high snow, towards the Wawel Hill. Behind him, the soldiers trundled on a little more, then halted at his command.

Ewa had a frantic quickness about her, a scared-animal ability to scamper off. Hands and knees acted in concert to part the snow, her race was improvident but effective and through the white clumps she moved in nearly a straight line, unhampered by her short fur coat.

Bora's metal-clad boots slipped on the ice under the snow. Height and a man's body weight worked against him in the race. His greatcoat was heavy and long, it impeded free motion. He lost balance and time while Ewa started up the incline that ran lush with grass most of the year, but was stark now and nearly unbrokenly white.

Already the guards from atop the Wawel bastions had noticed the escape and were crying out their own guttural warnings from above.

"Don't open fire!" Bora shouted at them, though the wind took his voice and they might not have heard him.

Ewa's neck scarf flew off and, like a blue disorderly bird snatched by the current, it was borne aloft behind her.

From this point, she could only hope to get to the closely guarded ramp that led to the gateway to the castle. Bora knew it wasn't safety she was looking for. Anger threw him into a fury to keep her from getting herself killed, out of spite and refusal to give her that choice, to be a part of her death.

"You have to stop!" he shouted at her. "I command you to stop!"

Ewa looked back, midway through the incline. The terrain was very steep at this point. The snow was piled high on this side of the hill, where it had accumulated due to the wind, and she stood in the middle of it nearly to her thighs. Her face was small and livid in the distance. She seemed about to renew her race, then let her arms fall to her sides, and didn't move.

Bora struggled to join her but did so quickly on his longer, booted legs. Ewa breathed hard, and so did Bora. Clouds of condensing vapour fled in front of them.

"I don't want to be arrested, Captain."

"There's no choice." Bora kept an eye on the dark, puppet-like figures of the guards atop the incline, armed with machine guns. "If you were to tell the judge about Retz and Helenka, you might get clemency from the court."

Ewa's painted lips were the only brightness in her pallor. "As if I'd speak to any court of my lover's incest with his own daughter. How perfectly German of you. No, thank you."

"Come along, then." Bora extended his arm towards her. She noticed, with a little surge of flattery, that his holster had remained latched.

"My son's dead, my lover's dead. You could let me strike you, and then your men would have to kill me."

"No."

"It'd be easier."

"Frau Kowalska, you're neither Tosca nor Clytaemestra. This is not the stage."

Bora's hand reached her elbow, taking it firmly. Except for the kiss, it was the first time he had touched her. He led her back through the convulsed snow without looking at her, the boyish angle of his face turned away from her as on the night in her dressing room.

The car seemed very small down by the slow, icy ribbon of the Vistula, there where the equipment had been finally unloaded and the road was clear.

12 January

On his way to the train station in the morning, Bora had been reading a letter from home, and did not at first notice the slowing of the car.

"What is it, Hannes?" he asked automatically, without glancing up.

"Street's blocked ahead, sir."

Quickly orienting himself, Bora saw they'd come quite near the station, driving through the working-class quarter that separated the Old City from Army Headquarters. Twenty or so feet in front of the car, a helmeted, gloved SS man had stood with his right arm raised, and Hannes was slowing down more.

Even from here, Bora could see that bodies lined the street: civilian bodies in bloodied nightclothes, and the SS had barbed wire, cars, dog. A truck parked in the street where snow had been trampled into mud. People already crowded under the tarpaulin, pinched white faces anxiously peering out in a double row. Entire families, it seemed, were being herded out of doors.

The helmeted SS man flagged the car down with deliberate, imperious slowness, so that Hannes' braking became a full stop.

Bora rolled down his window.

Just ahead, furniture and clothes were being thrown from balconies on the tenements' higher floors. A sewing machine came crashing down, attached to its skinny table, metal pieces flying. Papers sailed in mid-air and floundered like shot birds. The car idled at the edge of an unspeakable disorder of objects and people.

There was shooting going on inside the houses. Bora recognized the smacking reverberation of gunfire within four walls. Echoing cries followed, shouted commands. More gunfire.

"What is happening?"

He had to shout the words to be heard. The SS man answered from where he stood, near the sidewalk where the bodies lay, not bothering to draw close even though he certainly knew an officer was addressing him.

"Haven't you heard? We caught those who killed the Catholic nun."

"*What?*"

"It was the Polish swine who were hiding on the rooftops near the convent. The Army tried to cover it up, but *we* got them. Now it's just a matter of flushing their accomplices out. All trains have been cancelled, so you'll have to go back."

Staring, Bora folded his mother's letter and slid it in the cuff of his sleeve.

The SS man had turned away from the car. Blood flowing from the bodies was finding its way down from the street. When it reached the snow crust rimming the street, red flowers bloomed at the point of contact, a transitory efflorescence that flared out, and at once was no more than the mingling of blood and icy water into a pink slush.

"Move on and turn," the SS man wheeled around to order.

Hannes started out again at a snail's pace, aiming the car amidst the litter from above. Glass shards rained down, more debris.

Those who killed the Catholic nun. The Army tried to cover it up. Bora knew what it meant, what it all meant, and yet a dullness of body and soul let him keep watching without any visible reaction. Hannes drove hunched over the wheel, his big ears translucent in the cold morning light like those of a sensitive, mute animal.

A second roadblock manned by long-coated SS barred the sidewalk ahead.

"Turn left at the corner," Bora said to Hannes. And as the car prepared to leave the noise and confusion of the barricaded street, a drop of blood – from where? How had it jetted or spurted here? – fell on the windshield. High up, where ice coating the glass outside the wipers' reach stopped it from running, so that the blood sealed itself there, like a mark and an indictment.

The streets were deserted all the way from the turn-off to Rakowicka, where the low sun unfurled a chilly carpet of ice. On the brick wall flanking the garden of the old

Academy, yard-long SS notices had been posted, with split text in German and Polish. Black on the pale yellow, thin paper surface, it read, "Investigation into the death of Maria Zapolyaia, a Catholic religious woman, has resulted in the apprehension of Polish criminal elements. The culprits" – a list of names followed, among which, no doubt, was that of the battered prisoner Bora had met – "were tried, found guilty and sentenced to death. The sentence has already been carried out."

The Army tried to cover it up. Found guilty. The sentence has already been carried out.

Bora found that he could look at all this, hear all this, witness all this, and have nothing whatever to say.

13 January

The last person to come in for confession spoke English. Through the grid-lined window, Father Malecki understood well who it was, although there were no further signs of intelligence between them.

"*In nomine Patris, et Filii, et Spiritus Sancti.*"

"*Amen.* Forgive me, Father, for I have sinned."

"How long since your last confession?"

Malecki found himself sitting back in the recess of the ornate wooden box that separated him from the world, listening to the words coming earnest and low through what privacy the metal screen afforded the other man.

"Everything is different now, Father. Right and wrong, honourable and dishonourable – they're words and they are blurred to me until I sort them out again. No one can do it for me and it frightens me, it frightens me to have to choose. To have to pick one of the opposites when they're so blurred, and walk away with it not knowing if I have done well, if the choice was wise, when I don't even see the

306

rims of wisdom any more. It's gone empty before me, this great bowl of wisdom I was striving for and deluded myself that I was attaining, or even had attained in small part. There's nothing in it. *There is nothing in it.*"

"But it's not a sin."

Bora rested his forehead against the grid. "The mask fell off the world, Father Malecki, and no face stands behind it. I am sick at heart."

"Are you? This is the exit from Eden. Meeting the 'opposites', as you call them. Seeing that, contrary to your view from the Garden, they are truly good and evil, and the choice is yours, because you're a temporal creature with an immortal soul whose health depends on what you do *here*, what you decide *here*." Malecki was moved, because it seemed to him that Bora was silently struggling not to weep. "This, I tell you – whatever your choice, you will be crucified to it, nailed to it and bled white by it. You will live or die of it as surely as I speak to you now. More, others will live or die of it."

The shadow behind the grid pulled away. "I don't want to hear it." But Malecki was ready for the reaction. He stepped out of the confessional, rudely keeping Bora from leaving. He pushed him back towards the niche between the confessional and the wall, in the dusk of the empty church.

"Tell me, do you think the abbess was a saint? Is that what a saint is, someone cloaked in her egocentric God-love to the exclusion of everyone else, basking in God behind closed doors? Saints aren't so private, Captain Bora. They're crucified to the unglamorous daily crosses of their love for others, their anger and outrage and striving to create hope for others. They wear robes sometimes, civilian clothes sometimes – even boots with spurs on them. And they need to be as prudent and wily as God will advise, serpents and doves in the hands of men. *Do you understand?* I am afraid for you: I, who should be inimical to you and what you represent!"

"What a damn gift you have. Who can ever take it away from you?"

Having heard about Bora's reassignment, Doctor Nowotny had invited himself to dinner and to a private evening of Schumann piano music. "Well," he added. "A special Intelligence school and then the War Academy! That ought to keep you put until January 1941 at least. Will you have time to sneak home between lessons and tuck some *germ plasma* into your wife?"

"I hope so." Bora had just that afternoon taken leave from Father Malecki, and the separation somehow made him feel orphaned. He sat at the piano, careful to hide those feelings, and his melancholy for Dikta's silence over the holidays. "I miss her terribly."

Nowotny sank into the armchair, with a big glass of cognac nestled in his hand. "Good for you, good for you. Mail a telegram to Schenck as soon as you make her pregnant, so that he won't send you reminders of your marital duties." He laughed. "Easy to say. Who knows where we'll all be, two, three years from now." He listened to Bora play for a while, mellowed by the music into sentimentality. "This much I can tell you, Bora. You will put crime solving behind you and concentrate on your army career. If I know what's good for me, I'll sooner or later put this heavy smoking behind me. Our incomparable Schenck will keep reproducing like a rabbit. What else is there?"

It was little more than wishful thinking on Nowotny's part.

Within three years, he'd be smoking as much as ever. Schenck would die at the gates of Stalingrad before seeing his sixth son born, and Bora's left hand would be blown off by a partisan grenade in northern Italy. His wife Dikta would secure an annulment shortly thereafter. All of them, all of them, would lose a war more disastrously than anyone could fear. Gifts could and would be taken away.

Tonight there was Schumann, and mild expectation, and the mercy of not knowing.

15 January, afternoon

"There is one thing I would like to ask of the sisters, and that is the print that hangs over the door of *Matka* Kazimierza's old room."

Sister Irenka puckered her face. "That detestable little picture of Adam and Eve?"

"That one."

"You may certainly have it. Sister Jadwiga, fetch the print for the captain. Is it permissible to ask why you choose such image to remember us by?"

"Yes, but it isn't precisely to remember you by, Mother Superior. It is to remind myself of myself." Bora felt himself blushing, and for once did not resist the reaction. "I have after all failed at my investigation, and I need a reminder of man's pride."

Father Malecki waited outside the convent, smoking a Polish cigarette. He saw Bora put the print in the trunk, and was tempted to smile.

Instead, he asked, "Have you convinced them that you couldn't come up with a solution?"

"I don't know. They seem resigned to whatever comes."

"And I hear the SS are exhibiting the abbess's blood-stained habit in one of the Wawel's halls, along with the

Radom bullet as a proof of Polish guilt. So. What have we learned from all this?"

Bora invited the priest to enter the car.

"I can only speak for myself, Father Malecki, and it's elementary philosophy. Things aren't what they seem. Certainties aren't what they seem. There may be no certainties."

"Ah, but there is Mother Kazimierza's faith in some inner light."

"Yes. *Lumen Christi, Adiuva Nos.* We'll need it."

"We'll need it."

They drove in silence through the alleys of Cracow's Old City, under a cloudy sky that promised more snow.

"You never told me who Father Moczygemba was." Bora tried to smile.

"Father Leopold Moczygemba? A pioneer of Polish immigration to America. He built the church of Cyril and Methodius in Bucktown – Chicago's Polish quarter."

"And then?"

"And then he became the spiritual father of the Poles in Texas, but his flock chased him off when it realized the New World was not the promised land."

"There aren't any. Promised lands, I mean."

"Right. Trust in the one and only Promised Land, Captain Bora."

They knew they would not see one another again, and the feeling had a sharp, bitter taste for both of them. But they wouldn't speak of it.

Soon they parted ways at the end of Karmelicka Street.

Epilogue

OBJECT: *"Skylight" Dossier (ref. HOFER/ZAPOLYAIA), final informational to enclosed Appendices.*

TO: *US War Department Military Intelligence Division, Washington, DC*

ATTENTION: *LT. COLONEL WILLIAM C. DICKSON, US Army - Office G2*

CLASSIFICATION: *RESERVED*

(Omissis).. In conclusion, on the basis of information collected to date, and verified in place by the sources "Pedro", "Thomas" and "Karol" (see enclosed Appendices, *S.D.1, S.D.1-bis, S.D.1-ter*), the Cracow Office, as requested by Central Office G2 on date 20 January 1940, is able to confirm the substantial veracity of the information, ref. points 1, 2, 3, of present informational note.

1. The only copy of the final report by Wehrmacht Captain BORA (MARTIN-HEINZ DOUGLAS), ref: Object (*ref. HOFER/ZAPOLYAIA,* 7 typewritten pages, body 11, double space, on plain German Army stationery), was forwarded to the Central Office of *Amt/Ausland Abwehr* in Berlin. A first analysis of its contents (see enclosed microfilm transcription – *ref. "Pedro"/SD.1*) leads to the conclusion that it will be filed there, under the rubric Military Secret, 2nd class/Reserved, unless orders to the contrary are

issued: orders that, according to information gathered, source "Pedro" is not likely to be issued.

2. Similar filing is expected for the report written "pro veritate" by the Revd Father MALECKI (JOHN XAVIER), SJ, for the Vatican Secretary of State. In reference to this, the source "Thomas" (see enclosed marconigram – *ref. "Thomas"/SD.1-bis*) confirms that the Vatican Secretary of State instructed the religious person in question to maintain the strictest reservation regarding Object. As for details of the beatification process of canonization of Mother Kazimierza, the argument lies beyond the scope of the present informational note.

3. *SS Hauptsturmführer* (Captain) SALLE-WEBER sent an "urgent and reserved" message to the attention of *Reichsführer* der SS HEINRICH HIMMLER, with copy to Head of General Government HANS FRANK, reporting Captain BORA's "political unreliability", and soliciting the application of "appropriate punitive measures" in his regard. According to source "Karol", the *Reichsführer* HIMMLER, in consideration of the amicable relations the officer in question enjoys in the German Army *Oberkommando*, decided to insert Captain BORA's name in the list of Wehrmacht company officers under "strong suspicion" of anti-Nazism (see enclosed *S.D./1-ter/ref. "Kreisau-Counts"*), reserving for himself the decision to apply more drastic measures in the eventuality that *Hauptsturmführer* SALLE-WEBER's evaluation were to be confirmed in the future. Whether and how the discrepancy between Captain BORA and the political-military command cadre of the *Schutzstaffel* (SS) will become more acute and reach the breaking point, only time will tell. At present, no further factual elements exist in this regard, although the Cracow

Office, after attentive examination of the documents gathered to date, is inclined to conjecture that in the immediate future..*(omissis)*

The present informational note was written in date 22 January 1940, and approved by the US Consul General before its transcription in code.

Awaiting acknowledgement of receipt.

KEVIN J. LOGAN,
US Consulate General,
Cracow, Poland.